Davus

The black Squire

Or, A Lady's four Wishes - Vol. II

Davus

The black Squire
Or, A Lady's four Wishes - Vol. II

ISBN/EAN: 9783337067076

Printed in Europe, USA, Canada, Australia, Japan

Cover: Foto ©Andreas Hilbeck / pixelio.de

More available books at **www.hansebooks.com**

THE BLACK SQUIRE;

OR,

A LADY'S FOUR WISHES.

A Novel.

By DAVUS.

' A document in madness ; thoughts and remembrance fitted.''
HAMLET.

IN THREE VOLUMES.
VOL. II.

London:
SAMUEL TINSLEY & CO.,
10, SOUTHAMPTON STREET, STRAND.
1879.

THE BLACK SQUIRE;

OR,

A LADY'S FOUR WISHES.

CHAPTER I.

'Beauty provoketh thieves sooner than gold.'
As You Like It.

'KING HENRY. Stanley was once my friend, and came in time
    To save my life :—yet, to say truth, my lords,
    The man stayed long enough to endanger it.
SURREY.   . . . . 'Tis a king
    Composed of gentleness. . . .
DURHAM.   . . . . Rare and unheard-of ;
    But every man is nearest to himself :
    And that the king observes.'
        FORD—*Perkin Warbeck.*

'WHAT has come to Dicky Gryffyn ?' was the common question among his acquaintance. What, indeed ? Why did he, that used to sleep so soundly, now spend his nights in restless tossings on a weary bed, where sleep, if it came at all, came broken and disturbed ; and all the day long thick-coming fancies, now frowning, now flattering, set his brain seething and his blood throbbing, and agitated every nerve of his fevered body. Joy and hope, desire and rashness, fear and jealousy, possessed and harassed him by turns. Her kindness and beauty and feminine grace, her soothing voice, her words, her looks, imprinted in consuming flame, burnt into his young heart the ineffaceable name. His communing with himself on this one vital subject never ceased; and hope and fear, self-restraint and self-will, alternately swayed his soul. What took place within him one day took place every day, almost every hour. The alternations were rapid, but they came over and over again ; hot fits and cold ; ' To be, or not to be ?' was the ceaseless question.

He did think she had shown him some kindness. Was that a good reason for injuring her ? and his alliance could hardly do less : why be so selfish ? It was abominably mean even to think of winning her against her father's will. Had not her father's house been thrown open to him ? Had he a doubt about the way in which Mr. Palmer would regard his suit ? If a father treats a guest with frank confidence and unsuspicious hospitality, what sort of guest is he that will abuse confidence and requite a host's kindnesses by trying to rob him of that which he most prizes, and who would wound him incurably in his tenderest point ? For such breaches of the laws of honour and hospitality Dick had ever entertained the utmost abhorrence. He had never shared in any degree the opinions of the looser sort about heiress-hunting, and all the meannesses attending it. To be sure, with him it was not heiress-hunting—he only wished she were not an heiress ; but he would not be the man to bring trouble into a happy household that had done him nothing but good. He had not much experience of life, but enough to tell him that he was no match, in any respect, for Barbara Palmer. Had not Martel more than once hinted it to him?

'What business was it of his? meddlesome coxcomb! I hate him for it.'

He was right, though; nothing but unhappiness could come of seeking her, whether he won her, or not. Considering the terms of unsuspicious friendship on which, as he could not but be conscious, he was received into Palmer's house, there were but two courses open to him, in honour—his own feelings told him that: one was to stay away, and how could he? the other, to try his luck, and tell Palmer.

But then, Barbara—was he sure of her? Oh! how far from it! 'I am only sure,' he would shout, as he walked backwards and forwards through his solitary room, 'I am only sure that I love her as never man loved woman yet! Oh! heart! heart! heart! what would you have me do? Go rob my friend of his pet lamb; and, with the base betrayal, make myself happy—or my heart will break? Yet this will I not do: how can I? I would rather die outright, as I think I shall, or live in misery for ever. Suppose she should be willing to sacrifice her home, and kindred, and all that belong to her; do I love her so little as to injure her so much—to make a marriage all gain to me, all loss to her? Would I lower her in life? why, I worship her almost with idolatry! I could kiss the print of her foot on the

dirtiest road ! it would be clean from her touch. It
would be blessedness to me to drink from her shoe,
or to kiss the hem of her dress.   And would I pull
her down and discredit her ?   O fool! fool ! fool !
what a worse than fool am I !   But can I help it ?
would I help it, if I could ?'

Then he would break off into protestations that
he would never be raised, like a reckless speculator,
into discreditable affluence by the surreptitious
acquisition of a wife's fortune—and such a woman !
Not he ! He would none of it ; the very idea de-
graded his love. Love her he always must and
would, but with a generous love, at his own cost, in
a way that would not harm her.   All he would hope
was that he might some day, by some turn of fortune's wheel, be able to make for her some great
sacrifice ; what he could not exactly imagine, but
something that would let her see the consuming fire
that he had so manfully concealed.

When, by a train of magnanimous resolves like
these, he had worked himself into a very high state
of self-respect, he would, from this lofty elevation,
take quite another view of his position and duties.
How absurd and unpractical these romantic notions !
Sentimental rant, fit for romance-reading boys and
girls at school !—doing injustice to her and himself ;
for no one would ever love her as he did, or would
so devote himself to her. And all the happiness of
both to be wrecked by trumpery fashion !

These were not days to give in to aristocratic
assumption and insolent exclusiveness, and old rot-
ten feudal slavery. Democracy is abroad, and is

bringing folk to a level; that is, all educated and well-to-do people :—Of course not artisans and labourers, and cattle of that colour. Anyway, love levelled him and her, and all is fair in love and war. Were they not both of the same flesh and blood, with Adam and Eve for ancestors ? Her 'rank and fortune' indeed! What were they, after all, to be such a bar to the perfect happiness of both ? As to ' rank,' there was mighty little difference between him and the daughter of a parson, though he was a squire's younger son. He would be just a fool absolute to humour such fancies. Say he was not just her equal: who was ? Whoever married her must be her inferior. No one was worthy of her ; but who, like himself, could feel her superlative excellence ?

Then there was Mr. Palmer, who certainly at one time had been very kind to him, and for a while, at the time of his father's death, had been as a second father to him. It was to be feared he would take the matter very ill. But parsons should not be proud! And if he had been very kind, it was in a patronising sort of way. What right had Palmer to patronise him, Gryffyn? You may be friends with a man, or let it alone, but patronise! Not if I know it. When all was done, the old boy would see it in a better light, and come round, and get reconciled to it, and learn to like it. Why not? Such things happen every day. It is the course of true love, and could in no way be helped. In love, every man for himself. It was positive sin to let the dregs of feudal folly extinguish a passion that was God's own gift to man. Here poor Richard grew quite solemn, as he asked—triumphantly unanswered :—Would not everybody be the better for breaking through such servile, such unnatural bonds ? Flesh and blood revolted against them. He was not a man worthy of such a woman, if he were to throw away his chance of her for the outcry of a few formal old dowagers. Once done, the marriage would be, at worst, a nine days' wonder; and then what joy to have set at defiance Mrs. Grundy, whose business is talk, and who tells alike things done and not done, and mixes truth and lies in inextricable confusion. Do what you will, Mrs. Grundy will talk.

Mr. Palmer had very much retired from society. He had lived among grandees long enough to know their value and to give them up. He had never been so happy as now when he has few at his house beyond his own relatives and neighbours—squires, parsons, and himself, a common farmer. Well, no; not quite so common either. He was about as well born, and bred, and educated as most of the clergy, and certainly not worse off, whatever better. Yet there would be no great row if some parson were to carry off Miss Palmer. Her father, of course, would not like it if the clerical riever were one of the smaller fry, but he would put up with it and say nothing about it. To be sure there was Burgoyne. He had both a good private fortune and a living, and old Lance had sent him to the right about in double-quick time. He! he! he!

But—h'm!—the Reverend Burgoyne was a bird of one feather, and he, Richard Gryffyn, perhaps of another. At any rate, *she* had never smiled upon his reverence; and, by the way, why should he not be a 'reverend,' too? that was a new light. To be sure, he had preferred farming once; but he hated it now. He would sell his stock, and take the money into 'the Church.' He had some gift for theatricals, they said; he would *consecrate* it to a better cause: he would go back to college, and take his degree; why not? He had, indeed, thought of this once before, and had submitted part of his plan for approval to Martel, who had thrown cold water on it, and had cut some dull joke about 'debt and discontent, and bitterness of soul,' being bad stuff to make recruits of.

'Old sneerer I think he is "bitter of soul" himself; and I don't doubt he is in "*debt*," for it is not possible for him to live on his income; and I am sure he is discontented, for he always gives out that he is not. He has been very jealous any way, and very unfriendly about this matter all through: shamming blind, but giving nasty hints all the while. He is too fond of his great friends; but it's little I mind him or his preachments.'

Dicky had been saying this half aloud, with a good deal of hand action at times, as was his wont now; and he had talked himself into a ferment.

'Yes: I will go back to college and be ordained for all that jealous fellow.' And, oh! how he wished now that he had taken his father's offer of the living! He would get a fellowship and a college living:

but how could he wait for that ?—or how would he
get the other? Living or no living, he was not badly
off;—if he was not a match for her. She ought
to be a countess ;—a duchess, that fellow Martel
said ;—as likely the one as the other : but he would
not give her up to any man without a fight: why
should he ?

> ' Thou shalt not wish her thine ; thou shalt not dare
>   To be so impudent as to despair.'

'That is about what I am to be told, is it ?—we
will see.'

Besides, he could not go back if he would; he
must do, or die. There was but one way of escape,
and that he would never take :—must never go to
Finchdale, never hunt, never show himself at all.

And what would his neighbours say ? some were
jealous already, and resented his general absence
from farming society. And Mrs. Grundy, and her
doctors, and lawyers, and some parsons too, who were
not of the Squarson species, did in fact look upon
him with more favour and respect for the footing
he seemed to have in the ' *county* ' set. If he were
to be thus kicked out, as it were, what a fall in
their eyes ! and worse too, they would suspect the
reason, and perhaps cut their coarse jokes upon
him ! It was horrible to think off.

It was all very fine to make fun of Mrs. Grundy;
but would not Mrs. Grundy with her hundred
mouths and hundred tongues make fun of him? He
could not bear it ; he could not turn back; and he
would not. The line of life he had fallen into was

not of his own seeking: he had been drawn blindly
into it by overruling circumstances: he must go on
with it. Alas! that he must! But must he?
Would it not be better to back out, and have done
with it?

'Off with my painted honour,
While with vain hopes our faculties we tire,
We seem to sweat in ice, and freeze in fire.
What would I do were this to do again?
I would not change my peace of mind
For all the wealth in Europe.'

He would dwell among his own people; but
now her people must be his people. Well for him
if he had never quitted his father's substantial circle!
But to be kicked back into it!

Had she, 'the fair, the chaste, and unexpressive
she,' given to him—'oh! unfortunate he!'—'no en-
couragement? H'm! well: he thought she had: it
was hard to say; but he felt she had; and she felt
it too, or he was much mistaken. She had given
him many sweet words of notice, and many kind
looks of those beautiful eyes. She had quizzed him
constantly, to be sure, whenever he appeared to be
approaching tender ground. And sometimes she
seemed almost to have hinted to him—had she?--
that Miss Fisher might be found gracious to his
advances. No; he could not deny even to himself
that Barbara had kept him kindly at arm's length,
and had made fun of every nearer approach.

But—was there not something more then friend-
liness in taking that liberty with him? To joke
and to quiz him was an act of familiarity, and as
such he had found it pleasant; and he was pretty

sure that she meant it to be nothing else. Was he
to be such a lily-livered lout as to baulk the lady's
humour, and his own heart's one wish? The prize
was held out to him, and he would fight for it; he
had the will; he saw the way. The Church was
his vocation; he ought to have perceived it before;
never mind, he saw it now. And yet, and yet,
something told him that this was not the time to
turn. Why not? He would enter for the prize,
any way; and win if he could.

After going through this 'soul-searching,' as he
called it, time after time, with intervals of furious
raving, and always coming to the same stout and
disinterested conclusion, Dick's mind, exhausted by
the incessant strain of repeated debate and hourly
agitation, sank for a while into a state of contented
and confused repose. He had conceived an idea in
a puzzled period of anxious pain; he nursed it fondly,
and took greedily what comfort it gave. Though
conscience would stir uneasily now and then, he
managed to put her to sleep again always by the
same process. And his project, once formed, offered
a new object of exertion to a young life that, barring
this love affair, was beginning to pass too easily and
too tamely, and to pay the penalty in rust and *ennui*.
Here was an adventure that promised activity and
excitement. His mind was made up—at least, he
thought so. Thus he hugged himself to rest for a
season, and shuddered as he thought of the distracting pain out of which he had just fought his
way.

'Why not?' said he once more, as, dressing one

morning after a sleepless night—for his rest was only comparative, and was disturbed by many relapses—he received an invitation to spend a few days at Finchdale. 'It is a plain providence,' said he, 'which will just give me the opportunity I want. Why not ?'

He looked at himself in the glass with unusual attention, and, though generally well satisfied with what he saw there, he was startled to remark how little mental anxiety and a disturbed heart had done to improve either the complexion or the expression of his face.

'If this suspense is not soon over, it will soon be all over with me ; I shall be an old man,' said he, ' in no time. I see now why people bother me by asking whether there is not something the matter with me. But I flatter myself that, with such a load on my mind, I fight a good battle with appearances, and keep my manners in tolerable order, all things considered. I could not do it long, though. I must have it settled one way or other—do or die.'

CHAPTER II.

'Yes, I can be angry
Without this rupture : there is not in nature
A thing that makes a man so deformed, so beastly,
As doth intemperate anger.'
WEBSTER—*Duchess of Malfi.*

MARTEL had strolled with Mr. Palmer before breakfast to pay a visit of inspection to the stables. As they returned to the house, their path lay by the side of a box hedge that on the farther side spread within three or four feet of the aviaries, wherein golden and silver pheasants, and whole flights of canaries and doves, belonging to Miss Barbara, were kept. As the pair passed this spot, Martel, whose ears were sharp, heard plainly these words coming from the neighbourhood of the aviaries:

'Don't! you are quite mistaken. There! I hear some one coming; you'll make yourself ridiculous. How foolish you are! Go! go!'

These, especially the latter, words were said with energy—not exactly in anger, rather in a tone of good-humoured vexation; and the voice was the voice of Barbara. Who her friend was Martel could not see, not being of stature high enough to look over the hedge. Mr. Palmer, higher by the head, could see over it perfectly. Whether he looked or not, or whether he heard the words, Martel, who could not help glancing at his face, was not able to guess; he was looking straight before him with his usual calm expression of countenance.

Toward the end of breakfast, Martel heard him say quietly to Gryffyn, who sat near:

'I have ordered your dog-cart to be at the door at half-past eleven; that will give you time to get your traps together.'

'Thank you,' said Gryffyn; and Martel, who had not known that he was going, looked at him with some surprise.

The young man was intent on his plate, but Martel fancied that his ears turned red. When, however, the lad looked up, his face wore the bright look that till lately had been habitual to it; and as Dick had said nothing to him about his movements, his friend made no remark, but at the time named went to the hall-door to see him off. While he was examining something fanciful in Dick's smart harness, he could not help hearing Mr. Palmer say in his tranquil tone, as he shook hands with his departing guest:

'Good-bye, Gryffyn; I am sorry we shall not see you here again.'

No one else was near, but Dick, perceiving that he had heard the farewell, though a shade paler than usual, looked towards his old friend, slightly raised his eyebrows, and effected the most delicate of winks, and so drove off, carrying with him

his secret, whatever it was; but perhaps Martel
guessed it.

One glance Dick stole at an upper window, and
spied there a pale face, peeping at him from behind
the blind.

'A niceish nag, that of Gryffyn's,' said Palmer
to Martel, as they turned into the house.

'He is—*gone*, Barbara!' cried Kitty Fisher to her
cousin, as they sat stitching.

'Yes, indeed, Kitty dear.'

'What for ?'

'I am sure I don't know.'

'I thought he was to stay over Friday ?'

'So he was, dear.'

'Oh! Barbara, you know all about it, I am sure;
you are the cause of his going.'

'I am sorry he is going; but neither he nor
papa have said a word to me on the subject.'

'But it is all about you, though; you are the
cause, and you know it, Barbara. You have driven
him away, and you know you have; it is very cruel
of you;' and Kitty wept sore.

'Indeed, dearest, you are very unjust. I have
done all I could do, and more than I ought to have
done, to bring him here, and to keep him here; and
you know why, too, only you feel hurt just now,
and angry with poor me, your best friend, darling.'

'Oh, it is easy to preach patience; but——'

'Patience, dearest, is not a lady's virtue; don't
I know it full well ? But, darling, we must try to
practice it a little.'

'A little! Oh, it is so hard.'

'Yes, dear love, it is hard,' said the consoler, coming over to the weeper's side and kneeling by her, and patting and kissing her; 'we shall make it all right yet,' she said.

'No, no, no; it is all you he cares for: he does not care for me a bit; he hates me. Oh! oh! oh!' Sob, sob, sob. 'He will never, never, never, come back.'

'It is all cross purposes; is not it, dear? But cheer up, Kitty darling; never mind this, dearest: I told you you had my vote and interest: *it is one of my four wishes;* and you will see it will come right yet. The storm, if there be one, will blow over.'

'Storm! He will go and drown himself about you, who don't care one bit for him, that is what he will do,' said poor Kitty passionately, in a voice full of tears, and with streaming eyes.

'No, dear; he will not drown himself for me. He will keep himself for you: that will be much better.' And she sang cheerily:

> ' "Willie Foster's gone to sea,
> Siller buckles at his knee;
> When he comes he will marry me,
> Canny Willie Foster." '

And Kitty cried, and Barbara sang, and cheered, and pitied, and petted, and caressed, and coaxed, and at last comforted her. The forlorn maiden's tears did their work, and lightened her tender heart. And she began to tell Barbara that she had hope, and told her reasons with her poor head on her cousin's soft shoulder.

' Dearest, do you remember the day that he escorted me out hunting ?'

' Yes, darling, I remember very well, *he*—that unfortunate *he*—did.'

' Ah! but you never knew how carefully and beautifully he saved me from being run away with among all those horrid hunting-men.'

' Indeed, Kit; I did not think that old " Rockingham " had any runaway blood left in him, though he is a dear old beauty.'

Kitty did not stop to verify her perils, but went on with her panegyric.

' And when we got home he was so quick; he would lift me down himself, and how nicely he did it !'

' No doubt, dear.'

' Though, I hope, I am not awkward. And now, I must tell you—since he is gone and I shall never see him again'—(here Kitty sobbed a little)—'how— ugh! ugh! he—gave me—I am sure he did—the least bit in the world of a squeeze, as if he could not help it; but I am sure he did it on purpose.'

' Ah! how well you remember it all !' quoth her comforter.

' I remember he ate very little—nothing indeed— that day at dinner.'

' Not likely, dear.'

' Perhaps because he spent his time in stealing looks—I am almost ashamed to say it—at me.'

' Of course he did, darling,' cried the other earnestly, but not quite honestly.

' And I remember, as we rode, he said a woman

could never be handsome in his eyes, who was not good-tempered and feminine : I hope my temper is not intolerable.'

' The very sweetest temper in the world, my sweet pet,' whispered the consoler, pinching her subject softly.

' And that I am not very manly.'

' Indeed, dearest, there is not much of the man about you; it is the manly element you want, my dear, is it not ?'

' And he told me that he did not admire a very fair beauty ; he prefers a brunette.'

' That meant you, of course, darling,' said the comforter, who was a brunette of the brightest order.

Kitty, who was in her own way a very pretty girl, though dark too, was rather sallow, not to say yellowish ; her strong points were eyes and expression.'

'Dearest Kit !' said the other, 'how well you remember everything ! I did not think you were so far gone, or that our little Dicky was such a lady-killer.'

' I am not cold, like you, dear ; I cannot say that I have any aversion to the little Dicky—as *you* call him. He is not, to be sure, a grandee, or a count ; but he looks as much like a gentleman as any of our acquaintances now, does not he, dear ? and has as nice manners, and as cultivated a mind, and as refined sentiments.'

' To be sure, dear, all that; why not ? how well you express it !' spoke the consoler.

'You know how well he acted,' whimpered the
disconsolate. 'He astonished them all at Row'n-
shaw; did he not, dear?'

'Indeed he is a very nice little Dicky,' replied the
comforter.

'And not at all forward.'

Here a ripple passed over the consoler's face,
which happily escaped the eyes of the consoled.

'And how good he was to his father! every one
says so.'

'Yes, dear, and I am sure he will make a very
good husband some day: don't you think so,
dearest? that is, when he gets the wife to suit him,
Kitty dear.'

Kitty sighed, and went on with her estimate.

'And he has such a spirit! and rides so well!
they all say so; so brave! and so charitable too, all
the poor people about love him, I am told: and then
to send him away! and bid him come no more! I
know uncle did. Oh! it was *cruel*. What will
become of me?' and Kitty lifted up her voice and
wept again bitterly in her cousin's arms.

Barbara may have had her own reasons for
doubting some of poor Kitty conclusions; but, if so,
she kept her doubts to her self; and, telling Kitty
that Fulmere was not so very far from Finchdale,
succeeded in drying the tears of the little Fisher,
who was of a hasty and hopeful turn—in affairs of
the heart the affairs in which she most concerned
herself.

CHAPTER III.

'He loved Trulla, Trulla more bright,
Than burnished armour of her knight;
A bold virago, stout and tall,
As Joan of France, or English Mall.'

Hudibras.

'EVEN as one heat another heat expels,' and blisters remove inflammation; or as one nail drives out another by taking its place,—even so is it with love. Richard Gryffyn, smarting from its burn, seeks his relief in a new flame: and, having received Martel back into confidence, insisted on his going with him to see the wonder.

In the usual business way they went to dine with the lady's brother, a large, handsome, common-looking solicitor, in a large but equivocal sort of practice; ringed and pinned, and gaudily dressed. He had been sent to, rather than educated at, a great public school; but attracted by a natural affinity to its worst set, had carried away little beside knowingness, flunkeyism, and fast slang. Having an easy conscience, and a very brazen front; at political county dinners he was in his element seated himself as near as he could to the highest

20—2

places; made himself conspicuous by bustle, and put himself forward to do questionable work, if any were required by great people for party purposes; said things that no one else would say, did things that no one else would do.   His wife was his match, large, handsome, bold-faced, over-dressed, and under-bred.   A party was made up for the dinner.

There was an elderly cousin, a Captain Sharkie, who had once been lieutenant or midshipman in the navy, and was now a 'guinea-pig;' and found further occupation and profit by buying, and letting, worn-out and pestiferous tenements in popular places to visitors in a hurry to be housed.   This occupation afforded scope for his genius and constant interest to his mind, and, considering the expenditure,—amazing profit to his pocket.   Nobody indeed would take a house of his twice, or stay in it a year; but by assiduous practice, a nice knowledge of law, and the giving of his whole heart to the work, he had learnt so many tricks and shifts, that he managed one way or other to make each outgoing tenant pay double the rent he had contracted for.   He worked as partner in confederacy with other congenial spirits, who played into his hands with exceeding lubricity, by withholding their consent at the last moment, and then exacting fresh terms, and all sorts of insidious rules about notices to quit and so forth.   He was altogether a smart man with a great deal of experience, and his conversation was much relished —by his friends.

There was also a doctor, who never had a fair

trial in his profession, or he might have thriven, as others do, at the expense of his patients : but those who knew him best kept clear of him, thinking that he might kill more than he could cure; and the public, wary for once, seeing the general disaffection of his friends, took the alarm, and declined to become the subjects of his experiments. Wherefore since he could not operate upon men's persons by relieving their livers;—like a man of resource he took to operating more directly upon their purses ; and following the example of, and joining wits with, his successful friend, co-operated with him in letting unhealthy houses to the itinerant tribe who frequent the seats of idleness that they call pleasure. In this department he proved himself a very sharp practitioner, and bled his patients freely. His manner was pompous and plausible, and his society much valued by the set he lived in ; but outsiders who once had dealings with him, never wished to repeat them.

The captain was conspicuous in a splendid wig, his lady in a fine false front ; a false and dangerous pair, but reckoned 'very genteel' in the world which they called theirs.

The rest of the company was made up of an old hard-riding squireen, who aimed at wit, and bawled and blustered about hounds and horses ; told to a pint how much port wine he drank daily, and what he ate, and showed his old fangs from ear to ear to prove that he had not lost one. He was a bachelor, and a distant kinsman of the host, to whom he hung out residuary hopes, and received in return convenient attentions.

Then there was a squire. There are now, as there
have ever been, squires of two sorts—your Westerns
and Lumpkins, your Allworthys and Coverleys.
Our squire was of the Western tribe, many-acred,
little-cultured, and mannerless, who, not finding acceptance in his proper orbit, for which his habits
unfitted him, was welcomed into a lower sphere,
where he could play the great man. He spoke not
much, but would nod his head sideways, and wink,
and make with his tongue a clicking noise, that in
his adopted circle passed for wit, as he said ' Yes,
sir,' and ' No, sir,' at every sentence : not quite a bad
fellow, but very far from a good one.

There was, beside, a manufacturer, a bachelor, who
had a good stud of horses, and was a sensible and
good-natured man. Then a retired something from
India or the colonies, whose comical but most English ambition now was to get a footing in very alien
'*county society*,' and who, being a keen fellow enough,
seemed to be in doubt whether, in this sharp set, he
was not losing his way. He used clerical meetings
where bishops presided as a round in the social
ladder, and in his little speeches would inform the
clergy that he not only took interest in matters
ecclesiastical, but was also a sportsman, and kept
dogs and horses, as savouring of ' The County.'

These, with a Mr. Barleycorn, and one other who
had not yet made his appearance, were the gentlemen of the party.

The sisterhood of the house were of a piece with
their brother and his wife—tall, showy, coarse-fea-
tured, overgrown, and over-dressed women, distin-

guished by the names Beatrice Eugenia, Adeliza
Honoria, Georgina Josephine, and Rosamond Flora.
They played the very newest music, and sang the
very newest songs, and talked about horses and
lords and ladies; were excited about the balls and
entertainments of the high aristocracy, and were
altogether people of fashion.

Dicky's friend soon discovered, by the unreserved
behaviour of the rest of the family, that the chosen
was Rosamond Flora, the tallest of the sisters, and
the most Romanesque in feature. Some scraps of
her conversation reached Martel.

Had Dicky seen Lady Audrey Touchstone ? Was
not she exquisitely lovely ? So aristocratic ! so refined ! 'Mrs. Begum Martyn gives a ball to-morrow
night. The Bohuns, the Plantagenets, the Staffords,
the Brummagem Browns, the Lancasters, Yorks, and
Nevilles, are all to be there. Won't it be beautiful ?
There will be Lady Griselda de Guise flirting away
as usual, I suppose, with Lord Howard de Mont-
morency. Would not you like to be there ? The
Harold Robinsons are going, so are the Tallboys
Joneses. Won't it be nice ?'

'Are you going ?' asked the gentleman.

'Ah! no; we are engaged to the Randal Hark-
aways,' replied the lady evasively ; for she had not
been asked, nor was likely to be, inasmuch as
she had no acquaintance whatever with the ball-
givers or their party beyond an accurate knowledge
of their names, the Harold Robinsons and the Tallboys Joneses excepted : with them, indeed, she had
a dubious bowing acquaintance, how brought about

it is hard to say, but the result of much nice management.

The entertainment was really handsome, and would cost about twice as much as the best that the Palmers, or the Finch Adamses, or Lawrences would think of giving to any one. It spoke of money, and the gentlemen of the company talked of money and money's worth, mingled with a little electioneering business that pointed the same way. But if the company was rather short of ideas, the table flowed with wine; there were as many sorts as would have done honour to a wine merchant's stores. It was evidently meant to be the crowning glory of the entertainment, and it furnished much of the conversation—its fabulous qualities! and its fabulous prices!

'Where did you get this? What did you give?'

'Try this; it is drier; bottled in the year '98. A wonderful bargain. Very rare—in fact, only seen on royal tables, I assure you, between ourselves. The greatest luck in the world; you'll hardly believe it.'

Then the current turned to tailors.

'Try my breeches-maker—an infallible fit. I asked my tailor—Bryan Price, you know—whether he could undertake to fit me with breeches. "I dare say I could," said he, "but I always get my own from Pumperkell." Capital, was it not? So I went to Pumperkell, and he is simply perfection.'

'What do you think I gave for this coat? A new man, the best in London now, out and out— beats Bryan Price into fits.'

'You don't say so ?'

'I like Price's cut better than his, if THAT's his work.'

'H'm ! I know Lord Pinkeen employs him, and he's the best-dressed man in England, you know. He brought him over from Germany, and set him up. Lord Lyonville employs no one else now.'

'Awhr!' began Mr. Barleycorn, a rich young brewer of the first generation of profitable vats—'awhr ! Lyonville told me, when we were "out" the other day at Hoseby Gorse, that he would give Foxborough £10,000 or £15,000 a year if he would pass his examination. I—awhr !—told Foxborough that he was a —— fool not to go and pass. Awhr, erwh ! *whawt* more could a man want than £15,000 a year and the Life Guards ?' asked young prosperity.

'Don't Foxborough drink ?' asked some one.

'Awhr, erwh ! nothing but champagne.'

'Aye, but of a morning—at and after breakfast ? No man can stand that—certainly no one of nineteen years of age.'

'Awhr, erwh ! it can't do any harm. It is the very best that can be had for money; he don't care what he gives.'

'Nor how much he drinks, by all accounts.'

'Awhr, erwh ! he is not always drinking; he smokes a good deal.'

'That does not make it much better, my boy.'

'Awhr, erwh ! nothing but cigars, you know, at half a crown a piece—the best tobacco that can be had for money; he doesn't mind what he gives.'

' He must have a nice champagne and cigar bill !'

' Awhr, erwh ! money's nothing to him; he'll
have £365,000 a year. He ought to be happy,
oughtn't he ? What more could a man waunt ?'

'H'm ! he would want my new horse if he saw
him. Magnificent ! could jump a town !'

' Awhr, erwh ! Foxborough ought to see him ; I'll
tell him. Dare say he'll buy him if he is as good as
you say.'

' Or half,' put in another.

Horses, wines, clothes, and noblemen—our curate
gained a good deal of light upon these topics, and a
certain acidity of stomach ; but on the whole he was
satisfied. Naturally inquisitive, he had contracted
something of a bad habit of regarding men in the
light of curiosities; and he was especially interested
in the remarks of this flourishing Mr. Barleycorn, as
speaking the sentiments of the rising generation.
He was evidently regarded by the elders, too, as a
sensible and promising young man. When it is
said that he was decidedly good-looking, it is needless to tell how he was treated by the ladies of the
party.

The gentleman who was missing in the fore part
of the evening turned out to be Martel's recent acquaintance, Mr. de Coucy, who accosted him with
unexpected affability, talked of the little dinner at
which they had met—' Not this sort of thing, you
know '—laughed at their quaint host and his original
ménage, and, in short, made himself very agreeable
to one who, though amused, felt rather as a fish out
of water, devoting to him those portions of the even-

ing in which his attendance was not claimed by the
ladies.   They, indeed, appeared fully to appreciate
Mr. de Coucy's uncommonly handsome face and
figure, and very fashionable air.

'Is Bounceable your lawyer?' asked the squire of
the colonial, as they quitted the house together for
the inn, where they had chosen to leave their
carriages.

'No; is he yours?'

'No! sir; thank you, sir,' rejoined the squire,
shaking his head from side to side, winking and
clucking. 'No! sir; thank you, sir. I should have
to pay in my bill, sir, for all that champagne, sir;
and claret, sir; and all the other wines. I like to
drink them, sir; but don't like to pay for them,
sir. I employ no lawyer that swims you in champagne, sir; not if I know it.'

'I suppose it pays?' said the other. 'Draws
business from the foolish, fast young men, whom he
helps to get rid of their money.'

'And they may take his sisters in exchange, eh,
sir?' said the squire, and he winked, and nodded,
and clicked again.

'That was a son of old Gryffyn, wasn't he; that
fair-haired man?'

'Yes, I s'pose he's booked for one, sir.'

'If that sly parson fellow he brought with him
does not put him off it. I don't think he's safe yet;
and I do not think our friends were half pleased at
the other being there to spoil sport, eh? Who is he?
I see him with the Palmer set; wears black boots,
and rides a cob. Not very wealthy, I take it.'

'Not the sort of catch the Bounceable girls are looking out for, eh, sir? Poor curate; not a shilling, sir.'

'That other smart parson is more in their line; quite at home, too.'

'Staying in the house, sir,' said the squire, with a wink; 'getting tamed, sir.' Nod, wink, click.

This conversation, with cigars, beguiled the walk to the inn, where they had chosen to leave their carriages, for the sake of a glass of brandy and soda-water at the bar, to be tendered by a very elegant and affable barmaid.

'Well, what do you think of her?' asked at last of his companion the departing lover, as they were on their way home, in a very silent drive.

'She reminds me of the "Paradise Lost,"' was the reply.

'It's Eve, you mean,' smirked the lover, pleased.

'No; it's length. Who was the critic that said, "If length did not recommend it, nothing else would"?'

'Umph!'

'Now let me ask, in turn, What did you think of your company? Should you like that sort of thing every day, and all day, for the rest of your natural life? I dare say it would suit very well that handsome Brummagem dandy with the fine name De Coucy; but I will pay you the compliment to think you would like something very different.'

Poor Dicky groaned.

The upshot of it all was what the sharp colonial had surmised: Gryffyn, whom restlessness, anger, and an open door had tempted in, was seen there no more ; and the world of that clique said that he was a shabby upstart, who had made up to Miss Palmer for her fortune—it could be for nothing else —and had been very properly kicked out of her father's house. The Misses Cadoyer Bounceable were not going to take her leavings, not they, indeed —stuck-up minx ! What a scandal—that old Palmer should have sacked such a fortune out of the Church ? And as for that shabby, meddling Martel, what was he but a beggarly curate, who did not get as much wage as the Bounceables gave their footman.

So ended this little amatory episode in the life of Mr. Richard Gryffyn.

CHAPTER IV.

'But I, I darken my chamber;
  Black cloth o'er the casement I lay:
Some ghosts, who my being remember,
  Come to pay me a visit to-day.

'My old prime passion returneth,
  From Hades it comes forlorn;
It sits by my side and mourneth,
  And maketh my own heart mourn.'
HEINRICH HEINE, *by* JULIAN FANE.

BY reason of his youth and inexperience, Richard
Gryffyn was not yet duly installed in his father's
place as agent to the whole of Lord Mercia's wide
estates; but a part of the agency had been offered
to and accepted by him, on the understanding that,
when two or three more years had passed over his
head, the whole should be put into his hands. The
business arising from this quarter and from his own
farm gave to a novice plenty to think of, and was
doing much to divert his mind from painful contemplation of his unhappy attachment: and the
sanguine temper of youth was regaining its elasticity,
and already beginning to form schemes for some
distant future; but as yet, in his castles of air, the
presiding genius was still the lady he had lost.

One day, he had put up his horse at the inn of a small town, while he went about the business of his agency. On his return to the inn, as he was entering, a mail phaeton handsomely appointed, and grandly horsed with a pair of high-stepping power-ful brown cobs, and adorned with a cockaded groom and a very fine gentleman out of livery, rattled out of the old low-browed archway. Dick's eye was so taken by the horses that he had barely time to glance at the driver, who to that glance seemed to be a military man.

'Who was that?' asked Dick of the landlady standing at the door, having just dropped her curtsey.

'That, Mr. Gryffyn,' she replied, in lowered and solemn tones, is a gent as is going to Finchdale sir, a capting in the Landseers; a very rich gentleman as I am informed. I wouldn't go for to repeat it to everybody, sir; but I may tell you, Mr. Gryffyn, that his gentleman, who is quite a gentle-man and very haffable, did tell me that the capting is a-going on a very tender herrand, sir;—to see Miss Palmer,' she whispered, smirking and nodding; 'who is,—I dare say you may have seen her, sir,—a very beautiful young lady; and will be very rich, as I know. His gentleman tells me, as he believes that the capting is a sort o' cousin to her on the side of the late Mrs. Palmer; whose wish was that they should marry. And what could they do better, sir? He is a noble-looking gentleman as ever I see, and rich too: and she is as rich as she is beautiful, with ten thousand charms, which you gentlemen

seem to think as much of as of pretty faces; don't
you, sir?' And she shook her by no means ill-
looking ringleted head in a way sufficiently attrac-
tive, and proceeded for her hearer's delectation : ' A
very high gentleman, sir, is the capting, and
himmensely rich, as I am informed. To be sure,
money do seem to go to money somehow, don't it,
sir? Though I think it don't ought to : for them as
hav'n't got it, wants it most; don't they, sir? But
you don't want money, sir: you are one of the
warm ones. You'll excuse me, a-running on so.
But oh! good Lor'! what *is* the matter with you?'

Dick, unnoticed by the good-humoured, voluble
landlady, had during this harangue been turning
paler and paler; and was now trembling so violently, that but for leaning against the door, it
seemed he would have fallen.

The landlady, alarmed, flew to her favourite bottle,
and returned with a strong glass of very hot brandy
and water; which, hot as it was, Dick swallowed at
a gulp.

He had been subject to fainting fits, he said, as
he recovered himself; he had foolishly left home in
a hurry without his breakfast:—and that, he supposed, had brought on his besetting ailment : he felt
better now, and would go home.

So saying he turned away, and went to the stable
for his nag.

The ostler as he led the mare out remarked, ' that
the capting as has just druv away had been looking
at her, and asking whose she wor: he said he had
never seen a better sort for a little un. But little

uns is no good to him; he's a main heavy weight, is the capting; and a hout-an'-houter to ride; leastaways so his grum telled me: for I never seed un before, not as I know on. But his man—to be sure he does run on and drink gin uncommon; an' he does tell me they have got some of the best cattle in hall Hingland. The capting he never stands for price, not he: neither three 'undred nur four 'undred will stop him: an' now he's gone an' guv *five* hundred for a Hirish nag as 'll carry twenty stun, an jump the wall of a gaol—wi' it on 'is back. He bought un in Hireland just afore he come over;—an' they calls un 'Fan-me-cool,' or some such rummy name: an' the grum says as the man, as 'll foller the capting on that 'oss over stone walls had better hensure his neck. The capting is agoin' to 'unt 'ere this winter: you'll see the nag, no doubt; he's a roan 'oss, an a big un. They do say the capting's come to be married; but I only knows, as he axed me—how fur it wur to Finchdale.'

'Ah me!' groaned poor Dick in spirit; 'everybody knows all about it!' and doubling the ostler's fee in the softness of his heart he swung into the saddle, and rode home as fast as he could—to bury himself in the brown solitude of the old house at Fulmere.

His friend Martel lived there no longer, and had no settled abode, but roamed about the district, taking occasional duty here and there, as chance and the needs of the clergy called him.

On the day we have been speaking of, he happened

to be dining at Finchdale. A party had just sat down, leaving one place vacant on his side the table.

'Who is that with whom I have seen you riding several times lately?' asked the host of Martel, in the course of dinner, referring to a college friend of Martel, who had been staying for a while in the neighbourhood.

'Do you mean a great, long, red-headed man?' replied Martel, describing too accurately his friend.

He had no sooner uttered the unflattering words, than he saw his opposite neighbour, who was gifted with immense goggle eyes, opening them upon him to their full extent. Something was wrong with him, what could it be? He looked to Miss Palmer, who seemed to be smothering a smile; he was turning to his host, apparently in the same predicament, when, in the place by his side, that had been vacant, he espied, not indeed his too truly described friend, but a gentleman who answered exactly to his description : long and red-headed, and obtrusively large altogether. No wonder those eyes, like saucers, were turned upon Martel in mute amazement.

Our friend saw his slip, there was no place for explanation ; so with as unconscious a face as he could muster, he proceeded to tell Mr. Palmer who the friend was ; and before long he contrived to take a survey of the gentleman whom he had unwittingly depicted in such rude colours.

He was indeed 'great and long and red-headed,' but a very handsome man notwithstanding. His notable hair, of that deep, rich colour which, though some vainly call it auburn, few can refuse to admire, was cut short, and curled thick and crisp and close to his head, like the front of a red Devon bull. His eyes, full and blue, sparkled with fire, and his complexion was fair and ruddy. The features of his face were blunt-aquiline in outline, bold and regular; and his aspect betokened, if not intelligence, at least decision and nerve. The round, solid head was firmly set upon a bull-neck, and that again on broad shoulders, which were rather high, making his stature, which was an inch or so over six feet, seem greater than it was. Florid, big, brawny, and bull-fronted, if his shoulders had not been too high, and if his knees had not knocked inward, as was seen when he stood up, he would have been a grand model of a large man. Even as it was, he presented a very imposing figure, with, it may be, a little too much of the animal about it, and open, perhaps, to the prize-fighter's criticism on such conformations, as 'showy, but wanting stamina.' In short, he reproduced very closely the ancient German of Tacitus's drawing, with the 'stern blue eyes and red hair; large and robust, but powerful only in sudden efforts; hardly fit for wear and tear, and impatient of long toil.'

This rather striking person, with the detail of whose appearance Martel soon became better acquainted, after a considerate interval asked him, in the fashion of those days, to take wine, as it were in token of amity. He seemed quite at home, whoever he was. But his name Martel could not catch, till Miss Palmer found an opportunity to introduce him

21—2

as 'My cousin Captain Gibbons,' in saying which
she smiled slyly ; and Captain Gibbons pleasantly
tendered his hand, which the other received with
the like amused expression.

'Who is Captain Gibbons ?' asked Martel of Miss
Fisher in the course of the evening.

'Don't you know ?'

And then she told more fully and clearly the
story which had startled the ear and wounded the
heart of poor Dicky, when told by the landlady at
the inn.   For this was the veritable captain, pro-
prietor of Fin-ma-coul, and nephew of the late Mrs.
Palmer, who had wished for a marriage of the
cousins, and had in a manner, as it was considered,
betrothed them in her last illness, or, at least, had
expressed her wish definitely upon her death-bed.

'That,' said Miss Fisher, 'is the story ; but to me
it is only a rumour, for you know how impossible it
is to get Uncle Palmer or Barbara to talk upon any
subject where their feelings are deeply concerned.'

'Now,' thought the hearer, 'the murder is out.'

Often had he wondered why Barbara had no
serious flirtations, since he had reasons of his own
for suspecting that the goddess would have looked
with amaze upon any one, of the many that approached her shrine with incense, who could seriously have withstood the shock of her charms, had
she chosen to exert them against him.   But she had
been so cool and collected and impartially gracious,
and her stately father had shown so little encourage-
ment to young men, that our friend had suspected
there must be a secret.   It had surprised him at

the time, but now he understood what the father had said to him lately about his 'wish to see her married.'

So this giant Rufus of a captain was the happy man! Well, well! he was, to be sure, a handsome, fine fellow; but did he look like the man of her choice? Wonders would never cease! Who could have imagined it?

And being of a sceptical turn, he was not quite sure of it now: he had his doubts. Some of his reflections he kept to himself; others he expressed to Miss Fisher, who seemed, for some reason or other, inclined to make him her confidant.

'Oh, it was cruel,' she said, 'this concealment! Poor Mr. Gryffyn ought to have been told, if nobody else.'

'Then why did not you tell him, Miss Fisher?'

'Because, Mr. Martel, I am not in the habit of offering my confidences to gentlemen in such circumstances. And, besides, Mr. Gryffyn would never have listened to me,' added the lady after a pause, and half-blushing under the eye which was fixed upon her with as much of fun as sympathy.

'But you have not tried him, Miss Fisher,' said her companion, still looking at her.

'No, I have not tried, Mr. Martel,' retorted the lady.

'Shall I tell him that you pity his case, Miss Fisher?'

'You may tell him just what you please, Mr. Martel,' rejoined she, and looked so pretty as she said it that the poor parson thought there were in

the world worse conditions than being pitied by
Miss Fisher; and being naturally frank, he told her
so, at which she laughed and said he was a great
quiz.

Meanwhile Barbara held on the even tenour of
her way, to all appearance as calm and demure as
usual. Captain Gibbons seemed to pay her no very
marked attention; indeed, he might have been
thought much more occupied with Colonel Denny,
who was also one of the party. Denny and Gibbons
were, through the Palmers, slightly connected, and
had served together at the Cape before the former
had exchanged into the Guards. In his short service there the colonel had done some brilliant things
against the Caffres, which contrasting with the softness of his tone and manners, and his varied accomplishments, had rendered him in the eyes of Gibbons,
who had no accomplishments and very little softness,
quite a modern Sir Philip Sidney. Perhaps the removal of Captain Denny very young from his troop
in the dragoon regiment to London and the Guards,
with a seat in Parliament, did something to strengthen
his admirer's attachment. And then he had travelled
in Egypt and in the Holy Land, and altogether was
a knight of the old crusading sort in the eyes of the
red captain, a dragoon of the bluff, frank, unpretending sort, more addicted to bodily than to mental
activity, and to sporting than to more refined pleasures, but liberally open to admire in others virtues
of which he was destitute himself, and perhaps even
rating those virtues the higher because he had them
not. For the rest, he was choleric, and, when cho-

leric, rough and unfeeling, and apt to do things of which he afterwards repented. Brave as a lion, he was, like most brave men, generous—at least, when he was cool. Martel had opportunity of noting some of his points, for he stayed at Finchdale till the party broke up.

CHAPTER V.

'Away with him, away with him ! he speaks Latin.'
Henry VI.

' The People, ever rigid in exacting eminent virtue from their teachers, would be rude, but effective zealots of a ghostly discipline, from which they were themselves to be exempt.' —SIR JAMES STEPHEN.

' The Laity were thrown into the position, if not of judges of the priesthood, at least of punishers of its irregularities ; and such an invitation was of course readily and generally attended to. The occasion seemed to the selfish, the irreverent, and the profane, to legalise the gratification of all the bad feelings with which persons of those dispositions must *ever* regard the Church and her ministry.'—J. W. BOWDEN—*Life of Gregory VII.*

MISS PALMER was going on a visit; and her father would have been left alone, had he not persuaded Martel, homeless and houseless, to keep him company a few days longer. The rector was riding off one morning in a. hurry to the Bench, whither he was called by sudden and urgent business, when he stopped his horse to say to Martel that a visitor would arrive that morning—a refugee Hungarian baron—who was coming to him from his cousin, Brandon Palmer.

' You see, I cannot be here to receive him; so

please entertain him for me till I get back. You talk French ?'

'I can read it; but not a word can I speak. My father would not allow me to be taught it: he wanted me to forget France, and make England my home.'

'Right too; I remember. But it is awkward, just now, for the baron cannot understand a word of English.'

'Then, begging the baron's pardon for the comparison, I should be like an English ploughman I saw t'other day driving a French horse : he knew no French, and the horse knew no English; so the man Gee-whoa'd, and Com-o-the-whoop'd to no purpose. The horse refused to hear the voice of the charmer; however, the ploughman was a good-humoured, patient lad, and did not ply the whip much; but made himself understood as well as he could. His case would be just mine.'

'Well, I'll tell you what to do : whip up the baron with Latin. All the Hungarians speak Latin, I believe; so do the poor Paddies of Cork. Latin is the language of civilised Europe, ancient and modern. Yes, yes; Latin is the language of civilisation, and so we call it a dead language : the Hungarians and the Irish know better. Give it the baron in Latin ; you will find him answer to the whip.'

'But I do not talk Latin, as you know.'

'Having been at Eton and Trinity—why, wouldn't I know ? Never mind, show the way like a good sportsman ; there must be a beginning to all things. It will be capital fun, like fox-hunting ; go at your fence like a man, and you'll get over somehow.

Never fear; it will all come right. I need not say,
show the baron every attention that the limits of
your language will allow of. I wish you well
through it. Good-bye. I fear I shall be late now!'
and off he rode.

Not long after, the door of the drawing-room was
opened, and 'The baron' was announced. A small,
dignified, elderly man entered bowing. The curate
salaamed in turn. There was a pause.

'Parlez-vous Français, monsieur ?' said the
baron.

'Ah ! non,' said the curate, shaking his head.

They looked perplexed.

Martel remembered Palmer's hint, and stammered
out some shambling Latin, for which he would have
been flogged at school.

The baron, quick as lightning, replied, in a sentence
yet more execrable. Grammar there was none, nor
any inconvenient consciousness that it was needed.
But his fluency was marvellous, his *copia verborum*
inexhaustible; he poured out his words in a torrent,
all free and unshackled by number, gender, case, or
person.

In the fetters of grammar poor Martel hobbled,
and shuffled, and stumbled, and made many a lapse,
that at school would have cost his carcase dearly.
Their pronunciation, too, differed *in toto*—the baron's
continental, the curate's insular.

Here is a specimen of their uneven colloquy. The
Briton used the word 'Omnino.'

'O-o-h-m—n-e-e—n-o-o !' repeated the continental. 'O-o-h-m—n-e-e—ahh !'

'Omnēno,' returned the insular, sticking to his word, but yielding the pronunciation.

'Oohm—nee—ahh!' reiterated the unpropitiated baron, who altogether repudiated the word omnino.

'Om-ne-no!' persisted the curate, adding confidently, 'Cicero sic scripsit.'

'Cee-sar-ohh haud seec screepseet; Arhn-glee-c-arhnus seec deexeet! Monsieur l'Abbé,' retorted the baron.

'Je suis un pauvre curé,' put in the curate boldly, employing his scanty French to misrepresent his office.

'Ah! vous ête un abbé de Sainte Espérance—de Sainte Elpide; eh, monsieur?'

And so they went on mangling French and Latin, and laughing, and disputing through the whole day, which passed most agreeably, as they both declared. And Martel, who loved the excitement of novelty and was not averse to a difficulty, would ever after maintain that the day he spent with the Hungarian baron, without French or English, and one other that he spent with a deaf and dumb man, with only pencil and paper for their medium, were the two pleasantest days of his life. For the baron was a man of spirit and ability, as he had made the Austrians to know, by stopping their army two whole days in a pass which he had occupied with a handful of men.

Riding slowly home after his visit, Martel was overtaken by a nonconforming magnate, railway director, and so forth, with whom he was on friendly terms.

'You have a new nag,' remarked his friend, eying
it as he came alongside.

'I have not bought it; I have it on trial.'

'It looks as if it would do for next season.'

'Hardly that. I fear my dear old cob is quite
worn out; if so I shall never hunt again.'

'Are you in earnest?'

'Sadly so.'

'I am sorry to hear it.'

'May I ask why? I thought you gentlemen of
the opposition begrudged us clergy our enjoyment
of the merry hounds and hunter's horn, and the freedom of the brown woods and green leas.'

'Far from it, Mr. Martel. I count it among the
good things that you independent gentlemen of the
Establishment do. The hunting-field I hold to be
a great and most beneficial national institution, pro-
moting hardy habits in the nation. I was struck
t'other day by some remarks of a brilliant Irish
scholar that exactly express my opinions on field
sports. They are, as he says, "vastly superior to
pure 'athletics' in their effect upon the mind. It
were well to reflect upon this nowadays, when
boat-racing, and running, and jumping and pulling
weights, are bidding fair to take the place of our
old fox-hunting, and shooting, and fishing. The
Greeks knew very well what we ignore, that *such
sports as require excessive bodily training and care
are low and debasing* in comparison to those which
are content with ordinary *strength* and *quickness* of
young men, but stimulate them to higher *mental*
exercise—daring and decision in danger, resource

and ingenuity in difficulties ;" not to speak of special
training as weakening also the body for general
purposes. Now those are just my ideas, and I have
no notion of a sensible man yielding them up to
people whose ethics and theology never soar above
the lowest flight of the conventional. And then,
again, fox-hunting has immense value in another
point of view. Nothing is like it or comes near it
for bringing constantly together every class of
society, and binding them together in common and
healthy enjoyment. I should consider its decline a
great public misfortune; and I regret to see men
like you, who are bound to behave yourselves properly and to be reputable, quit the field, and leave
it to slang sporting-men and the idle riff-raff, high
and low, through whom the most English, and the
best of all European, sports will get a bad name. I
am not a Churchman, but then I am not a sacer-
dotalist; and I am not, as you hint, in opposition.
I regard the Church of England as a *National*
Church, which, in my opinion, it would be no longer
if the clergy were to become a separate and exclusive caste, with a different code of morals, and
different recreations, from those which are considered
fit for the laity. It will never do for us to run with
the hare and hunt with the hounds—to object to a
sacerdotal caste, and yet make clergymen feel that
there is one code of morality for them and another
for laymen. So I do hope you are not in earnest
when you talk of yielding to such vulgar dogma-
tism. I thought you were made of different stuff.
You know you should be a teacher in the matter.

The struggle to live sets man against man; their amusements should call them together again. Don't you think so?'

'Yes, I think so; and I think hunting does that much more and much oftener than anything else. I never said I was going to give it up to please vulgar or popular opinion, for which I care as little as most men. Why, the little hunting I have had has been the saving of me. There am I, the only man in the parish who has anything like a liberal education, however I may have profited by it. It is not in my power to enter into the amusements of my parishioners, nor can they enter into mine, unless in out-of-door sports. I remember a wise old schoolmaster, by whose lessons I did not profit so much as I might have done, telling a rich farmer, whose son was at his school, that the lad was capable of the greatest things if sent to college. "But remember," said the master, "if he goes there, that education will put a bar between his mind and yours that can never be got over. It is for you to know this now, and to think before it is too late whether you are prepared to make the sacrifice." The father was willing, and the son was lost to him—mentally. Without comparing myself to that man of genius, I may apply his case to mine, and say that between my parishioners and me there is the educational bar, in all but field-sports. There they are my masters, to teach me humility, and I have to learn lessons in my turn. If I know myself, which probably I do not, I should not lightly give in to clamour, and allow field-sports to be violently taken from me. It is a personal matter if I give them up, as I suppose I shall, though perhaps not this year, if cobby can carry me a bit longer. When she cannot, I must take refuge in a town. Should I suffer myself to be utterly isolated in a country village, with nothing to think of but my ministerial position, I fear I shall become possessed by egotistic fantasies, from which I am now, as I hope, preserved by a larger commerce with all sorts and conditions of men.'

'I hope cobby will last many years,' said the Nonconformist, adding, as he paid his parting salute, 'I think your nag has cast a shoe.'

This evil surmise proved too true; and, to have the lost shoe replaced, the parson turned into the shop of a blacksmith, who set his apprentice to work, while he affably entered into conversation with his customer. It began with horse-shoes, passed on to hunters, and thence to hunting, which the blacksmith pronounced the best of amusements for every one but 'ministers of religion.' They ought to attend to their own business. His hearer did not dispute the law thus laid down, but went on talking till they came to the subject of drink, 'which,' the man of the forge said, 'Parliament had ought to put it down.'

'You can't make men sober by Act of Parliament,' objected the parson, 'any more than you can make men religious by Act of Parliament. If you would have people sober, persuade them to be religious.'

'A man should be religious or not, as he likes,'

replied Vulcan; 'no one should meddle with another about religion.'

'What! not a minister of religion?'

'No; mind his own business.'

It turned out, upon inquiry, that our blacksmith was an atheist.

CHAPTER VI.

'Where Corydon and Thyrsis, met,
Are at their savoury dinner set,
Of herbs and other country messes,
Which the neat-handed Phillis dresses.'
                    MILTON—*L'Allegro*.
'To keep game-cocks, to hunt the fox.'
                    Old Song.

A SALE of highbred cattle in the village, wherein
Martel was now lodged, has gathered to it many of
the neighbouring gentry and almost all the bench
of magistrates.   Martel is known to, and had been
the frequent guest of, most of them; he seized the
opportunity of offering to them, in turn, convenient
refreshment and entertainment, and his offer was
very generally accepted.   He was. not the man to
ape finery.   There is a good round of cold beef on
the table, and a great frying of eggs, and rich rashers
of bacon hiss and sputter within hearing; dishes of
hot potatoes smoke on the tablecloth, white as snow
and coarse as a sail; there are knives (not too many)
with black bone handles; and steel forks (two-
pronged) to eat eggs with.   What matter?   They
are the best the house affords, and the company are

all honourable men, and men of the world, who know
how to take things as they come, and to be thankful.
Very merry they were over the failures to carry
fried eggs to their mouths upon two-pronged forks.
Ale from the public-house, and whisky from the
curate's stock, which is small and choice, washed
the dainties down.   That whisky and good Mocha
coffee, which appeared in due time, made the luxuries
of his home life ; wine he never has any, and beer
he cannot endure, for he is no Anglo-Saxon, but a
true Celt.

Such as the cheer was, there was no lack of it,
nor of appetite to discuss it.   Cattle sales are very
provocative of hunger and thirst, and plates were
emptied and filled, and emptied again; glasses
clinked, tongues ran freely, and all went merry as a
marriage bell.   No champagne luncheon, with ' all
the delicacies of the season ' in a hamper from Fort-
num and Mason, was ever more relished or more
quickly despatched.   What nonsense all that pon-
derous conventional expense, that weighs down the
enjoyment of many an honest gentleman's family,
who ought to know better than to be led by men
who, proud to find themselves in a new position, are
all for teaching Society the art of living like a
gentleman.

As for our friends, they ate and they drank, they
talked and they laughed, and were as pleased as
though they had been feasted on venison and Tokay
by my lord marquis, or with Tom Muggins the
hosier had supped turtle soup out of self-made
Josiah Bounderby's celebrated basin of gold with
his famous gold spoon.

Amongst the company had come Mr. Palmer, in quest of an Alderney cow; and with him Colonel Denny, who, declining to be driven back by Mr. Palmer, proposed to see Martel's church, and then to walk back at his leisure.

'Beside,' said he, 'I want to see your famous cob, of which I have heard so much. Yours must be a lonely life,' he remarked when all the company were gone. 'You seem very happy, however; you have "*resources*," you see.'

'Yes, indeed. Mine are not "brandy and water and cigars," as the cornet's were in country quarters; but mine do as well. I have my parish and books, and my pets, to which let me introduce you, and act showman.'

As they left the house for the yard, our curate's landlady set on him, begging that he would 'talk over' her brother, who, as owner of the premises, was going to cut down a noble walnut-tree that was the single glory of the place, under whose shade the curate's kind landlady and her hard-hearted brother had played when children.

'Spare that tree, *please*,' prayed the curate of Mr. Doughy, who was a baker and a preacher.

'Why? What good does it there?' retorted the utilitarian baker.

'Look at its beauty!' cried the sensuous curate.

'Isn't it written, "Turn away thine eyes, lest thou behold vanity"?' roared the Manichæan preacher, who looked fat and greasy and sensual; and his face was so obstinate, and his manner so dogmatic, that it

22—2

was but casting pearls before swine to argue against
his misquotation.

So Martel, whose hands were full of potatoes for
the poultry, merely said, 'Consider the lilies of the
field, and behold the fowls of the air,' and proceeded
to call about him his more docile feathered friends,
who flew screaming and flocking around, and settled
upon his shoulders and his head.

Martel was now in his element.

'There,' said he, directing the eyes of the colonel,
'there is a cock of the game for you ! None of your
lanky, leggy, Malay-crossed, modern prize game ;
but true old unconquerable Derby breed—short and
stout, and compact as a partridge. These trim,
tight-built dandies are the pure produce of a hundred uncontaminated descents, bred by the gallant
long-descended earls whose names they bear. His
" dauntless game-cocks symbolise their lord"—

   ' " First in the class, and keenest in the ring,
     Who saps like Gladstone, and who fights like Spring."

Colonel, did you ever before see a game-cock ?' cried
the clerical enthusiast. ' Look at that scion of royal
race, worthy the praise of Chaucer, and of Wordsworth, and of Thomson. What bird more beautiful
as he stands erect to display the metallic splendours
of his broad black breast ? See the comb, red as
coral, formed for a monarch's crown ! His black
bill gleams like jet, and the bold, rolling eye shines
with the quenchless fire of battle. How stout he
stands upon his strutting legs, short in the shank,
and green as the willow ! What king so gallant in

his knightly tread! how high he lifts his spur-clad nervous foot! how firm and proud he sets it down again! His neck of orange and his scarlet back glow like the red gold, and his long strong wings are barred with gleaming purple. His tail flows like a pennon, and as a gallant champion he sounds his clarion, challenging all comers. He is more glorious than the golden pheasant; and his many wives, trim in shape and rich in hue, rival the nut-brown partridge. He searches out the daintiest morsels, and calls his ladies to enjoy them, nor partakes of anything himself until they have first been served ; and should one be molested and cry out, nor man nor boy, nor cat nor dog, nor ox nor horse, could scare him from flying to Dame Partlet's rescue. If, indeed, there be anything that knows no fear, is it not a game-cock of the true *old* breed ?'

'And you are not afraid of being taken for a cock-fighter ?' asked the colonel, when the panegyrist paused at last.

'No, nor for a wizard either.'

'Nor a gentleman jock ? Where is the cob ?'

'Here she is,' and he turned to an ill-thatched hut of 'mud and stud,' with inside fittings to match.

'So that is the famous cob ?'

'You are pleased to call her so; but this I'll say for her, she is a good miniature likeness of the old Irish hunter, that, like the Irish wolf-dog and the Irish parson, is now nearly extinct; and the hunter, anyway, will never be replaced by an equal. I take it Captain Gibbons' Fin-ma-coul is one of a very few left.'

'He ought to be rare,' said the colonel, 'for he cost £500, and was cheap as dirt. At least they say so; and I am told a man should insure his neck who means to follow Ralph over stone walls when he is on the great Fin.'

'Then we who cannot afford the insurance must keep at a respectful distance. You know I have seen the great Fin, and I hope it is permitted my vanity to say that he is made exactly like my little Judy here, allowing for the difference between sixteen and a half and fourteen and a half hands. They have the same fine light head and neck, the same long sweeping shoulders, the same short back and drooping quarters, not pretty to look at, but first-rate for jumping. They have both the long arm and the shortness between the knee and the ground, the bone flat and the sinew free, with the downy fringe upon it of silky hair, ending in a full curl, the real fetlock, above the short, strong pastern, and the round, solid foot. There is a gay, light hazel eye for you! Isn't she a pocket-hunter?'

'That she is,' muttered the colonel, in contemplation, 'and a "well-lepped" one, as Paddy says. What is her age?'

'Untold. I mean, if all goes well, to see her out, and then retire from the field; neither she nor I can last much longer. Now if you will ride her home, she is a capital hack, and at your service.'

'No, thank you. I mean to walk off your capital luncheon; and if you would walk a little way with me, I should like to have a little talkee-

talkee as we go. I know you for a sturdy pedestrian; infantry or cavalry, all one to you.'

'Aye, aye; I am your man to walk and talk, talk and walk: *solvitur ambulando*, as we say in the classics. Ah, you smile; you know my failing. Who does not? Talkee-talkee, preachee-preachee. It all comes of my lonely life. I am bottled up; I must explode. If I lived in society, like you, I should be mute as a mouse. But you shall do all the talking to-day, and I will listen, you'll see. Come along, fat Fairy,' cried he to a graceful, delicate little Blenheim spaniel. 'You want exercise. You have been lying on my bed all this long day; and,' turning to his companion, 'I must introduce you to the colonel. This is my wife, and I have been rather lucky in my lot, for she is as cheerful and good-humoured a companion as a man can have, and very pretty too; isn't she? So come along, Fairy. Don't flirt with the colonel. Your only fault is your fat, and it is creditable to the house that one's wife should show feed.'

And so the three trotted off together.

CHAPTER VII.

' Don't deceive yourself, my dear Bateman ; it is not that
ours is your religion, carried a little farther, a little too far,
as you would say.   No ; they differ in kind, not in degree :
ours is one religion, yours is another.'—Dr. J. H. NEWMAN
—*Loss and Gain* (*a Novel*).

'BEFORE we start, let me see your church,' said the
colonel.

' By all means.   Some people would apologise for
it, as not restored.   I would rather see it as it is.'

' Aye, that " restoration," laughed the colonel, ' is
a word of large promise and very unequal fulfilment.
Old oak sittings " restored " with new deal, highly
varnished !   Good oak, good stone, good carving in
both, with perhaps a little marble, and crimson
Utrecht velvet for colour, are good enough for us
old-fashioned folk.   I am too ignorant to enjoy the
sight of a church that cost £40,000 or £50,000,
when I know the minister's endowment is but £50
a year, and he must either starve or be mulcted for
the public to an enormous amount.   " The labourer
is worthy of his hire " is my text.   Give us plain
Church of England folk, English simplicity, good
plain reading, good plain preaching, good simple

singing, enough of it to break the monotony of our
long composite service and its many repetitions, and
no more. To sing all is to be monotonous in a worse
way. As to a gorgeous ritual, I have no objection
to it in its proper place.'

'And where may that be ?' asked the curate.

'Where its cost may well be borne and constantly
maintained, without the victimising of clergy or
parish. Finch Adams and I were looking over a
church t'other day :

'" It is very *fine*," said Finch, equivocally.

'" Yaas," said the parson, with proud humility;
" it looks like the house of God, I think."

'" And I think it looks very like the house of
Mammon," said Finch.

'And I don't know but Finch hit the blot. The
passion for gorgeous display has spread with mercan-
tile wealth, which has created a demand for cost and
show ; it is a touch of the Materialism that sees no
value in anything that it cannot handle and feel the
weight of. I beg your pardon for saying so, but that
is my idea ; no doubt I am the cobbler, going beyond
his last. Only, you know, you clerical gentlemen
bewilder us poor lay folk with such contradictory
directions. " You can't go the right way if you do
that," says one ; " You will certainly go the wrong
way if you don't," says another ; and so, you see, we
are tempted to think you all wrong together. And,
indeed, things are told me that, however well lubri-
cated, I, as a layman, cannot swallow, not even when
rammed down my throat by a strong party of politicians.'

'Aye, aye!' quoth the clergyman; 'I know the
dose :

'"Be to Free-Trade very kind,
And clap a padlock on the mind."'

'But this padlock,' said the layman, 'this authority
—Catholic authority—can you explain it to me ?'

'I can quote Hallam : he says it is "A unit of
more or less value, followed by a vast number of
zeros." '

'Well, then, since you seem a little less frightfully
official and oracular than some of your reverend
brethren, may I ask you to unfold to me *whence* all
this innovation, and quarrelling, and calling of names
comes ? and what it all means ? I have been away
from England a good while ; and I come back to see
all sorts of new things that I cannot comprehend.
Palmer is a fair man, but nothing can be got out of
him ; he will never talk what he calls "Church
politics." I see you don't mind it, so please give me
a chart of the country. I gather that the change
began about 1830, or so. Tell me what started it ?'

'Well, you know, some people say that "change
was in the air;" there was "a spirit afloat," and so
forth ; don't you see ?'

'See ! No ; I do not see. I want you to show
me.'

'I do not know that I can ; but I will try, if you
have patience, for it is a long story, mind. It is
only *my* idea, you know, and I dare say groundless
from first to last.'

'I don't think that likely ; let us have it, any way.

Now that you have sacrificed duly to humility, please instruct me.'

'Ahem! since you have been so much away from England I have the more boldness. It is not possible to fix exactly the time, I should say that from the passing of the Roman Catholic Emancipation Act England was in a ferment; the clergy shared in the agitation, looking at things from their own point of view, for I believe them to be men after all. You know, I belong to the low, and grovelling, mere common-sense school of Paley and Whately. Well, the party *then* coming into power had for years, not unprovoked to be sure, systematically set themselves against the clergy, and written them down. And if they showed reverence at all to the Church, it was only as a standard whereby to try its ministers and find them wanting. In the probable change of government, the clerical class foresaw a yoke preparing that would press very heavily upon their order, and be very hard to bear. No doubt much of the degradation into which it seemed falling was to be traced to clerical faults. Pitt, and his preceptor Prettyman, better known as Bishop Tomline, had introduced into the Church a money ambition, which certainly did not mark the clergy in the days of Bishops Berkeley and Butler and the first Georges. Under George the Third, though the king was not the doer of it, it was brought to pass that he was accounted the greatest bishop, who netted the most money ; and he the best parish priest, who held the most livings. Five, and six, and even seven each, of the largest value, were for

a prey to the sons of some bishops. It was the
boast of one bishop that " He could give " (and he
did give) " to each of his sons so many thousands a
year, without putting his hand into his pocket." By
this bad ambition, most of the leading men in both
Universities were more or less corrupted; while the
body of the clergy, by these monopolies, was so im-
poverished and depressed, that to become a clergyman was held almost a degradation, unless riches
were the result. It is no great wonder that by the
new set which was coming into political power, all
clergymen were systematically slighted and snubbed;
and though their services were still sought for the
tuition of young noblemen, they were treated with
the least possible consideration. It was a standing
joke against the tutors that they had to dine with
their pupils at an early hour on cold meat. By the
mob in the streets the bishops were pelted with
mud; and with scornful words in the House of
Lords by Lord Grey, whose party could scarce raise
a friendly clergyman to say grace for them at their
dinners. No man, or body of men, acts from a
single motive; and the disgust produced by a social
condition, of which these are but the commonest
outward symptoms, crops out continually in the
writings of those high-couraged men who set the
Church of England in battle array, and led her
clergy to victory. For example, one would think
nowadays that the honour of the ministerial office
—the highest and the most sacred to which a man
can be called—needed no vindication; yet that true-
hearted priest, Keble, writes in a tone of apologetic
and constrained content :

'"Seems it to thee a niggard hand
That nearest Heaven has made thee stand,
     ○   ○   ○   ○   ○   *
The snow-white ephod wear ?
Why should we crave the worldling's wealth ?"

and so forth. In much the same strain did Newman write of Davison of Oriel : that he was " absorbed during the greater part of his life in employments which, *though sacred in their nature, and honoured by a special blessing, yet apparently might have been left to those who had not his particular endowments."* In short, without surrendering their churchmanship, and playing the courtier to a party, who set at nought their calling, the Fellows of Colleges in holy orders felt that they had no longer before them what they called " a *career."* Accordingly, we are told of Keble, by his coadjutor and friend, that he " went into the country ; but his instance served to prove that men need not in the event lose that *influence, which is rightly theirs, because they happen to be thwarted in the use of the channels natural and proper to its exercise.* Nor did Keble lose his place in the minds of men because he went *out of their sight,"* i.e., became the pastor of a country parish, or as the dons would say, was " relegated to a country parsonage." '

'Not a very appreciative estimate of the importance of a country sphere, as it seems to me,' observed the colonel.

'Well, letting that pass,' proceeded the curate, 'we learn from the same writers that, when the new Government actually took office, the more earnest of the dons with horror anticipated, in the distribution of patronage, the *authoritative* introduction of

opinions that were *not their own;* and the vital
question with them was, in their own language, to
keep the Church from being swamped, by getting
together a company of men able to hold their own
against the Government. " It is not we," said they,
" who desert the Government, but the Government
that has left us. *We are forced backward upon
those below us, because those above will not honour
us.*" With their party, and in some sense the whole
priesthood, thus politically weakened and threat-
ened, they compared the fresh, vigorous power of
which they read in the records of the mediæval
popes, and they soon decided that the principles of
the *Reformation* would not serve their purpose.
They were determined that " a great University
should not be bullied by a great Duke of Wellington," much less by an Earl Grey. They " had fierce
thoughts against the Liberals," and in University
sermons they boldly denounced " the National
Apostasy." They were men as brave and as hopeful as Wordsworth when, in the teeth of *Edinburgh*
and all other obloquy, he set steadfastly to work to
" create the taste by which he was to be enjoyed;"
or as " the great Duke of Wellington," when, with
a handful of undisciplined men for an army, with
the English Ministry frightened out of its wits, with
the Opposition furious against him, and heartily
with him only Lord Castlereagh and the Marquess
Wellesley, the author of the plan, he undertook to
drive out of Spain and Portugal the victorious
legions of France, by fear of whom the armies of the
Continent were half beaten before the encounter in

the field. Even so did Newman and Keble and Froude feel confident with the confidence of that big bully Achilles returning to the battle, and for their motto they adopted his not very modest words, " You shall know the difference when I am back again." Their special bugbear was the *Edinburgh Review*, which for twenty years had written down Wordsworth, and, worse, had written up Oriel, a college that, from Copleston's day, was a school of speculative philosophy, and infamous in their eyes for free thought. The greatest of the three complained that its common-room " stank of logic," and another of them asked if Arnold were a Christian. Dr. Pusey soon joined the movement, and as a Professor and Canon of Christ-Church, with a high patrician connection, gave it fashion and a name. The expression is true enough, there was a reactionary " spirit afloat ;" the atmosphere was charged with ecclesiastical " electricity ;" the temper of the eleventh century was in the air again. Men generally felt a want of something stable : there were Tories seeking a standpoint, old highbred Whigs secretly fearing the subversion of all things, brand-new Radical Plutocrats catching at a hold on antiquity. These did not fall in at first. The start was made by simple divines—divines in quest of some great principle to rally round—who flocked to the new standard from Oxford, from Cambridge, and from Dublin. But the most potent reactionary influence had come from Scotland, when the great " Wizard of the North" conjured up, for the admiration of the whole people, the splendid vision of mediæval feu-

dalism. Though "the multitude was mixed," it is
a mistake to imagine that the traditionary High
Church party, fed on the marrow of Bull and Barrow
and South, had much share in the movement; they
were most of them as hostile to it as Arnold and
Whately. The new men usurped their ancient title,
and nicknamed them "High and Dry:" good,
kindly, courteous, scholarly Archbishop Langley is
their "knight of the shire, and represents them all."
Hugh James Rose, to be sure, and, still more, Keble,
and a very few others, who were hereditary High
Churchmen, and had never been anything else, took
prominent places in the new party; but from the
Evangelical camp came the most headlong and determined leaders, Newman and Froude, as did afterwards Dr. Pusey, Cardinal Manning, and Bishop
Hamilton, influential from his position.'

'Now, how was that?' asked the colonel. 'I have
heard it before. I believe it to be a fact; and, if so,
it is a very curious one.'

'It is an undoubted fact, and, as you say, a curious
one, but very easy of proof for all that, and not, I
think, very hard of explanation. A remark made
by a chief of the "Evans.," and repeated to me by
a very good and much beloved member of their
brotherhood, clergymen both, seems to me to go to
the root of the matter. "I don't know how it is,"
said he, "but pastors of our school very often attach
their flocks to themselves, but *never* to the *Church.*"
And the Evangelical clergyman who repeated this
observation to me endorsed it with a sigh. Of
course I did not say to him what I say to you—that

the old Puritanic leaven of dissatisfaction with "the Church of England *as by law established*" is at the bottom of it. Such clergymen never loved her, and, as in the Oxford case, when they cease to look to Geneva they look to Rome, or if very lawless indeed, they seek Roman Catholicism without the pope.'

'But now go on with your sketch, please; I want to trace the course of things,' said the colonel.

'In my poor opinion——'

'In your opinion! On with you!'

'Well, my history, if not so well told as is history commonly, I think is, to the full, as true, or, as the French would more politely and more correctly say, as exact. Well, the new party set out by assiduously asserting and propagating what they held to be the old fundamental doctrines of the Church of England, meaning by them the counter-Reformation theory set up by Laud, while professedly their basis was "the principles and practice of the first centuries." The expression is loose; the earliest centuries were not their guide. Of Origen the best they could say was to express a hope that "so great a soul was not lost." The party's gaze was directed to the mediæval Church, and their hearts went with the great mediæval pontiffs—in particular with Gregory the Seventh, who had laid the Lord Greys of his day very humbly in the snow or dust. "Disbelieving a divine priesthood," writes the Coryphæus of the band, "men come to gaze with awe and reverence at the high station or splendid connections, or noble birth of the children of men." Against the exclusiveness of an aristocracy of wealth and station, and the showy cultivation of privileged society, which was the boast of the Whig circles and of the Grey and Holland House sets above all—against these patrician philosophers the Oxford party now set up another standard of exclusiveness, as they expressed it, "hiding themselves from those who were not worthy of familiarity with men of reverential and religious tempers." In short, my Lord Grey, when in his pride of place he bid the bishops "set their house in order," threw down a gauntlet that was fiercely taken up, though not by the bishops ; and the end of the strife is not yet. A far more liberal and wiser premier than he remarked bluffly and to the point, as his wont was, " It takes a vast deal to move the Church of England ; but when she is moved, no power on earth or under the earth can stop, her." '

' Forgive me if I stop you here for a moment,' said the colonel. ' Your mention of Holland House puts me in mind of Palmer. He was dining at a certain great Liberal house that shall be nameless, and heard the hostess shout out in her loud, overbearing fashion, " A glass of gooseberry wine to Mr. Nameless's tutor!" Our friend looked involuntarily towards the unfortunate object of the great lady's polite attentions, and saw, to his amazement, a clergyman whom he had known as one of the most distinguished scholars and divines in his University ; indeed, he was not long after made a bishop through the influence of the host, than whom, to do him justice, there was no man more generous, amiable, or accomplished. Palmer, who was looked on in those days as the heir of Row'nshaw, and was somebody in society on his own account too, though you would hardly think it now, was so offended at my lady's treatment of his cloth that he instantly put on his cold-water manner—you know how freezing he can make it—sat bolt upright, and looked straight before him, not deigning to take the slighest notice of any of the good things that were said by anybody, though the party was small and select, and there was a wit at the table, and many capital jokes were made by him and by others. Our friend was a perfect ice-house, and chilled and froze the whole company. As soon as the ladies left the room he called for his carriage, and never could be got to enter that house again, though the host and hostess, who were both connected with him and liked him very much, did all they could to engage him. Oh! he has a great deal of *esprit de corps*, has Palmer! Well, and so you think that—shall we call it jealous or professional feeling?—was an element in the great movement! Just a dash of worldliness, a grain of the earth, earthy, at the bottom of it, eh? Is that what you mean?'

'Well, no; I do not think it is. Motives are always mixed, to be sure; but I fancy few men ever have lived more free from dross than the great trio—Newman, Keble, and Froude; and I must add Hugh James Rose, who was the *beau idéal* of an English clergyman, and was as soon in the field of revival as any one. He could not, as Newman says, "go ahead across country, as Froude had no scruple

23—2

in doing, for Froude was a bold rider," on horseback as well as speculation. If any of them wrote at any time with more disdainful sharpness of wit than could be wished, we must bear in mind how justly the high-handedness of my Lord Grey and his set roused their independent tempers, not to speak of some provoking sneers thrown out by others who should have known better.

' " We can count you," said a busy, bustling bishop, of imperious temper and monstrous income, whom some of the same metal call "great."

' " We will have a *Vocabulum Apostolicum*," said the party, and started it, somewhat strangely, with —" Pampered Aristocrat," " Pauperes Christi," "Smug Parson," borrowed obviously from Byron's "Smug Sydney," of the *Edinburgh Review* and Holland House clique. They felt and quoted the language of Agobard, Archbishop of Lyons, uttered previously to the Reformation of the eleventh century :· "Such is the disgrace of our times, that there is scarcely one to be found who aspires to any degree of honour or temporal distinction who has not his *domestic priest;* and this, not that he may *obey* him, but that he may *command* his obedience in all things, alike lawful and unlawful, things human and things divine. So that these chaplains are constantly to be found serving the table, mixing the strained wine, leading out the dogs, managing ladies' horses, or looking after the lands." '

'Aye, aye ; I see,' said the colonel, ' a good deal of justice, and perhaps a spark of temper, in their ' Apostolic Vocabulary " and quotations. Now tell me another thing. How comes it that you clergy of the Reformed Church hark back so constantly on the old Roman line in matters not only of discipline but of ritual ? Excuse me, please, but is there any-thing in what Leigh Hunt said—of Milton, I think —that " a man thoroughly imbued with the Greek and Latin classic spirit is inevitably half a heathen ?" '

' I would rather say he is not quite a Hebrew. When a first-class classic turns clergyman, his old Pagan must mingle with and qualify his new studies in the Judaic literature, which is popularly assumed to be the sole proper nutriment of the purely cleri-cal mind.'

' As for celibacy,' put in the colonel, ' which is not a Jewish virtue, of course every fellow of a college has in effect taken the vow for the best part of his life, a vow to live in great comfort and good com-pany, without care. Plenty of the best of every-thing is good enough for him. Celibacy is to him meat, drink, and clothing, a robe of honour, and *otium cum dignitate.* Am I right in my Latin and my reasons ?'

' No doubt there is a good deal in creature com-forts, and in Latin and Greek, to account for aca-demic proclivities. As for the celibacy, it is easy to think a thing necessary for all that is very con-venient for one's self ; and as to the heathenism, a man must have imbibed something of pagan senti-ment who has spent the twenty-three first and most impressible years of his life in acquiring the thoughts and expressions of the Latin and Greek classic authors. If he becomes a clergyman, the books and mental habits of his youth act upon the theology which is infused, and leaven it, no doubt, in some measure. The man's imagination is filled by the great Gentile writers, and not a little of the groundwork of his mind is formed and fashioned by them; his head is furnished with their ideas; he is steeped in the religion of Æschylus, terrible, malignant, and persecuting; or from Sophocles he has learnt to see the irony of Providence; in Euripides, human nature as it is. He sees in the Gentile, as in the Jewish code, rites of expiation, a priestly caste, beautiful temples, and a gorgeous and costly worship, votive offerings, fumigations, lustrations, washings with water, incense, vestals for nuns. Endless ceremonies are part of the furniture of the classical scholar's mind. In this sense he is " mingled with the heathen, and learns their works." And so, when he turns at last to Christian theology, he is most ready to listen to those of the Fathers who use a language suggested by ancient usage in Jewish and heathen rituals, the offspring of old association.'

'But Milton! How about him? A classic, half a Pagan, if you please, *and a Puritan!*'

'The times and the man! times and the man! " Who to his reading brings not a spirit and judgment equal or superior, etc." It would need more than even the genius of Milton to substantiate half that the Puritan spirit has prompted him to say of the Greek and Roman poets and philosophers; though I do think Genesis, Deuteronomy, and Isaiah, as literature, superior to the Prometheus, or anything written by Æschylus or Sophocles, whom I hold to be religious poets in the strictest sense. But Milton's own just soul speaks out when he mentions the Hebrew prophets

> ' " As men divinely taught, and better teaching
> The solid rules of Civil Government
> In their majestic unaffected style,
> Than all the oratory of Greece and Rome.
> In them is plainest taught, and easiest learnt,
> What makes a nation happy, keeps it so ;
> What ruins nations, and lays cities flat.' '

As to " Political Science," Milton knew as well as another that the Mosaic Law is not political, but social. As to oratory, I believe in it greatly as a fine art ; but, for your orators, if politically inclined, I do not much believe in them. Orator is apt to be, as Hobbes says, another name for flatterer first, and for tyrant afterwards ; for any gentleman to " wield at will a fierce democracy " is rather a dangerous amusement.'

' Hardly " at will," ' said the colonel ; ' the gentleman is mounted on a runaway horse; he must humour it, and let it go.'

' I know Achilles is made a great orator, and the greatest bully of classic literature,' returned the curate. ' Ostracism is your only bridle, colonel ; there is no other protection for the endangered and much-suffering minority of quiet folk : one sort of despotism is tempered by assassination, and the other by ostracism. It is neither the despotism of monarchy, nor the despotism of democracy, nor

politics at all, but it is "Righteousness that exalteth
a nation ;" and Milton is right about the Jewish prophets, if one so humble as I might presume to say
so.   I am sure the man made a shrewd reply, whatever he meant by it, who was asked, " When will
you Radicals be satisfied ?" and answered, " When
we get the laws of the country as near as possible to
the laws of God." '

' Ah, the laws of God as he reads them, of course,'
said the colonel ; ' that reading is a difficult thing, for
all that is said to the contrary ; and I am sorry that
good Keble found so many followers in his misquotation of a prophet.   Any way, I wish there were a
good deal more study, as well as reading, of the Word
of God.   I doubt if you gentlemen of the pulpit are
strong in that point ; to be what I have heard called
a " *textuary* " seems to be the end and aim.'

' It may be,' replied the curate, ' that in our Universities the Latin and Greek studies are not fairly
balanced by our knowledge of Oriental literature,
without which a just knowledge of the Hebrew
Scriptures, even when written in Greek, as are the
New Testament and the Septuagint, is impossible.'

' To be sure, Martel.   "Christianity is a Greek
religion," says the classical divine ; and he is a Greek
scholar. What more do you want?' he asks, and I reply:
' A good deal more, unless he is to be very ignorant
of what he has to teach, judging even from my own
little knowledge of the East, Christian and heathen.'

' As to " Heathen " and " Heathenism," or " Gen-
tilism," ' returned the curate, ' I am bound to enter
my modest protest against what seems to me, a

generally used—a very loose expression—"It fits Plato and a South Sea Islander alike." For myself, I confess to a conviction that the Greek and Jewish religions, and all the spiritual good in any religion, are derived from the one source. All religion, all converse with things spiritual, all excursions of thought beyond the region of sense and the things seen, are the sound, or the corrupted, fruit of revelation, whatever force you may put upon the word :

> ' " Whether of actual vision, sensible
> To sight and feeling, or that in this sort
> Have condescendingly been shadowed forth,
> Communications spiritually maintained,
> And *intuitions* moral and divine." '

'What a frightful fellow you are to quote !' quoth the colonel; 'I wish I had your gift.'

'You would only have to lead my solitary life.'

'But don't let me interrupt you ; please go on ; you left off with Wordsworth, I think.'

'Yes; and I start with the belief—which I hold, subject to ethnic and scientific discoveries—that the Greek and Jewish and all other religions were originally derived from Divine revelation ; and, accordingly, I admit that the economy under which lived the heathen, the Gentiles, was, in its *primary* construction, as sound as the Jewish : it was, in fact, identical with the Patriarchal, the Mesopotamian, or Elder Hebrew economy—call it which you will. It had a like code of moral law with the Mosaic; it had rites, ceremonies, and sacrifices corresponding in the leading points to the Mosaic : and a like longing desire for a human redeemer seems to account for the mixed nature attributed to the heathen gods and goddesses. The *difference* between the heathen and the Mosaic economy, as I believe, lay chiefly in this, that the one was, to borrow St. Paul's figure, the olive of the fenced garden; the other, the wild olive of the wilderness : the one was more fenced against degeneracy and corruption than the other. But at the time of our Lord's advent, *both* were greatly corrupted and debased. I am going to quote again ; I love the shelter of a great name. Dr. Newman speaks right to the point : " The heathen religion is a *true* religion corrupted ; the Jewish, a true religion dead ; Christianity, the true religion living and perfect." Though he was too mediæval to accept the theology of Clement and Origen, their " broad philosophy carried him away," and enlarged his creed. Like a thorough schoolman he speaks of Aristotle as " most wonderfully raised up to be the minister to a Divine revelation," meaning the Christian. You, Colonel Denny, are a traveller : when you find the principal parts of that external form of religion which God gave the Jews, in practice also among the other nations from time immemorial, will you say, as some do, they were invented solely by man ; and God specially " *borrowed* " them for His own peculiar people ?'

'H'm—well, no ; if I suppose, as you seem to suggest, that men received a ritual from Adam, who had it—some way or other—from God, that will untie a good many knots that puzzled me when I have found substantial similarity in the religious rites and customs of the heathen in many lands ;

and their common agreement with Judaism in not a few points, and with Christianity even in some.'

'In the heathen religious rites and customs, you see,' said the curate, 'sparks of truth shining out through all the rubbish with which degenerate religious sentiment and groping superstition have covered them. Observation will not allow us to think that the heathen had all the truth which we find in their moral systems—by their contact with the Jews—out of those especially Divine oracles which were intrusted to Jewish keeping. There were other holy writings, besides those preserved in the privileged line through which the Saviour came, that contained corresponding inspired doctrine and precept. The family that kept these was not so chosen to Divine favour as the Jewish, nor was tied down in the same express manner to care and attention in preserving them. Wherefore, with the exception of the Book of Job, which, though bound up with the Jewish Scriptures, is not supposed to have been written by a Jew, and therefore belongs to the *Gentile* volume—with that exception, the Gentile volume has come down to us much torn and blotted and interpolated. Our divines seem hardly enough to have attended to this point.'

'But,' asked the colonel, 'may they not justly fear the consequences of confounding Jewish with heathen literature?'

'There should, I think, be no difficulty and no confusion; for have we not the volumes of the Jewish and Christian Churches as a test to try by? Is the nurture of the flower of the youth of Christen-

dom on the heathen classics defensible on any other
ground ?'

'H'm! is not your supposition, though I do not
know that I dislike it, rather strange doctrine ?   Does
not your proposition involve immense consequences ?
You are not propounding novelties to me as an unlettered soldier, *are you ?*'

'We will, if you please, pass by the pleasant joke
about unlettered soldiers, and I will say at once that
so far from starting novelties, I have told you what
Newman says; and you, who are a Kebleite, may
remember that Keble says much the same in his
hymn for the Third Sunday in Lent—that

'"Thoughts beyond their thought to those high bards were
     given;"

and

'"Fly from the old poetic fields,
     Ye Paynim shadows dark !
Immortal Greece, dear land of glorious lays,
Lo ! here the unknown God of thy unconscious praise."

But however, the idea, good or bad, is an idea of the
early philosophical fathers of the Church of Clement
of Alexandria, of Justin Martyr, and of Origen the
Great : theirs was that catholic school of Christianity
to which the schismatical exclusiveness of Montanus
is the opposite pole.   They were persuaded that
"Streaks of a brighter heaven behind their pagan
darkness were the wreck of paradise, and upbore
through many a dreary age whatever of good or
wise yet lived in bard or sage."   They taught that
the rudiments or creeds of heavenly wisdom *opened*
by the Gospel lay hid in the philosophy of the
Greeks as the kernel of a nut within its shell; the

essence of Greek philosophy was sound and whole-
some, and in accord with the light of Christ and the
spirit of Christian wisdom ; but it was wrapped in
a cloud of superstitions. The fountain of Greek
philosophy is the Divine wisdom, says Clement ;
but Christianity has a *completeness* and *perfection*
that is all its own. In short, the doctrine of that
ancient Alexandrian school amounts to this, that
philosophy had been to the Greeks what the Law of
Moses was to the Hebrew—in a more *privileged* and
secure way. Both in the outset were derived from
Revelation, and both were but schoolmasters to
bring men to Christ. " Pagan literature, philosophy
mythology, properly understood, were but a preparation for the Gospel ;" " The Greek poets and sages
were, in a certain sense, prophets ;" "He who had
taken the seed of Jacob for elect people, had not
therefore cast the rest of the world out of His sight :"
Newman again.'

' Ah, well ; you are an old soldier. You fight under
shelter whenever you can ; but you have got over a
good deal of ground, and left me plenty of food for
reflection. I reserve myself,—" epecho," as I think
your friends the Greeks used to say when I was at
Eton. I will think over all you have said.'

' *Quoted !*' put in the other.

' Well, quoted from the most learned and orthodox
authorities — of your own selecting — Anglican,
Romish, and Catholic. Thanks to your two sermons
that I heard at Finchdale, the subject is not quite
new to me, though some of the names are less
familiar than they should be ; for I profess myself of

the number of those who exercise their reason on such subjects. But we have not finished what we have begun with ; what you have said as yet would account rather for harmony than discord. What I want is some reason for your jarring and furious factions, which are scandals, you know, to Christendom ; and—between ourselves—no signs of zeal at all,—I mean, of *Christian* zeal. Tell me about this, if you can ?'

'I think I can, if you won't mind my being tedious again, and taking up the old story at the point where I diverged from it into what is to me a far more interesting inquiry. You will forgive my prolixity ; you know it is not given to every story-teller to be concise.'

The colonel laughed ; and the curate re-commenced :

'To return, then, to the Oxford movement, it was an *intellectual* outbreak, of which the University was the proper centre ; it was in great part a revival of the intellectual and the lettered spirit, which within the Church had declined, while it was spreading, and gaining great strength in the world around. The prime movers were persuaded that the exigencies of the day called for a studious and learned clergy ; they were taught by Mr. Burke, that, "If you divorce learning from religion, learning will destroy religion ;" and to learning they did not disdain to add literary skill, knowing how much learning is lost for the want of it. Bishop Sumner " appears to me to make parochial preaching a much easier thing than it really is," wrote the Tractarian,

Hugh James Rose, before the " Tracts " were started. "' *The limitation of rounded periods* ' "—you see I am doubly quoting this time.'

The colonel laughed again, and the curate repeated :

"'*The limitation of rounded periods*,' so that *dulness* shall not be mistaken for *simplicity*, appears to me to require great study and pains; and the '*interrogations and addresses*,' of which Bishop Sumner speaks, effective as they assuredly are, will become offensive, when not regulated by a just taste and knowledge of the best models. Bishop Sumner will, I fear, think the assertion extravagant; but I am well convinced that the village preacher of good sense might be much benefited by the study of Demosthenes, or of *any of the great masters, who to mighty eloquence have added a profound knowledge of the human heart.*" Be this opinion of Mr. Rose worth what it may,' said the curate, 'I will only observe that, though I should prefer the study of Bunyan, or Spenser, or Milton; and very great speakers, among whom is Mr. Fox, would recommend Homer and Euripides, Lord Brougham agrees with Mr. Rose about Demosthenes. Here, then, was the rule by which the writers of the " Tracts " wrote. No more finished work than theirs was in that day turned out of a literary workshop. Newman and Keble, at the least, must now be written upon the roll of " those great masters, who to mighty eloquence have added a profound knowledge of the human heart." Attracted by deep reflection, pure sentiment, and lofty imagination, dressed in the engaging

brilliancy of a perfect style, men rushed to a new
"Tract" by Newman, as to a new number of
"Dombey and Son" by Dickens.   The writings of
the great divine had the stimulating flavour of an
intellectual romance.   Bishop Blomfield, it was said,
used to call "The Christian Year" "The Sunday
Puzzle"; but people who could never read a page
of the bishop's lucid sermons, young and old, got the
"Christian Year" by heart.   "The style is the man,"
said Buffon; and these men proved good his saying.
And now, when the powerful and polished genius of
Newman and Keble had stirred to its depths the
Church of England, and made the State alive to its
force, a new start was made by a younger generation
who, taking advantage of the impetus acquired,
"cut into the movement," and drove for a point of
their own.   Dr. Newman has told us that he was
"Neither so fond of the persons nor of the methods
of thought of this new school, as of the old set; but
he had not the heart to repel them."   The leading
idea of the old set was the REALISING MENTALLY of
the invisible world, and of spiritual power, as against
material and physical force.   The leading idea of the
new set was the SYMBOLISING of things invisible by
things material.   The original movement has been
called—not very inaccurately—"intellectual"; it
was certainly not sensuous, nor even æsthetic, the
new men introduced into it the sensuous and material
elements.   Each generation takes its colour from
the climate in which it had been reared; the elder
had been bred under the influence of the military,
the younger under the influence of the commercial

spirit. They had grown up amid the wealth which
a long peace, purchased by their father's blood, had
heaped up; and, as natural and dutiful children of
the material industries, they almost inevitably learnt
to mingle with their ideal of religious worship a good
deal of material splendour. A gorgeous ritual was
their test of true worship. They would offer freely,
and have all Christians offer freely unto God of His
own: pomp and magnificence was a sign of the
Church's success. To the elder sort, habituated to
a simpler and more severe devotion, this was—to
say the least—distasteful and distracting; there
was ceremony and splendour which their eyes might
gaze on, but in which their spirits could find no
part. The luxury of the new wealth, that the new
set had seen perhaps in their early homes, but which
a few of them at least would deny themselves in
their own houses, they felt called upon to indulge in
their churches, and to be lavish of it in the house of
God. Their grand aim was to symbolise heavenly
by earthly glories; Christian privileges and Christian
graces by gold and silver, and precious stones and
radiant colours; materialising for the eye spiritual
truths, and justifying their practice by their use of
some chapters of the Apocalypse. Newman, having
followed a far other ideal, when he went, or was
driven, to Rome, took occasion to warn his recent,
though hardly welcome, allies that "the idea of
worship is different" in the Unreformed Church,
from the idea of it in the Reformed Church: "for
that in truth the *religions* are different." The new
party was not only not possessed by the idea of the

original party, it was urged on by one almost opposite. The first set were solely spiritual in their
views ; the second were largely leavened, not only by
material objects, but also by very strong *political*
opinions. The first move was made against
" Liberalism," considered as the worship of material
prosperity, and called " progress," and " the march
of intellect." The movers had a horror of politics
and politicians of all sorts, as of the earth, earthy ;
they believed in the divine right of kings, and had
no faith in democracies : in short, the party was
founded and built upon opposition to " Liberalism,"
though it was " forced " by the circumstances of the
time—most reluctantly—" to look *downwards* for
help." But the new set threw itself heartily into
politics ; wrote political and literary biographies
with a bias ; coalesced with Liberalism ; and retained
not a little love of the material industries, out of
which it sprung. The new school greatly affected
material magnificence, and shared as strongly as the
old party dissented from, the popular opinion that
" energy, displayed in bustle and ambitious desires
of function and prominence, is part of the high and
perfect state of the mind of man ; nor was it in-
disposed to divide all modes of life into the ambitious
and the selfish." '

' Never care for the new party, which I know ;
let us go back to the old party, which I prefer,' said
the colonel, hastily interrupting. ' I think I understand how it came to *take them up ;* but how did it
propagate and *disseminate* its principles so success-
fully and so soon ?'

'Oh! it partook of the wisdom of the serpent no less than the harmlessness of the dove. The excellent fraternity did not disdain to take a lesson out of the book of their very mundane and serpentine antagonists. As Brougham and Co. managed the Press for the Liberal cause in its infancy by filling every bookseller's shop with *Edinburgh Reviews* and pamphlets, and most of the London and all the country newspapers with paragraphs, and the boroughs with handbills, to enforce their principles, vindicate their conduct, elucidate their measures, and expose and be-little their adversaries, even so did Newman, Keble and Co., through their pupils and younger friends, take measures to spread their better sentiments. Then undergraduates, properly leavened, in due time became tutors and leavened others. What they had heard they taught in the University, and many went down into the country, and as curates leavened their parishes; they got down from London party reviews, party hymnals, party almanacs, party literature, and parcels of the famous tracts, and with these they filled the country booksellers' shop-windows, and contrived to have them reviewed and praised and quoted, or at the least censured, in the country newspapers; they introduced them into clerical meetings, and made proselytes, more or less, of their rectors and brother curates. That, in brief, is the history of the first movement, as I seem to read it, in their own words.'

But what were the bishops about all this time? What part did they take?' asked the colonel.

'Well, I suppose the more ambitious secretly fanned the flame, because the absolute authority of bishops was preached; but the wiser part looked to a disastrous issue, and poured all the cold water they could upon it. Their fear was that, if the doctrines buried in the grave of Laud were carelessly uncovered and approached with torches, the explosion would be as tremendous in its way as that which killed him and shattered the Church of his day. In short, the better part of the bishops—and that was by far the larger part—did what they could; but the spirit of change was afloat, and the Church was afire, and the more cold water they poured upon it the more did the fire blaze. And there were young politicians who saw in this a new element of political power that might in time be turned to their account.'

'I doubt you don't love bishops,' said the colonel.

'I love my own,' replied the curate, 'and all I have ever had over me. But I do not like a bishop who goes out of his way to tell his strong friend the public that his clergy want light—their horizon must be enlarged; they are too much insulated and wrapped up in their own interests, and must cultivate the society of laymen. I do not say this is untrue, but it comes ill from a bishop: he lives by the labours, and ought to share the cares, of his clergy. "Cultivate society" indeed! If he had ever tried to live on £100 a year, or on £200 either, as the hire of his labour, he would find *that* a very "insulating" income; and he has his own large one upon that very ground. No, I cannot admire that sort of rhetoric; it is inexact, unfeeling, and aggravating. Therefore, perhaps, I feel a loose, general sort of preference for noblemen bishops, like the Most Reverend Lord John George Beresford of Armagh. They are to the manner bred, and, though they have not more courage or honesty than other men, they have less to fear and less to hope: their established position and connections with society make them more independent both of mobs and of "nobs;" they have no need to put on magisterial dignity, or the dry, official manner that is so offensive; they can afford to be natural and frank and free; though even of them one here and there may be found somewhat ignorant, and as dry and dignified as a college don. But I have had the pleasure of being under one of the frank and free sort. He wanted to see me, and rode over to my lodging. Not having much to say, he would not dismount. I was dirty, and not fit to be seen by such a grandee; so I scuttled up to tidy myself instead of going out to him at once, and being very dirty, no doubt I stayed an unconscionably long time. At last my lord, having nothing else to do but look about him, espied me at the upper window brushing my hair. "Mr. Martel, are you ever coming down?" he sang out, with loud good-humour; "or will you keep your bishop waiting all day?" That is not the high-official, dignified, donnish style; but I like it, as the way of one gentleman with another. Beside, you can get your patrician at a cheaper rate; he needs less pay. Putting apart the highest motives, to be at the head of the most influential and cultured body in England, and

to exercise (begging a soldier's pardon for saying so)
the first calling that a man can embrace—this of
itself alone would be an object of just ambition to
the best, without the temptation of those many
thousands a year of salary which are held essential
to the maintenance of palatial dignity.'

'Ah! ha! are you there?' cried the colonel. ''Twas
but yesterday I was reading the "Diary of Sir
Charles Napier." The old soldier says just what
you say: "Oh, the riches of the Church!" he writes.
"Here is a bishop" (you see, Mr. Martel, it is my
turn to quote now)—"here is a bishop who has
lived a life of ease, and has £8,000 or £10,000 a
year and a palace! I, who have lived a life of hard-
ships, wounds, and banishment, have £1,000!" So
he writes what he calls "a Christmas sermon without the bishop; for if I went to Church I should be
thinking of his £10,000 a year."'

'Ah! there it is again!' said Martel. 'Oh, the
riches of the Church! aye, the riches of the Church!
Of course, all the clergy are bloated and overpaid!
I have received, what do you think, for fourteen
years' service, after spending on my education
£2,000? I have received just £1,400! Oh, the
riches of the Church! You see, Sir Charles Napier,
the general commanding a district, was the nephew
of the Duke of Leinster, so that £1,000 was enough
to support his dignity,' concluded the curate.

'And as you would infer,' replied the colonel, 'it
is enough for the dignity of a bishop of like extrac-
tion, eh?'

'Why not?' asked Martel. 'With frank nobility,

and without the lawyer-secretary always at the elbow, we should get on better. The clergy are not at school, you know ; only bishops and college dons don't know it, neither do they know that there are no oracles nowadays.'

' *You* are my oracle,' laughed the colonel; 'so tell me one thing more. This "Theory of Development" —what does it mean ?'

'Development—h'm ! Development—hah ! Well, Development is sometimes now called " the Living Voice of the Church," you know, by some clergy a.id some laity. But Development is a two-edged sword; it cuts both ways. It is used by the Tractarian, and by the gentleman who is termed " Latitudinarian " and " Rationalist " by dull folk who do not discern the signification of words. The Latitudinarian and Rationalist, I fancy, will desire no • better weapon than this " Theory of Development " and of " the Living Voice." He will ask, " Can the sixteenth and seventeenth centuries, but half awake from a sleep of thirty generations, offer anything to satisfy the hunger and thirst after a fuller, more comprehensive, and balanced sense of the words of Jesus—the longing after Christian excellence ? Could the perfect work of the Spirit be found in the *dregs* of *Papal* institutions ?" That will be his use of the doctrine of Development and of " the Living Voice." And how much of the " Oxford Tracts " will be left after a free application of that doctrine of Development ? Gentlemen seem to suppose that when they not only in 1835 started penal proceedings against their opponents, but have since systematically sapped

and broken down and poured contempt upon all the
landmarks of the last three centuries; when they
have pointed the finger of ridicule, and mocked and
scoffed and flouted and fleered and jeered at everything and everybody that savours of established
custom and old times, then they have nothing to do
but to cry "Stop!" to the upheaving wave of free
criticism; "hitherto shalt thou go and no farther!"
And the boundary-line will be theirs. Yet I have
heard tell of a dream that when the "Tracts" and
their school shall have had full possession of Oxford,
and may be supposed to have educated her for forty
years, a bishop of Oxford of that same school may,
in some charge, chance to declare that "a considerable number of graduates who hold offices in the
University, or offices in the colleges, have ceased,
according to his opinion, to be Christians in more
than name."'

'Oh, my prophetic oracle,' quoth the colonel, 'has,
to be sure, dreamed of a strange end to the doctrine
of development, and of "the Living Voice!"'

'Things as strange have happened,' replied the
oracle. 'One thing is plain, that the "Tracts" drew
forth other Essays, and "have taught" Oxford men,
and Churchmen generally, "not only to think, but
to think for themselves." Don't you perceive?
Some say the spirit of Luther is dead and buried.
I say the spirit of Erasmus is up and doing. Which
will win?—authority and policy, with "organisation" and pamphlets, or Milman and Dr. Arnold,
with only history, light, and ideas?'

'Light and ideas!' repeated the colonel. 'What
are they? What light? what ideas?'

' Well, to be grave, our Lord came into the world to be the *Light* of it; and that by restoring to it the original Divine religion that had been so long buried under men's superstitious inventions. What authority less than *His* could have taught mankind, so fallen from its Maker's image, that what is pleasing in its Maker's sight is such piety and such goodness as is shown in temperance, righteousness, and charity, in love to God and man ? What greater proof is there of God's providential watch over His Church than His having caused to be committed to writing, and preserved, the discourses, " the *very words* of Jesus Himself, the prime, indefeasible truths of Christianity ?" If Christ's doctrine had not been fixed in His own words Christianity would have soon become an empty name. As it is, we have a simple and perfect test. Nothing can be contrary to Christ and be right. It is not for us to strain the plain teaching of Jesus, under the notion of "developing" it by the teaching of His Apostles. We must interpret the message of the servants by the words of their Master, and all is well. It is to those words we must come back in all our difficulties ; and very specially so just now, to know in what direction "development" must be prosecuted. Stand still, I think, we cannot, if we would. So now you have my view of our brawls and squabbles; and, to give the "developers" only their due, things are in most respects far better than they were twenty or thirty years ago ; though, no doubt, the Whig abolition of pluralities and non-residence had no small share in the good

work of revival, and the old Reformation High
Church party had a very large one.'

'I see you looking over your shoulder,' said the
colonel. 'Must you turn back ?'

'When I have asked you one question, if you will
give me leave—that is, how you, a Guardsman——'

'Late of the Guards.'

'Once a Guardsman, always a Guardsman—and a
man about town, can find time to interest yourself
in the subjects you have encouraged me to prose
on ? That is a secret worth learning. Even I have
not too much leisure, and your time I should have
supposed fully taken up with clubs, and dressing,
and dancing attendance on parties, dinners, balls,
drums, and diversion, and grandeur in general, when
you are in London, and in smart country houses
when "the season" is over. I find it hard work to
make time for reading and thinking, while "vegetating," as our bishops kindly say, in a country village. How you men in society do it is past my
comprehending.'

'You reason,' replied the colonel, 'like a good
mathematician ; but, like the mathematician, you
start from hypothesis. In the first place, Guardsmen are better fellows than your question supposes ;
and, in the next place, if you count me a Guardsman, I do not go into "Society," as you call it. I
have long since had enough of it, as most Guardsmen have.'

'I have not a word to say against Guardsmen,
Colonel Denny. I never saw one that was not of
the right sort. If I were a soldier, I should like to
be a Guardsman, for certain.'

'Thank you, for the Guards. Then you will allow, I hope, that a Guardsman may be a Churchman, as well as a Christian, and that I may be interested in the concerns of the Church to which I belong. You will forgive my catechising you, won't you? You know my clerical friends are few, and Palmer—amiable, excellent, sensible man that he is—can never be got to say a word on what he calls "Church politics," which he says are as bad as, or worse than, any other politics. He told me that you were not so averse, and would not mind, if I could get hold of you; and Barbara was quite sure you would like it, for that she and you have had many a long discussion.'

'Indeed, we have,' said the curate; 'and how well she talks on that, and on all subjects!'

'Does she not!' cried the colonel, with an earnestness that struck his hearer.

'Is *he* the man then, after all?' said the curate to himself, when they had parted. 'I thought the big red one could never be her choice. Fine animal though he be, there is really nothing else to admire about him, except his honest admiration for the colonel, which seems not to be much returned: and no wonder, if my suspicion be correct. Rufus appears clearly to be the reigning prince at present, and takes his honours as a matter of course. I cannot understand it; time must show. But I do like the red captain for so looking up to Denny. It shows well in him, since in all else he is sharp, and narrow, and depreciatory, like other vulgar souls. Well, well, well; we shall see. "All's well that ends well."'

CHAPTER VIII.

'Simple Simon totters by,
Timid, and ashen pale, and shy ;
And as he threads the public ways,
The people turn, and stand to gaze.

' The lasses whisper, full of gloom,
"There stalks a man from out the tomb !"
Ah, no ! ye err, ye gentle lasses,
Not from, but to, his tomb he passes.'
HEINRICH HEINE, *by* JULIAN FANE.

'AH ! lawk-a-day ! How uncommon bad he do
look, sure-ly, sure-ly !' said one villager to another,
as poor Dick sullenly acknowledged their curtsies
and passed by. ' All unbraced,' said she, 'I do declare, and quite careless like ! Him as was used to
be so nice, and neat, and partic'lar ! He goes a-
talkin' to hisself. I do think he be out o' his mind,
poor lad, he do look so wild ! An' he don't get up
afore noon most days, they tells me. Lor' ! if his
poor old feyther, as was so proud o' him, could but
see him, poor old man, it 'uld break his heart; I'm
sure it a'most do mine. An' wus nor that. He do
speak so cross to his men an' maids—him as was so
civil-spoken an' kind-like ! Howsomedever, they

know what's up wi' un, an' don't mind now; but I doubt if they will bear it long, that I do.'

'Lork-a-mussy, Mary!' said a young man to a pretty young woman, who was luxuriating with the rest at the idle corner; 'I do believe, Mary, as I'm i' love wi' you; I do feel so bad like. How do I look?' added he, edging up rather close to her.

'Ha' done, yer great ugly bear,' said the lady.

'I do b'lieve it's all along o' love for you,' said the swain.

'Git along, yer great big fool,' retorted the fair Mary.

Yet Mary looked as if she did not think so ill of him or of his judgment.

'I know,' commenced another, reverting to the dame's remarks on poor Dick, 'I know he's turned uncommon sour, as sour as small beer in harvest; and I ain't a-goin' to stan' none o' his nonsense neither, 'cause his gell won't have him—not I! I'd sooner turn sodger, or be a factory "hand," as ain't a man at all.'

'Ne'er mind him, Will,' said the dame. 'Poor lad! he can't help himself.'

'There's summut i' that,' said grumbling Will; an' his feyther wor a good un—he wore that, he wor; an' this 'ere young un worn't half a' bad un afore this job; I will say that for un. Do as you're done by; that's my rule: them as does good to me, I'll do good to 'em; them as does bad to me, I'll do bad to 'em.'

'An' you call yourself a Christi'n?' screamed the dame.

'Awh! I *knows* better,' said he; 'but I'm like my betters; I don't practise it o' week days; I keeps it for Sundays. If a man behaves well to me, I'll behave well to him, an' I won't tell you no lies about it; that's more nor some folk can say. But, mind yer, I won't stan' gammon not from nobody, neither gre't nor small; so I won't. I heerd a man say t'other day as his dog bore malice like a Christi'n, an' I think he's about right—not as I say malice is right, not I—that's wus nor saying as he bore malice like a woman.'

'You git along wi' yer, an' let the women alone; and they won't have nothing to say to you,' retorted Mary promptly.

Next day the hounds met not far off. And some of our friends of the idle corner saw the subject of their remarks ride through the village betimes booted and spurred in full hunting equipment.

'That do look like old times,' quoth one of the dames, peering out from her door with village curiosity to see who was passing. 'Whenever I see him go a-hunting, I always do believe he's a-goin' to mend; he's bound to get over it, if he only keeps a-going among the gentlemen a-huntin'.'

'An' keeps away from the ladies,' put in a male bystander.

'Well, I dun know,' quoth the dame next door. 'I looked at him as he went by, an' thought if ever I saw death, it was in his face—I did indeed. I'm afeard he'll meet a bad acciden', or may be his death to-day—I am indeed.'

'Ha' mussy on us! how you talk, wench! Ye

turn one quite inside out—that's what you do—wi'
yer death, an' yer haccidens, and the rest on't!
Sich rubbage!'

'You'll see,' said the crone.

'No; I won't see; I don't mean to see nothin' o'
the sort,' quoth the more sober dame. 'Don't talk
sich rubbage; I can't abear to hear you. When our
time comes, we shall go all o' us; not afore nor a'ter.
Whatever ye may say, I say he's got the turn; an'
you'll see, he'll be just as he was afore.'

'I hope I may see it,' quoth the croaker; 'but I
think I see summut quoite different, an' I ne'er was
mistook.'

'Rubbage!' cried the other, frightened all the
same.

Meanwhile, all unconscious of prophecy and doom,
Dick rode on to the meet. If anything could cheer
him, his ride might. For

> 'Of all the brave sports that e'er man did see,
> Fox-hunting 's the fairest in its degree,'

when the wind blows softly from the moist south-
west, and thin clouds veil the sun, and the landscape
is clad in sober grey; and in pearly drops hangs the
dew upon the grass and upon every purpled spray
of the leafless hedgerow; and the damp sod takes
deep impression from the most airy tread of the most
elastic stepper that ever trod the green; and no jar
shakes the bones of the rider, or tests the tender foot
or strained sinew of the veteran leader of the van in
half-a-dozen hard-going seasons.

The day is perfect for its purpose of rural revelry.

The lord and the lady, the squire and the farmer, the
soldier and sailor, the lawyer and tailor, the doctor
and butcher, the banker and baker, the stockinger and
strong-minded parson, the ploughman and herdsman,
and glazier and sweep ; all the gregarious and eques-
trian tribes of men are gathered together, and mounted
on ten-pound ponies, on twenty-pound hacks, on colts
from the plough, on embryo hunters undergoing
education, on hunters made perfect and worth a
fortune : all the tribes of men are there, and most are
mounted—all save the unsocial and austere professor,
who prefers to spend his well-earned holiday in
exclusive enjoyments, and takes his solitary pleasure
sadly in the lone Alps.   There let him be ; and turn
and see, fair and fresh as the dawn, habited in
hunting-green, and mounted on that gallant grey,
the descendant in the fourth generation of genius
and beauty ; and see for contrast, lank and lean and
ghastly, as though he had been buried and dug up
newly to pilot her, sitting his horse with an ease and
grace that none can surpass, the finest rough-rider
in the three kingdoms, 'Cap Timson,' of Willesden,
rejoicing to rule the wild and wanton spirits

> ' Of youthful and unhandled colts—
> Fetching mad bounds, bellowing, and neighing loud,
> Which is the hot condition of their blood.'

Your Alpine clubmen claim to show more courage
and more skill; but rocks do not vary in their
tempers, are never sulky or frightened, never sick or
sorry, never grow tired and fall, or run away ; and
do not need one-hundredth part of the judgment and
discretion of 'Cap Timson' to deal with them.   If

you want to take off your hat to cool courage and ready skill, you could not find a man to represent it better than 'Cap Timson.' He is not on a raw colt now, but on a hunter, worthy to pilot such a queen of beauty.

Now please to turn to that knot of gentlemen: it has been 'chaffing' a county member about some small appointment, in the making of which he was concerned, and which has not turned out well. He learns public opinion there quite as well as in the columns of the newspaper, or in the House of Commons.

Having settled the member's business, the company are discussing the points of Fin-ma-coul. Fin is looking his best.

'What a magnificent horse he is !' said one; 'I suppose he can jump anything that is before• him, from a six-foot wall to six yards of water ? though your Irish nags are not generally grand at that.'

'I fancy he has done most things in Ireland before I bought him,' said the captain modestly.

'And a good many since, with you, Gibby, eh ? But you'll want him and all he can do to-day.'

'Why to-day ?'

'Because I see that little Gryffyn, as usual, on the look-out to cut you down !' said the Honourable Allan Fitz-Osmund.

'Confound his impudence !' cried the captain angrily; 'I'll break the little beggar's neck ; see if I don't. I don't mind a little jealous riding more

than another; but I am tired of this sort of thing;
I have had too much of it.'

'Never mind, Gibby; it's a case of Cupid!' said
another.

'Or of cupidity,' said a third; 'for the lady is
rich.'

'Well, little Gryff means to ride, I can see; and
he has his eye upon you, Gibby,' said the Honourable
Allan. 'He's a feather-weight, and game, every
ounce of him. What'll you bet he don't take the
shine out of you, Gibby? Will you give fifty to
one? or twenty to one? or ten to one?' asked the
honourable, who, poor and sharp and expensive, was
always on the look-out for crumbs to be picked from
the tables of his richer neighbours. 'What *will* you
bet?' he asked again.

'As I mean to break the beggar's neck, I shall
make no bet on the subject,' replied Gibbons
roughly.

'Well, look sharp,' said the other, still 'chaffing';
'you have cut him out, haven't you? or have you?
See he don't cut you out to-day. He means
mischief, I can tell you. Your nag looks fit to run
across country for a man's life; and he'll have to
run for your credit, mind, if we are in for a good
thing to-day; and something tells me we are.'

'Something tells you a good many things that are
all wrong, Ozzy,' retorted Gibbons.

'Little Gryffyn's nag is as thoroughbred as Eclipse,'
said another, yet keeping up the fire; 'and he has
gone like a bird this season. I like the little man

for his pluck; I'll be shot if I don't. I have a good mind to make him my agent.'

' A disappointment is a rare thing to make a man ride,' said another.

' Try it yourself, then, Giles; it'll maybe cure you of craning and funking.'

A very palpable hit, which raised a general laugh and turned the conversation of that dandified clique.

' I say,' said Captain Golightly to Franklin, in another set at another corner of the covert, ' did you ever see a man so changed as our friend ? so quarrelsome, so jealous and savage ; and he used to be such a cheery little Dicky, always good fun. He has nothing to say now but to snap and to snarl, and very nastily, too. What's it all about, Franky eh ?'

' He is, indeed ! quite another man,' replied Franklin ; ' dull and ill-conditioned enough, just now ; acid as vinegar. You never know a fellow. I did not think it was in him, so bright and merry as he used to be, singing and joking for ever.'

' And what's it all about ? You know, Franky ; I am sure you do ?'

' He never told me.'

' But you guess. Come now, out with it ; what is it ? Something very bad, to turn him so sour. He is just the opposite to what he was. Case of desperation, eh ? Lost his pet bird, and the yellow-boys ? Goldfinch, and that sort of thing ? Doesn't see the pretty finch, now ; does not haunt the dale, you know.'

'Perhaps not.'

'But hang it, man, a mere refusal would not so sour the milk of human kindness, as the poet says. Hasn't been kicked, has he, eh? They do say old Palmer is a terrible fellow; took him by the shoulders, put him out of the door, and spun him down the steps like a top. Is that true, old fellow, —eh?'

'It is very like Palmer, to be sure,' said the other. 'You know him, of course?'

'Not I; but he is a tremendous fellow, they tell me. Uncommonly strong; can break a poker across his arm, and all that sort of thing; and a perfect dragon about his daughter. He horse-whipped Burgoyne, that I do know; and if he had not been a don, a squire-parson, and that sort of thing, the bishop would have pulled him up for it, and had his gown over his ears.'

'Of course,' sneered his friend.

'And let me see,' proceeded the captain, musing aloud; 'don't they say he gave you the sack too, old fellow—eh?'

'I tell you what they do say,' retorted the other, 'that you dream a good deal, and don't know when you are awake or asleep; and that accounts for your getting such an uncommonly bad place in every run for all your fast nags. There! listen! the fox is stirring; we shall be off directly. Look out!'

Near to the spot where the subject of these discourses sat moody but watchful, lamenting his lost love, and 'filled with folly and spite,' was an elderly sportsman in scarlet, with black cloth on his arm, bewailing to Sir Alfred Ashwood and Finch Adams, Lawrence, and some other intimates, the lost partner of his life.

'Oh, my poor wife!' he was repeating again and again, as the tears trickled down his weather-beaten cheeks.

This gentleman, suddenly lifting his head and pocketing his handkerchief in haste, rose in his stirrups, looked intently for a second, then put his fingers to his ears, and screeching: 'Tally ho! Gone away! Tally ho!' gathered up his reins, put spurs to his horse, and galloped off like a madman.

'I am afraid our friend is a bit of a humbug,' said Sir Alfred.

'Not a bit of it,' said Finch Adams, as they followed more leisurely, and watched the turning of the hounds. 'He was very fond of his wife, and he is very fond of hunting. She has been dead these six months, and the fox has just gone away; he'll make it all right again, and pipe away at the first check. Meanwhile he forgets his trouble; for that is all nonsense about "black Care sitting behind the horseman," if he is riding to hounds.'

So saying, he put his horse at a stiff stake-and-bound fence, and took his line.

The hounds had hardly settled to the scent.

'Can't you find a place?' was heard from the other side of a fence so thick and high, that nothing could be seen over, or through, or beyond it.

'There is old Brewin pounded,' said Golightly, going at his ease, to Franklin, going in like manner.

Then came a gate, and a crowd at it, and a fumbling at the latch.

'Those cavalry men can never use their hands,' grumbled a peppery old stager.

Then there was a rush, and the gate banged to again, another fumbler and more grumbling.

'*He* has not even the excuse of being a military man,' sneered the vexed old Nimrod.

And now there was, for the better sort, no more opening of gates ; the pace was mending.

'There is little Dicky !' said Golightly, 'to the front, riding at the red captain, as usual. If we cross the vale, as seems likely, we are in for a clipper, and then they will see which is the better man. Which will you back, the little un or the big un ?'

'If I were going to bet, which I am not, I should back the red un at two to one. Little Dicky's of the right sort and of the right weight, and his mare is of the right sort too, thorough-bred as Eclipse ; but the red captain is on his Irish horse—about the best hunter that ever jumped a fence—and Gibbons is an old hand and a first-rate workman,' replied Franklin.

'See !' cried the other, in metaphor confused, perhaps by his haste ; 'there goes your friend Martel on his cob, bucketing away like a bird. What a good little crettur it is ! If she were half as big again, I would back her against either.'

'Aye ; she is wife and family to him, and all his property,' replied Franklin.

And then the pace for a while stopped the inter-change of ideas between these two sportsmen. But

Captain Golightly's prophecy did not seem in the way to be verified; within ten minutes the fox was lost, and covert after covert was drawn without finding another at home. By one o'clock the day had cleared up into warm sunshine, and 'the field,' grown hopeless of sport, had turned careless, and got broken up into sociable knots; some smoked, some sang songs, and sitting on the banks by a wood-side, while the hounds silently and vainly rummaged it, plucked violets, and enjoyed the subtle infinite charm of a premature spring day, and the free country life of the foxhunter.

When at last they had given up the wood as empty, and the hounds on their way to another copse were trying a patch of hill-side gorse from which nothing was expected, the red captain, who had no rustic enthusiasm for the sunny delights of a fine March day, and was but a keen, indefatigable sportsman, who had as yet done nothing with Fin-ma-coul, kept a sharp look-out for the chance of a run; and Dicky, who would in other times be as ready as any one for smoking and singing songs and picking violets, never let Gibbons out of his sight.

Suddenly, while the many were scattered and unobservant, the fox stole away. The master, a true foxhunter to the core, who spent twelve thousand a year on his hunting establishment, and would, as he said, gladly have given as much more to keep the field free from crowds and from jealous and unruly riders, took care that as little noise as possible should be made. So away they slipped, the few men who were on the alert, and among them the two foes.

It soon became clear that they were in for a good
thing. The scent is excellent, the ground is in prime
order, and the hounds scud along like the wind, with
heads up and almost mute, and nobody within a field
of them. The nearest were the huntsman and the
red captain, and a very little behind, to the right
and ready for a turn, was the master. They were
running over large, rich grazing grounds of a hundred
acres each, enclosed with strong ox-fences; but for
the first fifteen minutes, no very extraordinary
obstacle stood in their way. Then they saw that
the fox was making for the famous farm, whose
fences no one had ever been known to cross without
a fall at one or other.

And now they begin to pull their horses together,
and settle themselves for the struggle. The master
had come to the front, next to him came the red
captain and little Dicky, taking fence for fence and
stroke for stroke abreast. The mare being thorough-
bred on this sound ground, might have passed the
Irish horse, but Dicky was bent on keeping his man
in view; and close behind them came the huntsman.
At a tremendous stile, with a wide ditch and foot-
board, and bad taking-off and bad alighting-ground,
the master got his first fall, and his horse got away.

'Keep with the hounds!' he roared to the glad
huntsman, who seemed to hesitate about catching
the loose nag.

At the next fence Dicky, who was now with the
red captain in front, saving his mare from a fall over
the back-rail of an ox-fence, was fairly *pulled* over
her head.

The huntsman, who was now alongside of the red captain, came into trouble next. In rising, his horse's breast caught the first flight of a double post and rail, and they tumbled through it, by rare good luck, without hurt to either. And at the very last fence of that fatal farm, the Great Fin, whose only fault was the Irish one of jumping sometimes a little short, got his feet in a dyke on the off-side, and gave his owner his first fall.

In spite of all this there was no stop or stay, only a changing of places at each disaster: the four kept pretty close together, and near the hounds. The master had recovered, and remounted, his horse in a few seconds; Dick had scrambled upon his mare while she was yet moving; and the other two got on their horses again as they rose to their legs, in so great haste were they: the fox so near, the time so little, and the run so hot.

When they emerged from those renowned enclosures into an easier country, their places were again pretty much what they had been before that course of danger was entered; only the huntsman led, and the master was the last of the four; the red captain was second, and Dicky, whose mare, though she was thorough-bred and had all the endurance of her sex, was small, and began to suffer from the extraordinary stretch and exertion called for by the huge fences she had just got over, came third.

Horses, however good, are not made to gallop and jump for ever: under the mare's flank, so shrunk it was, you might hide your hat; and even the Great Fin looked as though he had not been fed for a month, and he was lathered as for shaving. Luckily for all, the pace slackened, and there was a momentary check ; with the others, Dicky and the red captain jumped off, and turned their horses' heads to the wind, and their own backs on one another.

Within three minutes the hounds struck the scent, and were off again in full cry. The course for a little way ran along a green lane that bounded the hedgerow, along which the hounds were hunting their fox, and which soon led them to a gently sloping grassy hill, on whose distant top loomed, cold and grey, a well-known park-wall, six feet high, of solid stone-masonry. Presently the fox was viewed topping it. The red captain, mounted on his Hibernian—expert, might have sung :

> ' He thinks nothing at all
>   Of a six-foot wall ;
>   That's the man for Galway.'

But what were the rest to do ? The hounds swung round a little to the right, where the wall had lost a few stones, and a gap that they could compass appeared. The huntsman and the master followed them. Gibbons, confident of the powers of Fin-ma-coul, and glad of a chance to give this pestilent boy a lesson, slackening his pace, held on the straightest and shortest way in the direct line of the fox, sure that the lad would not be so infatuated as to follow him. But Dick was a man of another metal ; his blood was up, and he would have faced an auto-da-fe.

As Gibbons slackened his pace Dick came up on

a level with him, and was now riding abreast, and very near him; and, to the captain's amazement, showed no sign of turning. The experienced man saw at a glance that the mare was pretty nearly beaten, and that the boy knew nothing of the art of riding at high walls, and he hoped that at the last moment Dick would have the sense to turn tail. When, instead of that, he saw the lad going to the front with his face hardened like a flint, and sitting well back, with his hands down and with his spurs touching his mare—and she, with her ears cocked forward, showing no symptom of refusal—much as he had been exasperated by the young man's most provoking and insolent behaviour, he took a pull at Fin-ma-coul, and shouted:

'Are you mad? For God's sake, hold hard! You'll break your neck to a certainty.'

'What, a captain, and afraid!' barked Dick, short of breath and wild with fury, and he drove his mare at the wall.

A rush! a shower of stones! two steel-shod hoofs, and a tail toppling over! a heavy thud! a groan! Then the Irish horse, with the cleverness of long practice in wall jumping, tipped lightly the coping, and landed safely in the park. There lay the mare motionless, and partly under her Dick, with his neck broken, as it seemed, and stone dead.

Gibbons' heart leaped into his throat; he would have given all he possessed to have had his angry words unsaid; the evil threat rang in his ears like the voice of a fiend: he felt as though the boy's blood were on his head, and for a few moments he was paralysed. He was recalled to his senses by the fallen mare, who suddenly stretched herself, made a great struggle, rose to her feet, and shook herself as if perfectly recovered. For an instant hope returned.

' It is all right after all, thank God,' he uttered in fervent joy.

But the young man lay still. Captain Gibbons was not intellectual, and but half educated, so far as books are concerned; but his feelings were the trained and sensitive feelings of a gentleman, and he was helplessly agitated.

CHAPTER IX.

'In the morning thou shalt say, Would God it were even!
and at even thou shalt say, Would God it were morning!
for the fear of thine heart, wherewith thou shalt fear, and
for the sight of thine eyes, which thou shalt see.'—*Deut.*
xxviii. 67.

'DIDN'T I tell 'ee I saw death in 's face?' said the
croaker of the day before.

'But there wa' n't no death in 's face, so you
couldn't ha' seed it,' retorted the more cheerful
spirit.

'Didn't I see un wi' my own eyes carried up the
street feet fust i' the carridge last night, an' his
mare, poor dumb thing, behind, a hangin' down her
head, for all the world as though she were a-
weepin'?'

'I don't know about weepin', nor I don't know
about feet fust; but I do know as he ain't dead;
an' I'll never believe as he's agoin' to die, not till I
hear the bell go for un.'

'Nor you needn't believe it then, missus,' said an
elderly man standing by.

'No! how's that, Jem?'

' 'Cause I heerd the bell go for me years ago ; an'
you see I ain't dead yet.'

' Ye heerd the bell go for ye years ago ! Whoy,
what nonsense ye're a-talkin' !' said one.

' May be it wa' for his marridge,' said another.

' Noa; it wa' for my death. I wa' laid out, as
true as I'm standin' 'ere. It wa' afore you come to
the parish. There's Tom Low an' Bill Glads 'll tell
'ee the same, if ye ax un. I wa' in a trance like, ye
see ; an' they thought I wa' dead, and were agoin'
to bury me. We lived, then, in that 'ere corner
'ouse, there ; an', as I lay, I could hear folk a-talkin'
about me at the corner, as plain as I hear you now.
An' some said good, an' more said bad o' me.

' " He wa' an uncommon bad un," says Bill; " I
never knowed a wussur ; he never had a good word
for nobody but hisself; an' a deal o' that, surely."

' " Not sich a werry bad un," says Tom ; " not no
wuss than the rest o' us, whatever better," says he.
" I've know'd un do a many a kind thing; an' he'll
get his reward now."

' " E'es, he'll get 'is reward," says Bill, an' he set
up a-laughin' like anythink.

' Uncommon pleasant it wa' for me, as I lay ex-
pectin' to be screwed down every minute. I couldn't
speak, nor move, nohow. I thought Tom were a
good-natured fellow, an' so I do now; for I wa' n't
a very good un then, I know.'

' But you are now, Jerry, ain't you ?' said another.

' When I'm not compared along o' sich a hangel as
you, Mick.'

' Drat your rubbidge ! Don't stan' there a-sniggerin', when the poor young gentleman is maybe a dyin',' said the kind dame.

' Didn't I tell yer he'd die ?' quoth the crone.

' An' that's just why he won't,' snapped her friend. ' I'll never believe it till I hear his bell; an' not then.'

' I know he's got three doctors ; an' if that won't kill 'un, I know nothin'.'

' I know you'll kill me if I stop a-listenin' to you ; but he'll none die for all your talk : he'll go when his time comes, an' not afore;' so saying, she turned into her house, and banged the door on her loquacious friends.

Meanwhile, one doctor was with our poor friend, and another had just left him, having both spent the night by his bedside; and then they shook their heads together and used many hard words, which no one else present could understand.

After a fortnight of assiduous and costly attention, the two doctors were able to declare their patient on the high road to recovery ; they paid him fewer visits, and left nature and rest to restore him. There was a broken collar-bone to be healed, and a broken arm and rib; and there had been a concussion of the brain.

The Palmers and all the people about had, throughout the critical period, made daily inquiries, and showed sympathy in every way ; and, now, all his friends and neighbours came to comfort him ; but Dick refused to be comforted, and sulked, and would see none of them : only to Lord Mercia admittance could hardly be refused. As he sat upon the sick

man's bed, a sight to do good to sick eyes, bright
and free and kindly and gentle as a woman, he
seemed to fill the room with the jollity of his ample
person, and the wonted overflowing splendour of his
array: his vast waterfall of silk necktie, his huge
jewelled breast-pin and chain, his fine waistcoat
all thrown back, and his bright blue cut-away coat
thrown open too, and the white zephyr overcoat,
most fly-away of all. It was not the sort of dress
that many men could wear becomingly; but Lord
Mercia would not have been himself without it.
There, on Dick's tumbled bed, the great earl spread
himself, all affability, and talked, and stuttered out
news, and hopes, and comfort, and consoling praises
of Dick's management.

The lord had been round to look, while Dick was
laid by, and had seen everything; and nothing could
be going on better; and Dick would soon be about
again. And was there any alteration he would like
to make? anything he could suggest? about the
estate? or his own house, eh?

No, there was nothing; and Dick would say
nothing, nor smile, nor even give thanks, nor look
pleased; but lay sulky as a wounded bear. And
the kind earl, baffled in the hope of rousing and
cheering his young agent, went down the stairs
stuttering to himself:

'Too bad, too bad; they have behaved abominably
to this poor boy; abominably, abominably. I don't
know who it is, don't know who it is; but they
have nearly killed him among them. It can't be, as
they say, that gentlemanlike old fellow, Palmer;

I know him better than that—better than that;
nor yet that nice girl of his—I'll never believe it—
never believe it. I can't understand it, can't understand it; but they have done it among them,
somehow—great shame,, great shame. He'll get
over it, though, and be none the worse for it; but
it'll be a long time—a long time.

Meanwhile, the young man lay with his head
shorn of its amber looks, with one arm swathed to
his body to keep in place the broken collar-bone,
and the other bound up in splints, while the broken
rib barred change of posture. His mind was sorer
than his body. It's only relief came with the brief
visits of fitful slumber. Then, begotten of an
agitated heart and brain, a vision of joy and beauty
hovered over him with airy charm. Most lovely
in her parting smile, she seemed to haunt his
hot pillow. Again and again he views her with
rapture; again and again she glides away, and in
an instant is gone, flitting with the light wings of
departing sleep. A cold, stern form, red-haired and
blue-eyed, usurps her place, and, lo! he is awake
and wretched.

In youth broken bones soon unite, and bruised
flesh is soon sound again; but the wounds of the
young spirit, what but time can cure? Dick was
soon up and about again; and, though he still refused
to see any friends, he could wear out his days in business, and get rid of them in a sort of stunned and
weary forgetfulness of anguish. But when the day was
gone and work was over, and Hesperus came ' bringing all good things, home to the weary, to the hungry

cheer,' he could neither rest nor eat, nor read, nor forget himself; but sat moping and pining, a desolate young man in a lonely house, thinking of what he had lost, and refusing to be comforted by all the good that was left to him.

Sometimes struggling after a hard Stoicism, sometimes yielding to a soft despair; sometimes hot with angry pride, but never bowed in trustful submission to say, 'Thy will be done,' he would at last throw himself upon his bed, to lie tossing through the night, while the blood rushed through his veins with the accelerated pulsation of fever.

One day he disappeared. At first it was feared that he had made away with himself; but, upon inquiry, it turned out that he had made arrangements with his bankers for supplies and secrecy, and with clerks and bailiffs for the working of the farm and the agency.

CHAPTER X.

'The bishop of our diocese is to me an incredible man, and has, I will grant you, very much more money than you or I would give him for his work. One does not even read those charges of his, much preferring speech that is articulate. . . But what think you of Bobus of Houndsditch, of our parts? He, sausage-maker on the great scale, knows the art of cutting fat bacon and exposing it, seasoned with grey pepper, to advantage. Better than any other man he knows his art, and I take the liberty to say it is a poor one. Well, the bishop has an income of five thousand pounds appointed for his work, and Bobus . . gains, from the universal suffrage of men's souls and stomachs, *ten* thousand a year. . . It is not good sausages he makes, but only extremely vendible ones. . . He is not an excellent sausage-maker, but a dishonest, cunning, and scandalous sausage-maker ; worth, if he should get his deserts, who shall say what ? . . The bishop I, for my part, do much prefer to Bobus. The bishop has human sense and breeding of various kinds : considerable knowledge of Greek, if you should ever want the like of that ; knowledge of many things, and speaks the English language in a grammatical manner ; he is bred to courtesy, to dignified composure as to a second nature ; a gentleman every fibre of him, which, of itself, is something very considerable. The bishop does really diffuse round him an influence of decorum, courteous patience, strict adherence to what is settled, teaches practically the necessity of burning one's own smoke. . . While Bobus, for twice the annual money, brings sausages, probably of horse-flesh, cheaper to market than another.'—T. CARLYLE.

' MRS. HUBBARD ! Mrs. Hubbard !' bawled the curate from the top of the stairs ; 'what have I done, Mrs.

Hubbard, that there should not be a button on any
one of my six shirts ?   And my boots are not clean !
my stockings I cannot find ! and where in the world
have you put my coat and waistcoat ?'

'Ah ! dear sir, whatever would you do without
me ? You ought to be married, Mr. Martel, and
have some one to look after you.'

'Too much luxury, Mrs. Hubbard. I should have
all my buttons on, and my hair combed too. I
would deny myself, don't you see ? It is enough
for me to have you, Mrs. Hubbard, to take care of
me.'

'La ! sir, you are helpless-like. Why, here are
your things right under your very eyes ! It is my
belief, Mr. Martel, you read too much. You are
always reading, sir, when you are at home—at
breakfast and dinner, and tea too ; and I do believe,
Mr. Martel, that you don't know what you eat or
drink ; and you don't have your meals regular and
comfortable ; they don't do you no good. I'm sure
so much study is bad for your stomach, an' it can't
help confusing o' your head. You han't got no
method about you, Mr. Martel. There was Mr.
Bulmarter—he was a curate, and lodged here before
you—why he never read nothing, an' he was all
method ; and you know, sir, you have no method at
all : you let your meals go anyhow, an' I never know
when you'll have 'em.'

'Well, Mrs. Hubbard, if I have no method, I have
you, Mrs. Hubbard, and that's as good or better.'

'Indeed, sir, if it were not for me, you'd never
remember your dinner, I'm sure ; for you go out,

and you forget to tell me when you'll be back, and
you come home late or early, Monday or Saturday
night, as it may be ; and you might be murdered,
and no one know anything about it. And I believe
you would often go without your breakfast and
never miss it, if I did not make you remember it.'

'Aye, indeed ; you are a wise wife and a virtuous
woman, and a crown to your husband. And now
you have done the buttons, like a good body as you
are, will you kindly tell Jim to have the nag at the
door in eight minutes from this time. I have only
fifty-eight minutes to dress in, and ride eight miles
to meet two live bishops at dinner ! no less, as I am
a live curate ! And think, Mrs. Hubbard, what will
be done with me if I keep bishops waiting for their
dinner !'

'La! sir, you don't say so; two live bishops!
What like is a bishop, sir ? I never came near one
since I was confirmed, and then I couldn't see him,
nor hear a word he said, for I was put in quite a
back seat. The fine ladies, you know, had taken
all the front ones; they will have the best, sir, of
course. But I did get one peep while he laid his
hands on me, and I should like to see one once
more.'

> ' " Be bishops all unseen, unknown,
> They must, or you will rue it ;
> You have a vision of your own,
> Oh ! why should you undo it ?"

Your confirmation is a pleasant · memory, Mrs. Hubbard ; you keep it.'

'I will, sir ; and I will go now and tell Jim.'

'Do. Ah! what like is a bishop?' muttered
Martel, thinking aloud after his hermit-fashion, and
then our bothered curate went bawling a-top of the
stairs after his boots.

It was no easy task to draw them on in a haste
upon hurried feet in the dogs days.

'Sure I am "swell-foot," and this boot is my
tyrant, ill-called Wellington,' groaned he, tugging
viciously at it in the sweltering heat.

After much scurrying to and fro with petulant
complaint on his part, and soothing good-nature on
the part of his landlady, he is at last started on the
cob, Miss Judy, with just thirty-eight minutes in
which to do seven miles, and present himself starched
and spotless before the awful eyes of their right
reverend lordships.

The thermometer is standing at ninety degrees in
the shade; the roads are deep in dust; the flies
torment Judy; Judy herself is out of temper and
fidgety, and shies; and, though fast and sure, is
terribly rough in her trot. What is our friend's
chance of putting in an appearance at once timely
and tidy? Would you, gentle reader, at ease in your
cool and judiciously-shaped chair, with your room
at the agreeable temperature of fifty-five degrees,
like to change places with our curate, and mount
his rugged cob, in order to dine with two bland
bishops?

For a curate who thinks well of himself, and
would like preferment (and where is the curate who
does not, and would not?), to be invited to meet a
bishop, much more two bishops, is like a magnified

going to court. His wishes to look and behave his best. But with the best intentions he may conspicuously fail. Our friend is of frail flesh, and, at his best, is much subject to the influences of weather.

This particular day was broiling hot; he had been at the most unseasonable moment summoned into the parish, and delayed in dressing; he had to scuffle; his clothes were mislaid; his shirts buttonless, his boots tight; his impracticable cob shook him, and kicked up the dust, and covered him with it as with a plaster; the heat took the starch out of his shirt-front, and turned his neatly-folded white neck-cloth into an unclean-looking rope. Conscious of what was going on, he suffered martyrdom during his ride in no patient spirit: the way seemed the longest he had ever taken; but he reached at last Mr. Ratcliffe's rectory, retired from the village street amid fine elms, behind a high wall.

Martel entered the house, red as a lobster fresh boiled and dripping from the water. Beside being hot and red and dewy, his face was caked with dust; his neat black suit, the costly production of a West-end tailor, about which he was rather particular, was powdered like a miller's working suit, and to make bad worse, he was five minutes late at a punctual house on a state day.

The decorous old gentleman-like servant who opened the door looked at his dress, first with amazement, then with horror, last of all with pity.

'Dear me! sir; dear me! and dinner, sir, has

been ready these five minutes; their lordships are
both in the drawing-room, but master would wait
for you.'

'Very kind ; I wish he hadn't.'

'But, really me ! we must do something, sir ! If
you would be so good as to step this way with me
we will try and make things a little tidier, sir ; you
must be uncomfortable.'

After five minutes' retirement, Martel emerged,
cleansed and refreshed ; soiled indeed and barely
presentable, and very cross. He felt somehow that
he was injured, and was in his most perverse mood,
with a decided disposition to be disagreeable, which
was not unusual to him in like circumstances. He
was not a man to be much put out by such things,
otherwise than in temper. He felt more a sense of
injury than of discomfort, as he walked through the
cool, well-ordered black and white ranks of men,
generally rosy and spectacled, who lined the drawing-
room, to make his host the clerical excuse of being
called away into the parish at the last moment.

'Ah !' said the elder, shaking his head good-
humouredly ; 'you young men nowadays leave
everything to the last. It was not so in my young
days ; we took Time by the forelock ; you know, he
is bald behind. But you have saved your dinner.
Let me present you to the Bishops of —— and ——.
You know the Bishop of ——, do you ? To be sure
you do—I forgot.'

'So you are at Sarsby for a time, are you ?' said
the bishop, shaking hands ;—' for a time,' he repeated,
with perhaps the faintest suspicion of reproach, or

reproof; for he thought Martel more given to change than became him, and possibly discontented, which would have been wrong, you know, in a curate.

The late comer had but a moment to glance over the room ; but he perceived there were no ladies to beguile the attention of clergymen from their bishops ; not even the lady of the house appeared. It was a huge man's party, a sort of convivial chapter. The black cloth and white necktie, which stand for the tonsure in the Church of England, were indeed the evening dress common alike to laity and clergy; but the aspect of the assembly was clearly ecclesiastical for all that. A certain decent stiffness of carriage, a decorous but independent formality of manner, proclaimed the country clergy, the backbone of the English Church. No black squires were there ; that sort of gathering is not much in their line.

The host, though garbed like the rest, and neither a giant in size nor a model of beauty, had among them an air of distinction, and looked what he was —not rural, or civic, but cosmopolitan, and a man of original genius.

There seems no reason why a bishop, barring coat, apron and shorts, should differ from another man outwardly; but it so happened that the prelatic members of the party, beside their distinction of dress, had other distinctions to be noted by a curious eye.

The one to whom Martel was newly introduced, small of stature, looked every inch a man of mind. His finely-formed head and serene blue eye, and his delicately-cut classic features, added to the orthodox coat, apron, and shorts, might, without any announce-

ment, have sufficed to make Martel suspect that the
little man in whose presence he stood was, with
one splendid exception, neither voluminous nor
wordy, the most learned and judicious bishop on the
English bench.

Beside him stood the other in like vesture, otherwise unlike enough. Something over the middle
stature, he had a dark complexion, regular features,
and a long, solemn face, lighted up by large, soft,
black eyes. Gentle and benign simplicity pervaded
the whole man, and bespoke him one of those rulers
of the Church who never fail in any age to be alike
called, and felt by all, save some mad bigots, indeed
fathers in God; were not the expression in any
exclusive sense anti-Pauline, one would say, here is
a true ' *saint*,' if ever his generation saw one. His
kindly, unpretending manner had not a grain of that
sugared softness so much affected in certain schools ;
rather had it with great plainness the refined easy
freedom which early habits of good company are
supposed alone to confer. His handsome face clean
shaven, and dark, suave, and grave, well became a
father of the clergy, such as Martel, whom he had
ordained, but whose organ of reverence was not over-
sensitive, had ever felt him to be. He did not, as
he had hinted, quite approve of Martel's frequent
changes of cure ; they seemed to him to indicate an
unsettled mind. He rather inclined to approbation
of the contented quiet which bishops have since
called the ' vegetating ' process. But, then, he was
quiet himself, and shrewd, and had a poor opinion
of bustle and fuss, and ostentation of every sort ;

and, simple and sincere himself, prized simplicity and sincerity and modesty in others.

Take this pair of bishops as they stood, aproned and gaitered, two better specimens of the Christian gentleman could not be found in any Church in Christendom. Both were born in that class not to be measured by money, called 'middle,' but composed of the middling gentry and of the educated professional grade.

The one had taken the highest honours of his University, and, at the age of twenty-six, was selected to be the private secretary of a cabinet minister of the same age, who was regarded with fond hope as the young Octavius of the high aristocracy; a hope which, on the whole, he did not disappoint. The ministry was short-lived; when it broke up, the ex-private secretary was soon made master of his college, and, not long after, called to a bishopric.

He never reached the topmost round of the ecclesiastical ladder; but it was well-known that a premier, famous for the fitness of his episcopal appointments, had made up his mind to raise the ex-secretary to the primacy, should the See of Canterbury fall vacant during his tenure of office. Fate forbade his elevation to the archiepiscopal throne; but the bishop made himself a great reputation. His administration of the diocese was fair, and mild, and discreet; his charges were models of good advice: men of every school of thought went to his visitations to hear, and anxious to profit by his wisdom. No one was ever offended by narrow party utterances, or wounded by one-sided and unjust censures, or made to laugh by pompous platitudes.

His official addresses were supplemented by the publication from time to time of valuable studies of the ecclesiastical history of the first three centuries, as illustrated from the writings of the Early Fathers, and as illustrating in turn the Articles and Liturgy of the Reformed Church of England. The patient labour, the learning, the penetration, the sober and balanced judgment, the nice skill and the unacademic acquaintance with the noble vulgar tongue evinced in these works, no one has ventured seriously to question. But, as some one says, the Church is apt to be but a smooth caricature of the world; and in sacred as in secular debates, when very solemn men cannot controvert, they can be merry and jest: and the bishop did not escape the jocose charge of having made Tertullian feel uncomfortable by thrusting him into the Thirty-nine Articles, and of having made all the Early Fathers Anglicans. In writing he was direct, and terse, and clear, and a master of plain statement; yet being a wary, non-party man in public life, he was accused of having 'the art of saying nothing in many words beyond any man that ever existed.' However that might be upon occasion, it is certain that he had, in great perfection, when it suited him to use it, the art of saying much in few words.

The story goes that at a visitation a churchwarden, red with anger as one of his own turkey-cocks, burst into the vestry upon the bishop, and without cere-

mony or preface demanded : ' What power, my lord,
has an archdeacon to enforce his mandates ?'

' What power, sir !—power !—has the archdeacon !'
repeated the bishop, caught unawares, but not asleep.
' I cannot tell you, sir, all the power that is possessed by an archdeacon !'

Orators tell us that in speechifying, action or stage-
play is everything. The prelate's acting was perfect,
and cooled at once the hot churchwarden, who,
silenced and sobered, left the vestry with a very
serviceable idea of the unspeakable potency of arch-
deacons.

But if the bishop was a cautious and careful man,
in nothing was his care and caution more manifested
than in keeping clean hands. Of everything that
borders on self-seeking or nepotism in the dispensa-
of patronage, he was as spotless—some said as cold—
as the new-fallen snow.

Touching ecclesiastical advancement, a relative
might have said to him, as a brother once said to the
great Butler, ' Methinks, my lord, it is a misfortune
to be related to you.' Though short of that prelatic
giant, he was a very wise and good bishop, and
though small of stature, of great reputation ; and
he looked every inch a great man, as he stood shorter
by the head than most of the men assembled to
meet him in Mr. Ratcliffe's party.

His brother bishop was a man of the same age, a
graduate of the same university, a member of the
same college ; less distinguished, but enough so to
gain a fellowship at a small college. After some
little, and not happy, experience of a forlorn and

benighted country parish, remote from towns and civilisation, to the incumbency whereof his family had presented him; he resigned it, and was recommended for an engagement as tutor in the household of a very great personage ; and there he lived several years valued and happy. And when time came to quit that sphere, he carried thence an exceeding simplicity and kindliness, which proved those virtues to flourish sometimes to the full as well in the highest as in lower places.

Not in the three grades of the Church's ministry could be found a man more humble or more friendly. He had lived in honour among the great long enough to appraise them at their real value ; whereas those who have no experience of them always over or under rate them. To his special patrons he was devotedly and most justly attached.

He was not greatly learned, as was in one way his right reverend brother, and in another his reverend host ; but he was of a quietly observant habit, meditative, and very shrewd of judgment. Mild and patient, he was never hurried, and very seldom misled. Nature had furnished him with a dry caustic vein of wit, over which he kept careful watch, holding the free exercise of it to be little becoming a good Christian, still less a Christian bishop.

Some without much wit have piqued themselves on saying things smart and tart ; he with a great deal of wit was remarkable less for it, than for the gentleness with which he used it. In both these prelates there was abundance of paternal authority,

in neither of them one grain of that dry, undignified
formality which so frequently disfigures the manners
of men in office, whether clerical or lay.

Having seen what manner of men they were, we
may without harm venture for distinction's sake to
call them, after the sources whence they rose, respec-
tively the politician and the courtier; though no
one could be less politic in the sense of time-serving
than the one, or less courtly in the sense of fawning
than the other. Without doubt their several courses
of life had rubbed off, by contact with men of the
world, certain angles of the ecclesiastical character;
and the polish acquired made them all the more
useful for good in the sacred seat of the ruler.

Into the courtier's diocese, during some years of
his episcopacy, had crept the spirit of party, and the
few violent men of each side, judging from their
own conduct, were loud in asserting that the diocese
was in disorder, and that the bishop did not 'govern
with vigour '—not that the complainants wished to
be governed, or would submit to be governed—but
that the bishop should be their cat's-paw and their
tool.

To the confusion of all dragooners and centralisers,
when, after many years, the Government inspectors
made their report on the state of education in
England, it came out that in no diocese were found
proofs of more efficient activity among the clergy in
education and in all good works.

The bishop's maxim—from acting on which he
was not to be bullied or driven—was that if the fire
of strife be not stirred, it will go out; and if you

give things time, they will come round. Many
prelates have been more widely known, and many
more loudly belauded; but to the thinking of those
who were near to see with eyes not blinded by
party fury, no more perfectly Christian ruler has
held the crozier in our days. With our courtier, as
indeed with many more, whatever worldly scoffers
may say, the 'nolo episcopari' was the simple
truth.

'Much as I love my calling,' he would say, ' I have,
as a matter of taste and feeling, or rather till use
wore it away I had, a positive repugnance to all
that state pomp and precedence, ecclesiastical as well
as civil, which is, I dare say rightly, considered
proper to us bishops; and it was well known that
my wish was not to be raised to the bench. And
so after many years' service in different spheres and
capacities, I was put on the list of—of—for a good
living. You will hardly credit me when I tell you
that, even on such an application, one of the good
livings of eight hundred a year or so was not to be
had, at any rate during the two years that I was permitted to wait for it; and I was at last compelled
to yield to the pressure upon me, and suffered myself
to be put on the bench, though I feared I should
wear but poorly temporal dignities, for which I had
no taste.

'My feeling on my elevation was,' "Je ne suis pas
à la hauteur des circonstances." But the man who
would fulfil the will of God must follow the leading
of His Providence. All this happened long ago, and
I thank God I have been very happy where He

called me to be. I was never uneasy about my own weakness, for I had seen often enough the strong fail and the weak succeed: weak or strong, man labours, and God gives the increase. And I hope He has enabled me to do some good, if not in other ways, at least by following after the things that make for peace in these days of bitterness and strife. But at first '—the good bishop would ramble on—' at first I felt sadly out of place. My man was my master. I had lived, to be sure, among great people; but I had lived among them as a little person, and to be waited on was never my idea of comfort or independence: I could do things more to my mind myself, as I had been brought up to do. But being made a bishop, I was taken possession of by a gentleman, whose feelings I would not hurt by declining his services or resisting his authority. There was nothing for me but to evade them as much as I inoffensively could. I used to get up before he came to me of a morning—for he was not a very early riser—and he would find me dressed. At first I do believe he despised me a little for not needing his help; but we soon got used to one another, and have lived together very comfortably ever since: I am quite satisfied with him, and I hope he is not very dissatisfied with me, though he is rather particular too.'

But, while the manner and habits of the two prelates have been told in detail, the host, a not less remarkable man, has been waiting for introduction to the reader. He was at the same college with his two silk-aproned guests. Of the three friends he was probably the ablest, and, in his way, not the least distinguished. Son of an attainted and ruined family of rank and ancient note, but so fallen that few, even of his intimates, knew him to be in blood, if not in law, the representative of an old baronial house, he by some means or other, like so many more, found his way from an obscure provincial grammar school to the University, where he won a fellowship and independence.

But for long, of his own free will and act, he remained very poor. Instead of emptying his own head and filling the heads of others and his own pockets in the way of tuition; he spent his money in buying books and his leisure in reading them. For several years he went on thus, gathering knowledge and collecting a library, and his outlay on rare and valuable books, despite his fellowship, kept him poor.

After a while, ceasing to reside in the University, he took a curacy not far from London, whence he wrote letters occasionally on public topics for the newspapers. One of these caught the eye of an enterprising foreign secretary; who sent for him, and, finding him full of talent and information, employed him on a delicate secret mission, which kept Mr. Ratcliffe on the Continent for several years, among people of the highest condition. Of the nature of his employment no particulars were ever made public; all that was known was that he had acquitted himself with credit and success.

On his return to England he distinguished himself in London by some ingenious and profitable inventions connected with the printing-press; and his services were liberally acknowledged by a share in the profits, and a gift of a house in the West End. These handsome additions to a large college living of some eleven hundred a year, which about the same time fell to his turn, placed him for the rest of his days in easy competence; and, with his lettered habits and childless state, made him pass even for a rich man.

He was probably better off in reality than either of his friends on the episcopal bench. His society was sought after in the best London circles, and in the country he entertained in turn his less fortunate brethren, all the curates and rectors of all colours in his neighbourhood; living in habits of intimacy with the most cultivated in the county set, and on easy and friendly terms with all. Of the county dons, some perhaps were a little jealous of his superiority of mind, in private carped a little at his unconscious mention of the greater people he had known, and cavilled at his stories as told too often, now that he grew old. He was now in his sixty-sixth year, after a struggling youth and laborious manhood, a prosperous, benevolent, happy old man, who divided his time pretty evenly between town and country, honoured, and with 'troops of friends,' entertaining the little and entertained by the great, at ease in circumstances, robust in health, at home in his pulpit and in his parish, a staunch, but tolerant, Churchman, well known and well liked by moderate politicians of both sides.

Martel's acquaintance with him had begun long

since in an application for his curacy, with the then unusual stipend of £180 per annun, without deductions or parish expenses. The application concluded with a request—suggested by the inconvenient silence of many rectors—that Mr. Ratcliffe would confer on the would-be curate at least the favour of a reply.

The curacy had been disposed of; but the old gentleman's very kind reply began with :

' I am not one of those who neglect to answer gentlemen's letters.'

When Martel afterwards held a curacy within reach of him, Mr. Ratcliffe was among the first to invite him to his house ; and his invitations, beside formal ones, he repeated as often as they met. This happened frequently in the market town, on Saturdays, when Martel would invariably decline, and the kind old gentleman would as invariably shake his head and say:

' I see, I see; you young men put off your sermons till the last moment. Bad plan, bad plan; we never did so in my day. Bad plan; change it; take time by the forelock.'

CHAPTER XI.

' He sympathises with the feeling of the day, in thinking
that energy, activity, bustle, extraordinary development of
intellect, are parts of the high and perfect state of the human
mind ; and that, to be a freeman, is to have the power and
will to encroach upon others.   He divides modes of life into
the ambitious and the selfish, as if thereby exhausting the
subject.'—J. H. NEWMAN—*Essays*, vol. ii.

' In truth, taking the corruptions of that day at the worst,
they were principally on the surface of the Church.   Scandals
are petulant and press into view ; and they are exaggerated
from the shock they communicate to beholders.   Friends
exaggerate through indignation, foes through malevolence.'
—*Ibid.*

' In Scotland, Dr. Laud, much to his regret, found no
religion at all ; no surplices, nor altars in the east, or any-
where; no bowing, no responding, no devotional drill exercise; in short, " no religion at all that I could see, which
grieved me much." '—T. CARLYLE—*Cromwell.*

THE bishops at the host's end of the table are in
post-prandial discussion, and the courtier is
speaking.

'What I think most injurious to sober vital
religion in this new and popular system of inviting
observation by pushing and puffing and display and
rivalry and emulation—sometimes with wrath and
strife—in meetings and congresses and so forth, is

its unreality. Notabilities and grandees, lay and clerical, just air their vocabularies, and nothing more. What can have a worse effect on the poorer clergy and the people at large, than to see a great meeting, with half-a-dozen bishops on the platform, and Canon This and Prebendary That, and the holders of the larger livings, and some affluent college tutors, and, perhaps, a cabinet minister, and one or two lay lords and rich commoners with twenty or thirty thousand a year each; and then to hear long speeches full of magnificent ideas, urging all people to self-denial and liberality and Christian zeal on account of the necessities of the Church; and the supreme importance of the work set forth in glowing terms. And all to end in what? Why, a contribution from all these rich and zealous and eloquent men, amounting to—perhaps in all—twenty pounds! It sounds ridiculous, but it is no joking matter. Of course orators are prone to indulge in sublime imaginations, for, you see, it is their trade, and theory costs nothing, since they have not to put it in practice. They shut their own eyes to the inconsistency, and think that no one will see it. But they do a vast deal of mischief.

'"What you preach," say the hearers, "is absolute asceticism; and your practice is just that of the rest of us. Your doctrine, as tested by your very respectable and rational way of life, is proved un-practical and impracticable."

'I am speaking only of the platform oracles; but the clergy generally are led, almost driven, whether they will or no, to copy their superiors. And so they come to me, and hold meetings, and put me in the chair. And I am expected to make a speech, and praise their activity and zeal in coming so far to do good. And then I am bound by all the laws of truth and justice to say a word for the number of quiet, conscientious, modest clergymen who stay at home and mind their own business, and stick to their own parishes, and look after their families, and perhaps educate for future usefulness, their children whom they are too poor to put to school, and in short do the main work of the Church. You know if every man minded his own parish and his own household, there would be no need for all this advertising and all the meetings where we come to tell or to hear something new. It is not for us to advertise and cry, " Lo, here ! or lo, there !" but in quietness to mind our own business, each in his own sphere. A " roaring trade" may do for those whose highest Church ideal is formed on principles of commercial competition ; but the aim of the Christian is not to stir up variance, emulation, wrath and strife ; not to separate men, but to bring them together—and to promote equality, not to raise distinctions. I am constantly urged, by this party and by that, to step in the moment anything goes wrong with them, and to play the bishop and set it right with the high hand. But I have lived a long time and seen a good deal, and have observed that in general the best way to settle a disturbance is to let it alone, and give things time to come round, and men time to cool. If you do not stir the fire, you know it will go out. And so we get along—not badly, I hope ; and we do not make much noise in the world, but are quiet and mind our own business, as we are bid to do.'

'That is not the way people do things nowadays,' said the other bishop. 'The spirit of the times cries, " See how much we are better than our fathers!" This England of ours, that has been some fifteen hundred years in building, we must pull down, rebuild; and everything in it must be turned upside down.'

'Even to the cases of nouns and the tenses of verbs in the Latin grammar. I am sure I could not find my way through it now,' put in the courtier, reflecting on his past labours as a tutor.

' Well, you know Plunket is right when he quotes Bacon, and says, " Time is the greatest innovator of all ;" while man may sleep or stop in his career, the course of time is rapidly changing the aspect of all human affairs : all that we can do is, to watch his progress and accommodate our ways to his flight; arrest his course you cannot ; but you may vary the forms of your institutions so as to reflect his varying aspects. If this be not the spirit which animates you, philosophy must be impertinent, and history no better than an old almanac.'

' Aye aye, Ratcliffe; very good, and very true ; but following in the track of Time is one thing, and hastening the wheels of his chariot is another,' replied the courtier.

' Too true,' replied the host; ' too true. The fact is, we are a good deal under the sway of the *novi homines*. And " how use doth breed a habit in a man !" There is your new man, the Right Honourable Phenax Stumper, born and bred to bustle and to show. His father, a most worthy man, was first the porter and then the partner in a commercial house; and as he honestly filled the till, he rose to a new position in life—new estate, new gardens,. new hothouses, new carriages, new liveries, a new coat of arms, and a new spelling of his name.'

'And new ancestors,' boomed the deep voice of the courtier.

'*Diruit, edificat mutat quadrata rotundis* describes the man at home and abroad, in private and in public,' went on the host. 'He buys an estate, grubs up all the hedges and fences, and resets them in squares and straight lines; cuts for the brook a brand-new channel and cures it of meandering, though it frets and wastes its banks much more than before: he covers with a decent culvert the sparkling stream from the fountain, which the old folks had loved to watch as it brawled along its rocky course through the village; he pulls down the old house and builds a new one, on a new site and a new plan; cuts his old friends, and gets new ones.'

'I hope he does not cut his poor old father and mother among the rest. Did you ever read of John Bounderby in Dickens's " Hard Times " ?'

'I should be sorry if I had not,' replied the host ;. 'every one ought to read that parable for the times. Those are the habits of mind your new man brings with him into public life. He deals with matters of state and the affairs of men as the tailor of Laputa dealt 'with Gulliver's clothes: he took exactly his altitude with a quadrant, and his dimensions with rule and compasses, and sent his suit home a complete misfit.'

'Well, you know, that is the sort of treatment our poor old Church of England is coming in for, under her new doctors. Devotion now means ritual; and decency and order gorgeous decoration. We all know that pomp and magnificence may be accessories of *religion*, and among rich people consistently; but are they essential to it? It is a new thing, with us, to be told that there is no religion where there is no splendour. Beautiful buildings, rich colouring on wall and window, and "dim religious light," ornaments of gold and silver, and tinsel, studied attitudes and tones, histrionic art and scenic effect, may, and often are, accompaniments of religion. But so is the wild hill-side, for a congregation accustomed to it; and what I, for my part, should like less, the white-washed wall and the barn-like chapel. All these things depend for propriety and fitness upon circumstance, and custom, and the fashion which comes and passes away with the other things of the world. I do not put my faith in decoration or in the destruction of it.'

'One cannot deny,' said the host, ' that pomp and magnificence are proofs of a Church's prosperity; only, as Mr. Hallam observes, it may be a prosperity that comes of " processions and all that we call foolery, but which is not the less captivating to the multitude for its folly." '

'I know there are gentlemen who (assuming their premise) ask, why are the poor and ignorant more religious and devout in the Church of Rome, where doctrine has been corrupted, than in the Church of England, where it is cleared of corruption ? And they make answer that the ignorant are taught by the eye rather than the ear. But I say, if they be ignorant, send the schoolmaster to educate them ; raise them out of their ignorance ; do not sink your religious teaching to the lowest barbarian level ; that is neither good for the teacher nor the taught.'

'But it is what the sectaries do in another way— they also neglect the reason, and they minister sensationalism to the senses,' remarked the host ; 'a worse error by far. To create a sensation, they employ fanatics, who create besides disaffection and ill-blood. For you know that morbid excitement, which is commonly called enthusiasm, mostly means egotism and intractable temper. There are no more dangerous and deadly weapons that selfish ambition can lay hands on than religious enthusiasm and religious demagogues, if I read history aright.'

'I do not know,' said the courtier, 'whether it is enthusiasm or ignorance that prompts the sentence ; but I do not like to be told that the old system, which brought us all up as Christians, is an incubus on the country. And as for those who, having been nurtured and taught all they know by the Established Church, are the first to turn round and throw stones at their mother;—why, I have no patience with them ; *mala mens, malus animus.*'

'Yes, indeed, *mens* and *animus* are pretty much alike. Quip, who can never be grave, cuts jokes upon his cloth ; and Proseon, who never saw a joke, takes them for earnest, and goes away raving at the careless clergy,' said Mr. Ratcliffe, laughing.

'Well, well,' returned the other, 'we English are not alone under unfavourable judgment; the Latin priesthood gets worse handling; we are told it has been a hotbed of impurity for hundreds of years, embracing all the centuries since the enforcement of celibacy began ; and the German clerisy fares rather worse than better, so we may be thankful we are let off so easy.'

'Have you ever read Wesley's sermon on the text, "No man taketh this office to himself"?' asked the politician. 'The Wesleyans have left it out of the later editions of his works—not unwisely —but it is worth your reading, for several reasons. He tries the clergy from the institution of the Jewish priesthood downwards to his own, and finds them all guilty, save those of one or two brief periods, among them the English clergy since the Reformation. Some people are now challenging any age of the Christian Church to show a clergy so secular and lax as the body into which you and I were ordained, in deplorable ignorance of its character. You see how doctors differ.'

'Particularly if they are fond of physicking,' added the host. 'But what pleases me most in these critical young gentlemen, is the modesty with which they ask, "How is it we are so much in advance of our generation?" "We are, as one may say, the flower of England;" "designed to set to right a generation accustomed only to bit reforms and rules of expediency," like poor Paley's, which, by the way, are generally misunderstood or misrepresented. "I should *like* this;" "I should be *sorry* to think that;" "My *grief* is poignant" about this; "it is *painful*" to imagine that; "*I* have done;" *I* have found;" "*I* feel,"—is the new test of all excellence, and the rule of right and wrong; and, on the strength of this egoism, men would revolutionise, or, if not, quit, the Church of their fathers. It is "*Sum pius Æneas*" all over; can you stand that?'

'I never liked Æneas or the Æneas-like character,' returned the politician. 'Talking of turning things upside down, do you ever go to the Bishop of Babel's public dinners when you are in town, Ratcliffe?'

'I went once; it was enough;—nothing but running down and crying up of this man and that, and schemes for the renovation of all things. I used to enjoy very much his predecessor's public days, and went to them whenever I was in the way of them, for one always found there good conversation and good manners.'

'The present bishop, between ourselves,' said the politician to his old friend, 'is much changed since I first knew him. He began well, and would have made a divine, if he had not muddled his head with reforming politics and the revolutionary tendencies of things.'

'Tendencies, indeed,' quoth the host, looking out of the window to speak to his gardener; 'you see that thistle-down; as Coleridge says, "its tendency is towards China, but it will never get there, nor many yards from the place where it grew."'

'You and I,' sighed Policy, ' have lived to see the
vanity of political vaticination; but our brother is
all vaticination——'

'And holy innovation,' added Mr. Ratcliffe. ' By-
the-bye, we hear a good deal about slovenly ritual
in churches; did you ever happen to hear of
slovenly exegesis of Scripture ?'

' Our friend, you must know,' replied Policy, ' sent
me the first book he published; it was not a large
one, but it was a good one, and I told him so. But
I ventured to add that our pious theologians dis-
liked all principles, the application of which would
cost them trouble; they preferred the short cut,
and he must not expect their approbation.'

' Then he paid you the compliment of taking
your hint in a way that you hardly looked for. No
one can suppose that he ever bestowed much time or
trouble on anything that he published since. Did
you ever read his later books ?'

The bishop shook his head, and there was a little
pause. Most of the company had been engaged in
conversation with those who sat next them; there
was not much noise; the few who were near the
shrine naturally wished to hear the oracles.

Our curate, who sat at no great distance, towards
the middle of the table, was one of these. He had
been thinking it all a deadly dull affair; he was
put out by his ride and the discomposure of his
array; and, having a testy sort of temper, was in
his most perverse mood. He had caught very little
of what had been said, but heard distinctly the
question about ' the books.'

' I have his " Family Prayers," ' quoth he, softly, slowly, but in a very clear, audible tone, ' and by striking out every other word, and then every other sentence, and substituting logical sequence for disorder and conjunctive particles ; and then translating his Latinised six-foot words into Saxon monosyllables, I have reduced the volume by two-thirds in bulk ; and the style is not now so very tedious and windy. I had thought of asking his lordship to allow me to print the abbreviated form, with a respectful dedication to himself ; but perhaps he would not take it well of me.'

This was uttered placidly, and with an appearance of great simplicity ; but, somehow, all at once a solemn silence seemed to hold the room ; the company, low-toned before, were turned into mutes ; one bishop looked up at the ceiling ; the other looked down on the table ; the host smiled, and seeming half amused, half vexed, raised his eyebrows with an air of resignation, as much as to say, ' You have done for yourself.'

Suddenly the awful stillness was broken by an explosion of laughter, which, beginning with one voice, soon swelled into a roar from the whole lower end of the table. Their lordships amazed looked for explanation, but none reached them ; the secret of the mirth was kept at the other end of the room ; indeed it was hard to tell it at the time.

What had happened was this : one of the clergy attempting to pull out his handkerchief, and apply it to his nose for a pastime, as the manner of some is, during the uncomfortable lull, drew out and flourished

before the company the full length of a pair of long
and not quite clean stockings. The day had been
so hot that he had on the way taken them off, and
put them into his pocket, to relieve his poor feet;
and had put his feet back bare into his boots. All
went well and comfortably with him, till dearth of
conversation drove him to have recourse to his
favourite nasal abstersions; and when he would
have produced the snowy, spotless, creditable cam-
bric, there came forth instead the sullied, obnoxious,
misplaced hosiery. However the hilarity of his
neighbours was promoted, and he being a gentleman
of original humour, gave a very lively and entertaining account of the accident.

When the rest of the guests were gone to their
homes, the two aged prelates paced the garden-
terrace, enjoying the sweetness of the earth, steeped
in the cool dews of summer night, and in the silvery
light of the moon. The grey tower of the old
church threw its shade over one end of the terrace,
and owls flitted softly to and fro, and hooted from
its high windows and battlements. All things
looked softer and more beautiful after the glare of
an August day; and the two old men, whose busy,
useful lives had been simple and pure, felt the charm
of the scene as they discoursed of the days that were
over—days when, with their host, they had oft at
even, on the banks of Camisis, paced the chestnut
groves of Academus, discussing and digesting the
lore of past ages, and dreaming of honour in the age
to come. And now they were talking of their old
companion; of the fallen fortunes of the poor

scholar; of his high spirit and love of letters; how
he had not made his fellowship the downy bed of
sloth, but had spent its income in books, and had
built himself up to the stature of a man of learning.
And then they looked at the resting-place he had
won, the old-fashioned, ample mansion, with its
well-kept garden within walls well-stocked and
high, and admired the venerable avenue of elms.

'Our friend is a very independent man,' quoth
one.

'Yes, indeed; as he says in reply to all offers of
advancement, he has wherewithal sufficiently to
support himself as a clergyman; and he might add,
as I happen to know, though not from him, that he
gives away, in careful quiet charities of one kind or
other, three times as much, in proportion to his
means, as any layman in England that I ever knew.
Our friend is no hunks; he deals with every penny
he has as with a trust.'

As they spoke, they were looking up at the comfortable house suited to hospitality, that gave
outward tokens of having passed through the hands
of many successions of prosperous tenants. For the
living of £1,100 a year was of that magnitude which,
at their University at least, falls only to the option of
Fellows who have passed middle life—men, now and
then, of scholarly distinction—but, at any rate, men
who, by celibacy and a certain sort of prudent self-
denial, have saved a purse, and secured some com-
forts for the latter days.

And the speakers too had prospered. Born in a
middling rank, they had spent half their lives in

palaces, and had kept their simplicity. They had
changed their lots, and their locks were turned to
grey, and their grey hairs covered experienced
heads; but their hearts were not changed from the
days when they had paced the college grounds as
poor scholars : or, if they were changed at all, it was
only by enlargement.

After they had spoken of their host, they proceeded
to discuss a person who would have been very
much surprised to hear that they had given him a
thought—no other than our old friend Martel.

'He is in your diocese, Ratcliffe tells me,' said the
politician; 'and that he reads, and is a scholar.'

'Whether he be a scholar I know not; but I
believe he reads the books that scholars read—at
least I am told so : but to my knowledge he has
restored peace to three different parishes, which the
clergymen had to leave for a while, because they
had, at great cost to themselves, effected restoration
of their churches, and redistribution and enfran-
chisement of the seats in them.   He is not what is
called a popular man either.'

'That I can conceive; but you consider him—a
good clergyman ?'

'Yes, indeed; his chief fault is that he is too fond
of hunting, and that is what makes me doubtful of
his scholarship. I do not mean to say that he
hunts very much—I know he does not; but he
should not hunt at all.'

'It is a great fault in a poor clergyman, dependent
on his profession, as Ratcliffe tells me Mr. Martel is,'
said the politician.   'It is a different thing altogether

with the black squires who hunt. It is not that
hunting is not lawful to a clergyman as well as to
the layman; "Vani erimus, si putaverimus, quod
sacerdotibus non liceat, laicis licere," says the acute
Tertullian; but for a poor clergyman it is inexpedient, highly inexpedient. We are not a caste ;
and clergymen of private fortune may choose to do
out of their private pockets such things as may become
a good Christian laymen. But the Church does not
profess to keep hunters for her ministers, and Mr.
Martel must learn to deny himself that luxury
before he will appear to me a fit subject for promotion.'

'He seems to have rather a severe critical taste
in composition,' added the politician dryly. ' However the small living, or starving, that Ratcliffe
asked me to give him, is already given away to a
gentleman, in whose parish I lived for some months,
while repairs were going on at the palace. He is an
elderly and a worthy man—not very learned, to be
sure, but really the greatest master of variety in
style that ever I met with. I never heard from
him any two sermons at all alike ; those he preached
while I was in his church were as distinct from one
another as though they had been the compositions
of different men : great variety of style indeed !'

And the prelates chuckled, and went to bed.

CHAPTER XII.

> ' Like the thresher that doth stand
> With a huge flail, watching a heap of corn ;
> And hungry, dares not taste the smallest grain,
> But feeds on mallows and such bitter herbs.'
>
> B. JONSON—*Fox.*

' Rectories were reduced to vicarages, the greater tithes going to the abbey fund, the smaller tithes left as a miserable stipend (often not more than a sixteenth part of the revenue of the benefice), to the minister, who took the monk's labouring oar under title of vicarius. Thus originated that divorce between the property of the parish church and the minister of it, which continues, in most instances of vicarages, to the present day.'—J. J. BLUNT—*Reformation,* ch. iv.

' Though ordained a priest, he has done no priestly work, and has always been somewhat angry when any one has suggested to him that he should take a part in any clerical duties.'—ANTHONY TROLLOP—*Clerical Fellow.*

> ' Why should he not as well sleep, or eat, by a deputy?
> This might take idle, offensive, and base office from him,
> Whereas the other deprives him—of honour.'
>
> WEBSTER.

ALL this time our perpetual curate had no settled cure ; he was taking what is called occasional duty —now here, now there, now for a shorter, now for a longer time ; for a month, for a fortnight, for a week, or a month or two; running hither and thither, as the needs of the clergy called for his aid. Made aware at last of Mr. Ratcliffe's baffled attempt to get him beneficed, he began to bestir himself to find a permanent curacy.

'I hope I am not "avaricious,"' he would say : ' I seek only to keep body and soul together—and soul includes books, and something to ride for society's sake.'

Whether care about money be a virtue or a vice, he had it not; but to his temperament the very dependent position of a curate growing elderly was peculiarly galling. Frequent change had given him some semblance of that independence for which he sighed, but prudence suggested a settlement; and hearing of a curacy in a distant county, he set off to inspect it.

Some previous knowledge of the rector made him think that he would succeed in his application if he made it; but before making it, he visited the out-going curate who was still in charge. He found him in a cottage in the midst of a garden of cabbages eked out with weeds. The inside matched the out-side of the abode, and painful poverty marked both. A slip-shod ragged little maid of twelve or thirteen, steeped in soap-suds, opened the door; the lady was ironing in the sitting-room the house-clothes which, with Cinderella's help, she had just washed; and her little daughter, some seven years old, came skipping in, with little else on than a shift and a blanket, as merry as a cricket.

The lady—for she was a lady, despite her homely

dress and useful occupation—laid aside her iron to welcome Martel ; and presently her husband entered —a dark-haired, emaciated, melancholy young man, whose bloodless lips and pallid complexion told of too much anxiety and too little food.

With a black squire for his rector, such a forlorn state of slavery would have been impossible, even though the value of the living had been but two hundred or one hundred a year. Its income was, in fact, over nine hundred, but it was a college living.

The rector was a valetudinarian, who had been Martel's college tutor, and had driven him and most of the men away from the lecture-room by the dreariness of his lectures and the tartness of his tongue. When nearly fifty years of age, and without parochial experience, he succeeded to this good living, where he never performed nor was fit for performing any of its offices. But he said to himself, ' *Qui facit per alterum ipse facit;*' and he became very sensible of his duties, when they were to be discharged at the cost of another.

He paid a curate a tight hundred a year, and worked him hard for the money ; out of which the poor deputy had to pay an inordinate rent for his wretched tenement. That oppressed gentleman happily possessed some eighty or hundred pounds a year of his own, whereby he escaped absolute starvation. At the time of his marriage, he had also in the Irish Court of Chancery about five hundred pounds, due to him since his father's death nine years before ; but by the wear and tear of the court, and the waste of time, it was dwindling away rapidly to nothing.

There was no suit, nor dispute, nor doubt about anything of any kind ; but simply '*the law's delay*' had withheld it : while once he had been sold up for a debt of not half that sum, that had been owing not half the time.

All the charity that he of necessity dispensed in visiting the sick of a large and pauperised parish, had to come out of his own scanty funds, for the liberally-beneficed and unworked rector contributed not a farthing ; he pocketed the whole balance of eight hundred a year as his right, after furnishing the parish with the services of a curate.

He was a bachelor. and had two sisters living with him to keep his house. Of low origin, and not young, they were hungry flatterers of their brother : took great care of him, which was right ; and of his pocket, which was needless ; and to feather their own nests, which was natural ; and worried the curate and his wife, which was cruel. They would effectually have stopped any extra outlay on the curate or the parish, if their brother had been at all disposed to it, which indeed he was not. He did nothing whatever but write treatises on dogmatic theology and Church tradition and discipline ; and of course, in virtue of his large living, was a rural dean, and had a canonry. Martel, who had known, and not regarded, him as his college tutor, soon learnt all the conditions of the cure from the curate.

He pitied the poor man very much, for he was ill, and was required by the bishop to remain till a successor was secured ; but our wanderer could not be persuaded to see the rector, or to entertain for a moment the thought of becoming his slave. He was prevailed on nevertheless to accept a night's hospitality at the cottage, where, before he left, a little incident occurred, that under other circumstances would have amused him. There is a knock at the door; his reverence the curate opens it. A gentlemanlike personage, very well got up in a quiet suit of brown tweed, makes a civil bow, and puts into his hand a card inscribed 'Captain Browne.' A Mr. Browne had just married a sister of the curate, who concluded at once that this was some relative, who, in passing, had come to pay his respects to his new connections. So the stranger was shaken by the hand very cordially, and conducted into the house, where he was introduced to its lady and the visitor.

Captain Browne however made no allusion to relationship, but talked pleasantly about the gentlefolk in the neighbourhood, with many of whom he appeared to be acquainted; and at last explained in an easy, incidental manner that he was not Captain Browne: the real Captain Browne had been wrecked on the adjacent coast; part of his cargo was saved and at hand. There were valuable and lovely things of all sorts, very little the worse for salt-water, but not quite fit for the regular trade, to be sold privately at nominal prices. The narrator of his sad losses had, out of pure friendship for Captain Browne, who was a most excellent and honourable man, volunteered his services as salesman; he was always ready to do any good he could to any one, and here was an opportunity of benefiting good Captain Browne, while he could at the same time offer 'really wonderful bargains' to all the ladies in the neighbourhood. Here he bowed to the lady of the house as though she had been a duchess, and put up his hands quite gracefully.

'The fact is, you know, the things are damaged in a commercial point of view; and, if they could be sold here at merely nominal prices on almost any terms, the cost of removal would be saved; and the extent of the loss would be known at once.'

His manner was frank and courteous; and though his tale, as he unfolded it, was a little confused; there was so much to explain; and "he was a perfect stranger," and "had never done anything of the sort before;" he "had been led into the undertaking purely by good-nature," &c.

If his story was perplexed, the bargains were clear; and the lady was deeply interested. Her dress did indeed need replacing, and here was a grand opportunity; it seemed quite providential, as one might say. Her lips said little, but her eyes spoke much. Her husband was moved; the gentleman saw it; seized the propitious moment with something like practised dexterity, and rushed out of the house to back his eloquence by a few samples of the good things he had provided. His dog-cart, a roomy vehicle, was, in fact, left in the lane, a little out of sight.

He was gone but just long enough for the lady to say: 'I *should* like to have a new dress; it is such an opportunity as we may never have again.'

Her husband sighed, smiled, and agreed.

The cargo was, of course, from China; as they

had heard, the '*Chinese*' silks were reduced not at all in value by the mishaps of the wreck, but were brought down, one might say, to nothing in price.

Captain Browne's kind representative returned laden in quite a business-like way with silks, cloths, fans, slippers, silk stockings, gloves, all at no price at all. Only, of the stockings, slippers, gloves, and such-like things, that go usually in pairs—cheap and tempting as they were—no pair could be had, for only one of each was brought, just as a sample ; the rest would come to-morrow, if encouraged. The price of these odd articles was, in truth, as he said, ' ridiculously low.'

The price of the silk dresses was not mentioned specifically ; but, of course, they were cheap too, like the other things ; real Chinese silks at almost the price of cottons, no doubt. They were beautiful, certainly, and were greatly admired, and, at last, though it was hard to put such a question to such a gentleman, the price was delicately hinted at, in an interrogative manner.

It did seem rather high, to be sure, but the silks were so good ! Of course, like all the rest of the cargo of the wreck, they were ' *ridiculously* ' cheap for their *quality*—that was it : they would never need renewal ; they would just wear for ever.

The lady was a true woman, and was enchanted by, and almost committed to, a love of a silk dress ; and, though its price was three times as much as she had hoped it would be, it was very hard to part from it. It was impossible to think of bargaining with such a perfect gentleman, merely selling the goods of a friend, and offering such 'ridiculous' bargains, as he 'said candidly.' And so the dress was bought, and the curate stifled a groan, and paid like a man—with his last five pound-note, Martel sadly suspected. It was not often that poor lady had a treat.

But would not the gentlemen seize the opportunity too? There was, at a perfectly laughable price, some very rare frieze cloth, especially affected by the officers of the 'Blues,' as the gentleman said, though he omitted to state whether it was manufactured in China for Oriental wear, and brought thence to be wrecked with the unfortunate Captain Browne.

This question did occur to those who were invited to buy it: but how could one show such inquisitiveness to a gentleman so candid and liberal, acting a part that no doubt was most repugnant to his taste, gratuitously, on behalf of a suffering friend.

The curate, however, had no more money; and Martel was wondering where he had seen that man, or his likeness, before.

Would they not avail themselves of some other cheap lot? Then Captain Browne's friend must be gone upon the captain's business; but to-morrow he would call with the pairs of which he had exhibited the ravishing oddments; and, for the lady, he would bring some cocoa-nut oil to cleanse the silk, that would wear for ever, of all the stains that could be contracted in its endless existence.

'At what time should he call, that he might find them at home?'

They appointed an hour, and waited for him; but, somehow, he never appeared again ; only, he was heard of as having made similar visits to many houses in the district.

The silk, that had cost four pounds, turned out to be worth but two, and would hardly wear long enough to need the cleansing cocca-nut oil. So Captain Browne's friend and Captain Browne's wreck passed away, and were numbered among myths.

Martel, much moved by their distressing circumstances, having accepted their urgent hospitality for one night, and having waited to see the failure of the promise regarding the cocoa-nut oil, took his leave of the good curate and his wife with a mind full of indignation against his quondam tutor, comparing college dons with the fox-hunting black squires—Palmer, Finch Adams, and Lawrence—each and all—vastly to the disadvantage of the better-paid holders of college preferments ; he vowed inwardly, in fine indignation, that he would rather starve, or beg his bread outright, than play jackal to ' that mathematical old ruffian,' and lend a hand to bolster up a system so iniquitous. He left the place, confirmed in his preference for squire-parsons with small livings and private fortunes, great or small, who give much, and receive little ; do much, and talk little, as he asserted.

To be sure, he was not quite fair in assuming that all black squires were like Palmer and his friends, and all college dons like his old tutor. No one knew this better than himself, when he was in a right frame of mind; but now he was soured and discontented.

He was growing old in curacies; and a nervous restlessness, which had, perhaps, its root in his nature, but was fed by unusual anxiety about the future, impelled him to desert the country, which he had so often pronounced to be the better place, and to seek employment once more in a town, and this time under a popular preacher. The stipend offered was some temptation ; a good one, as these times went, being, in fact, the whole proceeds of the living, some £120 a year ; and our curate submitted, for the first and last time, to a ' *trial*,' which issued in his acceptance.

To do him full justice, he was now attracted mainly by the novelty of the sphere, for his curiosity was as notable as his general carelessness about money, and he was rather taken by the reputation of the incumbent than by the amount of stipend, it is but fair to say. For once he was ambitious of doing work on the grand scale ; but, most of all, he was attracted by the character of the rector, a gentleman who is worth a passing notice.

His vocation he conceived to be preaching; his heart was in his pulpit, and, beyond the occupation of that, he had never derived or sought any benefit from his living. He was at ease in his means, and he was unmarried, so that he could give undivided attention to his calling, which he did in his own peculiar fashion. His '*theological*' furniture was poor and scanty ; he was not full of exact defini-tions, but he knew his Bible and men's need better

than most preachers, and, though not nice as to the
manner, he knew well the way to make an impression.   His presence was hardly striking; his voice
was rasping, and, one would say at first hearing,
not well managed, and his taste was tawdry.   But
the fire, the life, the spirit, that he threw into his
delivery, the glow of his chariot-wheels, as the discourse rolled on, the absorption of the whole man,
as his speech proceeded, atoned for everything.   He
would not do the work—according to his idea of
it—negligently.

He was perfectly honest and open; he never
pretended that his sermons were originally of his
own composing; he attempted no sort of disguise
or reserve on the subject : but, by judiciously selecting them, by manipulating them after his own
method, by poring over them, and biting his nails
over them, as his admiring churchwarden and
landlord remarked (for he lived in lodgings); by
ruminating upon them, chewing them over and over,
usque ad nauseam, as he used himself to say; by
digesting them and assimilating them, he took them
once for all into his own proper mind, made them
his own, a part of himself; and, despite the common
knowledge how he came by them, produced a sense
of rightful property in the minds of his enthralled
hearers.   They knew full well that the original
writers never made one hundredth part of the
impression that was made on them by the eloquent
plagiarist.

He knew every sermon '*by heart,*' in the fullest
sense; he had present to him, throughout, every

break and turn of the discourse; he knew exactly how to express every shade of its meaning and every touch of feeling. He laboured on them as Garrick, or Kean, or Siddons, or Rachel, laboured in their vocation. He worked up his feelings to high-water mark, and poured them out with all the nervous energy of his system. It was an exhaustive effort which no one, who has not long wrought himself to it, is capable of making. He was rapt, he was possessed, he toiled in the utterance, till the perspiration would stream from him on the coldest day.

One night he had preached a sermon full of figures, culled from the Revelation of St. John and Daniel's prophecy, on the coming glories of the New Jerusalem, walls of adamant, streets of gold, rivers and seas of crystal, gates and floors of emerald and ruby, all apparently taken in the most material and literal sense, under the enlargement on which Martel had sat amazed, disapproving, and enthralled —after all this, the curate could not help saying to the rector at night:

'If you would give me a thousand pounds to do it, I could not preach that sermon.'

'Nor could I,' replied the orator, 'without the excitement of a crowded congregation.'

Whenever and wherever he preached, there was a crowded congregation, if only his coming were known beforehand. He had been in holy orders some fifteen or twenty years at the time when Martel became his subaltern ; and beside all the immense toil of mastering and assimilating them, he had preached

his sermons over and over again so often, that upon
some of them, as he would say, he might celebrate a
centenary ovation. Thus by constant repetition and
experience, he had reached in his peculiar style
perhaps the perfection of delivery. But this success
bred in him a fastidiousness that led to his oratorical
ruin. He found that he could by no labour give to
a new sermon the force and effect, the *actio* in fact,
that would satisfy him; and at last he could not
bring himself to preach any new one at all : he could
only repeat for ever his old and perfected discourses,
and his people were well content that he should do
so. Wherever he went to preach, if the distance
were not too great, they followed him in crowds.

One night a mob collected round a neighbouring
church long before the doors were unlocked, pressing
towards the entrance. At that church, though well
served, such an assemblage was most unusual.

'What do you want ?' cried the sexton, putting
his head out to see.

'We're come to hear Mr. Willen preach.'

'Yer fools, git along wi' yer: it ain't Mr. Willen ;
it's only old Billen.'

And they went their ways.

Now Mr. Billen was a very learned man, and he
too was followed by the few, who were thoughtful
and cultivated; but to the many he was unintel-
ligible, or at the least unendurable. 'How much of
the learning of the Church of England is lost for
want of the study of elocution ?' is one of Bishop
Berkeley's ' Queries.' However our orator thought,
though his people did not, that he should not preach

old sermons for ever; and with new ones he could not content himself, so he gradually ceased to preach at all.

Under him Martel was pretty sure to get excitement enough, since he was specially to give attention to the pulpit. By it his rector had acquired extensive influence for good; by it he had made a great and lasting impression, as he supposed, upon large masses of people, who never grew tired of hearing him. He valued his pulpit accordingly, and other clerical offices mainly in subordination to it, as the special and exclusive means of preaching the Gospel. As to new lights and tracts for the times, he simply laughed at them, and went on his way, taking his curate so far as he could with him.

Martel did as he was bid; by his rector's advice, and like the great Dr. Donne, he chose his texts, or at least his subjects, and began his new sermons on the Sunday night; and had them on the anvil, and hammered away at them without ceasing throughout the remainder of the week : and though he learnt the truth of what a great Roman Catholic preacher had told him, that—since not only the man's tongue should preach, but also all his members, looks, and motions—it was impossible for any English clergyman to do justice to his sermons, boarded up to his middle in an Anglican pulpit like a jack-in-a-box, and effectually debarred from preaching as he should do, with feet, and hands, and all his body. Despite this palpable drawback, our friend succeeded in getting himself so possessed by his discourses and so excited in their delivery, that, being of a highly sensitive

organisation, he managed to expend in nervous
energy upon the day of rest, the vital power proper
to the whole week's consumption. It was a delightful discovery. Always at heart thirsting for
emotional dissipation, he could now, for the first
time, drink of it to the full without let, hindrance,
or reproach.

He felt himself a homeless man, marked to have
no household ties, no 'fair spirit for his minister;'
and now a preaching spirit took possession of him,
and cheered his loneliness. Febrile irritation of the
frame through fasting and the heating of the brain by
the long strain on it, disturbed his judgment, and
went near to make him that which his friends
would last expect, an enthusiast. For a day before
preaching, he would eat insufficiently in order to
maintain an excited state ; and he thus worked
himself up to a frenzy of susceptibility; so that without knowing it he was not far from 'the gift of
tears,' which distinguished our Oliver Cromwell and
Gregory the Seventh, and other fanatical geniuses.
Yet his strength appeared to be doubled,—to be inexhaustible.

His rector approved, and thought he '*would do,*'
when experience had given him the self-command
that should rule and direct his emotion; his flock
were attentive, and talked of a new gown, and all
seemed to go well with him. He read, he thought,
he wrote, he preached, and read and thought, and
wrote and preached again—week after week, month
after month, without pause or variation. Work
never killed any one, he was now sure ; the more he

did, the more he wanted, and the more he felt able,
to do. Now he was sure that he had mistaken his
way in life; now he found out that incessant toil,
provided only it brought excitement, was the true
happiness and the vocation of man here below. He
doubted not that he had discovered the grand secret.
He had been too inert and contemplative to enjoy
life, or to serve life's ends.

Only just at this time one little thing began to
trouble him; for all his work, he did not rest o'
nights as formerly. His sleep went from him
gradually more and more: he went to bed late;
he went to bed early; but whether he lay down
late or early, he could never close his eyes till the
cool of daybreak. He drank tea, he drank coffee,
he drank water, he drank wine and water, nay, he
even drank brandy and water, but it was all the
same. This he did not much heed at first; he
began to fancy that he had made another discovery :
that sleep had been over-valued and was needless.
He thought there was a fulness of blood to the
head, and he reduced his scale of diet. After a
while there was no need for this, for his appetite
failed him; his nerves grew irritable and his mind
grew anxious; and he who had, beyond most men,
been able to throw behind him the care of the
future, became haunted by terrible fears for his
temporal prospects; which, to be sure, were as bad
as possible.

He was a curate without interest; he was getting
on in years; his health was failing him : what if he
should break down ? Where was he to go ? What

was he to do ?   How was he to live ?   The three or
four hundred pounds that were still left him of the
original six hundred, he might spend on doctors and
on maintenance for a while.   And what was to come
next ?   He was not in the army ; he was not in the
navy ; or in the Indian, or the Civil Service ; he had
not a business that could be managed by deputy.
There are pensions for soldiers and for sailors, for
civilians and for bishops, and great rectors; but
there are none for small rectors, or for curates.
When his health was gone, and his money gone, he
had nothing to look to but the workhouse, and to
be described in the newspapers as the 'reverend
pauper.'

When once this idea got hold of him, no reason,
no theology, no preaching, no, nor even prayers,
could exorcise the demon.   He preached against
care for the morrow; he read and prayed against it,
and was consumed by it.   People soon told him he
looked *dreadfully* ill; and that did not tend to
make him better.   The spectre of ruin haunted him
as he rose up, and as he lay down, and as he went
by the way.   The demon was a dumb devil; the
possessed would open his mind to none of his friends ;
he ceased to write to any one.   In a happy moment
his better angel suggested the doing that which
ought to have been done at first.   Martel went to
an experienced physician, and told him of his in-
creasing inability to sleep.

The doctor, who, though not of his parish, often
attended his church, having examined his frame,
and questioned him closely about habits and studies,

drew out of him, by little and little, his mode of preparation for the pulpit.

'We will track our enemy home,' said he. 'Sleeplessness comes of an óverflow of blood to the head; that from incessant exertion of the brain; that again of too much thought; and that, in turn, of too much sermonising. They are all good things, taken in moderation—use of the brain, thought, and sermonising. But we have taken too much of a good thing. Excitement is pleasant; so is brandy and water. You are taking too much of this pulpit preparation; I wish some of your reverend brethren had just half your complaint. Your brain is overtasked, and your feelings are overwrought; there has been an excessive strain on your nervous system. I should say you are a person naturally apt, when excited, to run into extremes. And it is a terrible thing—I say it as a doctor—it is a terrible thing for any man, much more for an excitable man, to have to prepare and preach two sermons a week, to the same people, all the year round. I do not mean "sermonets," or "friendly addresses"; but two *sermons*, which are composed, and not borrowed, and to which the heart and mind are thoroughly given. In fact, I maintain it to be *physically* and *intellectually impossible* for most men to continue to do as you have done, *without frequent and long intervals of rest.* A week now and then won't do; and you have not even had that relief. You are strong, and sound; but you have been taking too much out of yourself. In the first place you work seven days a week, and that is against all law; in the next place, though sound, your organisation is highly nervous, and you have been practising upon it. And, then, let me tell you that, setting all the rest of your work out of question, the concentrating your mind upon a single subject, such as the writing of sermons and getting them up to *preach with excitement*—upon your elaborate system—is the most exhaustive kind of labour. I know where you get your idea; and you are not the first man that has been misled and has misapplied it.

'Our friend the rector is healthy and well, though he has for many years worked upon the system that you have adopted from him; and he has done his work well, such as it is—no man better. But, don't you see, old hand that he is, he has never, for any continuance, preached two sermons a week. I knew him when he had not such a stock of sermons as he has now; he took plenty of holidays, and rarely electrified us more than once a Sunday. He has always used the help of a curate; and now, you see, he has given up the pulpit and desk also to you, altogether; more's the pity. He thinks himself delicate, which he is not; but when he does work, he does it with a will, with might and main; there is no doubt about that. I have never heard any one come near him in the art of making impression on an ordinary audience in town or village. The secret is, he gives himself wholly to it, heart and mind; not every one can do that.'

Martel nodded assent, and the doctor proceeded:

'In the preacher's (if I may venture on the comparison), as in the actor's, or singer's, or any other artistic vocation, almost as much as in the common routine of what is called " business," the rank and file are mechanical ; they work ' (excuse me if I say it) ' technically, and are not wasted by keen sensibilities, nor consumed by the fire of emotion ; they never draw upon their sensitive system, and know nothing about nervous excitement and exhaustion, and are proud to tell you they have no nerves. I could tell that of the clerical sort of them by their sermons.'

'People tell me,' said Martel, 'that work never killed any man.'

' *That sort of "work"* never did,' replied the doctor ; ' but where men are of the genuine artistic temperament, and draw largely on the nervous system, they need frequent and long vacations to recruit.'

' I don't know that I have anything of the artist about me ; I only know that I have never before overdone myself. I have always worked by fits and starts,' said the curate.

' And that has been the saving of you,' replied the doctor ; ' nature, that gave you an emotional constitution, taught you to work in that way. I have carefully observed, and have never found a popular preacher of the Lacordaire sort, whose habit it was to preach twice on the Sunday. I have a young man on my hands now (at least, I have just sent him away), who, after two years in the Church, came into a living of two thousand a year. He was not, to be sure, " of the true old enthusiastic breed," who are not content with " working," but aim at doing

work of the best quality ; he is just a common kind
of young man, but he is zealous, and, in his way, has
worked hard in his large parish, and has stimulated
himself with missions, and processions, and choirs,
and decoration, and endless labours of that rather
mechanical species. And what is the end of it ?
Why, in less than two years, he fancies himself—for
it is a good deal fancy, but he dwells on himself,
and fancies himself·used up, and has to come to me ;
and I have sent him to Italy for twelve months, or
more. I am sorry that I can't send you to Italy,
nor find you a substitute to give you a thorough
holiday. But you must give up our friend's work,
since he won't share it with you ; and as you cannot
afford to be quite idle, you must go, for a while,
where there is less stimulating work, and you will
soon be well again. Only, don't try that experiment any more. You are of inflammable material ;
and you are not so young as you were, remember
that.

    ' " Est modus in rebus, sunt certi denique fines,"

is sound advice for a divine, no less than for a poet,
though it comes from a heathen.'

    So saying, the good-natured doctor refused his fee
and rusticated his patient.

    Martel was confounded, and more distressed than
at any other of the many disappointments that had
befallen him in the course of his ministry. But he
soon called reason and humility to his aid. After
all what did it matter, though he was laid by just as
he seemed to himself to be in the way of doing the

most good ? He was laid by, indeed, only in seeming. The Author of all good knew what was best; and, if He used His services at all, He did not need them to work out His plan.

'Lead, kindly Light, amid the encircling gloom,
 Lead Thou me on.

I loved to choose and see my path : but now
 Lead Thou me on.'

One must not only be content, but be glad, to be led by Providence; if he might not produce immediate and self-flattering impressions, why, he would go back to his old jog-trot system of exposition step by step, and might, if more slowly, yet perhaps more surely, build up a knowledge of the truth in the minds of some. After all, his main business was to instruct Christians in the right understanding of the religion of Christ, and not exhort heathens to accept a Christianity which was strange to them.

'If only one now and then, here and there, had his mind enlarged to a fuller perception of the light of truth, why such were the pick of the flock, and as such were centres of several circles to radiate light around. As Fuller says with equal wit and wisdom: "Preaching is, in some places, like the planting of woods, where no profit is received for twenty years together; it comes afterwards. If God honours me not to build His temple in a parish, yet I collect metals and materials for Solomon, my successor, to build with." Or I may plough, another sow, and a third reap; who knows? We may take comfort that whatever be man's judgment, God measures us not by our success, but by our endeavours.

' Who and what am I, after all, when I think of Thomas Scott, the great commentator, with his thin congregations to hear the results of his stupendous labours; or of F. D. Maurice, with his select band, come to glean suggestions for their own more popular harangues; or of J. H. Newman, whom the bishop's wife went to hear, and pronounced "humdrum," while dignified dons declared that "He had made a simple failure;" or of the preacher—to be classed with Jeremy Taylor—whom the Bar assembled at the assizes heard, and some deemed him wondrous wise, and some said the man was mad. Anyway, I trust it is not selfish to hope that I shall not be as Fuller's "rider, who opens awkwardly a gate for others, and shuts himself out." '

Such was the sum of the reflections with which our curate schooled himself into comfortable acquiescence under this disappointing dispensation. And doubtless he derived a double benefit—from the efforts he had made, and from their frustration.

Having thus, by a struggle, cleared his mind of clouds, it soon returned to his old friends, whom in his brief season of absorbing excitement he had rather forgotten, and in his hour of disappointment had hidden himself from them; so, having left all their letters unanswered, had not heard news of them for a long time.

Now, with reviving friendship, he thought that of all things he would most wish to be curate for a turn at Finchdale. Was it possible? One would say no; but that it had happened to him to wish for the cure of two different parishes, whose soft scenery had so struck him in passing, that he had said to himself, ' If there's peace to be found in the world, the heart that is humble might look for it there;' and those parishes had come to him, though the peace had not.

Once too he had conceived an intense desire for the solution of a particular passage in the Old Testament, upon which all the commentators that came in his way had preserved a discreet silence, as is their wont in difficulties; but in an unsought and unexpected way, there had fallen into his hand a rare book that untied the knot, and set his mind at rest. And so there had grown up in him a sort of ' *mesmeric superstition* ' on the subject of ardent wishing, as some of his friends said, or a boundless belief in special providences, as he would say himself.

And now he wished for the cure of Finchdale, which, for all his boundless belief, certainly did seem to him like wishing for the moon. His friend the rector was, as he hoped and believed, perfectly well, and he had never worked by deputy, or employed a curate, and very seldom left home at all.

CHAPTER XIII.

'Nous revenons toujours
A premières amours.'
'We dance like fairies in a ring, and our whole life is but
a nauseous tautology.'

'Yes; books are a nice little amusement. When I
go with my wife to the seaside, I always take my
little books with me.'

This was said in reply to Martel's apology for
having his room so littered with the articles in
question, that a chair had to be cleared before his
visitor could sit.

His books were his stock-in-trade and his com-
panions; he could not get on without them, he had
said: but what his visitor had replied surprised
him, for he had not suspected the gentleman of any
literary tastes. He lived in the parish, and his
occupation was that of usury and money-lending in
a respectable sort of way. If time had been given
him, he would have explained that '*the little books*'
which relieved his seaside leisure were his account-
books, and he was drawing one from his pocket in
illustration of his remark, when the name of another
gentleman visitor was unintelligibly announced by

the little waiting-maid, and the usurious visitor retired to make way for another.

'Packing! I declare, and ready to bolt!' cried the new-comer, who was none other than Colonel Denny. 'I am glad I have caught you. You have never written to any one this age,' said he as they shook hands; 'but we have heard of your doings, and over-doings, and all that: and so I am sent to look after you. We are told that you are to take care of yourself, and to take it easy; and so as Palmer is suddenly called off to Ireland to look after his property, which is going to the bad, we have all agreed to think that if you have nothing better to do with yourself, you might like to come and keep the house warm at Finchdale, and see your old friends in the parish, and preach over again to them some of those good sermons that we have heard of. You see a little bird has sung to us all about you.'

'Well, well!' said the curate at last, after looking long at his visitor in delight and astonishment, 'well, well! wonders will never cease. I was a believer in special providences, and I am so now more than ever, if that be possible. Why, you will hardly credit me when I tell you that this is the very thing I was wishing for, and thinking I was all the way to the moon from it! I am very thankful to Providence, and to you all. You see my household gods scattered about me. When am I wanted? When shall I come?'

'The sooner the better. Palmer wants to be off as soon as you can relieve guard for him, and Barbara goes with him.'

'Will next week do ?'

'Exactly.'

'Done with you, then ; if all goes well, so be it. And now, Colonel Denny, tell me all about them.'

There was not much to tell, and the little was soon told.

At last Martel, who had been expecting something else, asked :

'Where is Major Gibbons ?   I saw his promotion a while ago in the paper.'

'Ah ! poor Gibby !' cried the colonel cheerfully ; 'you have not heard, then ?'

'Of his promotion—yes.'

'Aye, in her Majesty's army ; but not of his other promotion ?'

'I saw he had his majority ; that is all.'

'Oh ! but he has got more promotion than that.'

Martel was all ears.   Like most single gentlemen that ever knew her, he was reluctant to think of Miss Palmer as married : a kind of hopeless, senseless jealousy shot through his heart for an instant.

But the colonel went on, to his hearer's surprise, very gleefully laughing :

'Poor dear Gibby ! he has not been in luck lately. After Gryffyn's affair, you know, he left his old quarters, and went into Wales—of all spots on the earth for hunting ! There he was riding at a cramped place, as he loved to do, when the Great Fin, to save a fall and his own credit, brushed the poor old boy's leg against a tree, and broke it.   That was no joke : but that was not the worst of it,' continued the colonel, chuckling, 'for Gibby is a hard, healthy fellow, and his leg was soon all right again. But after the accident, he was taken to the house of a small native squire—what they call a "county-man"—who lived near the spot.'

'And was nursed by the daughter, of course,' quoth Martel.

'And of course married his nurse,' quoth the colonel; 'and she is what they call a "girl of the period!" Poor Gibbons!' and he laughed the low, gurgling, musical laugh which was peculiar to him. 'However, I am told she is a very pretty girl; and for the rest, you know Gibby is not particular, and would rather not be bored by too much "culture," and "refinement," and all that. But, poor Gibby! with a "girl of the period" for his *fiancée*! Can't you fancy him? What a come-down—eh! Just the man, though, to be taken by that sort of thing in a snug country-house, with nothing to do but to smoke cigars and talk about hunting. Of course she likes smoke and hunting-talk; she is a "girl of the period!" I only hope she is good-tempered and a good girl, and he will be as happy as a prince with his "girl of the period." But it is a come-down—eh! He is a good fellow at bottom; a very good fellow is Ralph, with his "girl of the period."' And he laughed his low laugh merrily again.

'But I do not quite understand whether he is married, or to be married,' said Martel.

'You shall hear,' said the colonel. 'You know he was very grateful for the nursing, and full of admiration for the nurse, and expressed it all vigorously, and so forth; but he could not make

up what he calls his mind. He was at all times
dreadfully afraid of being taken in; so when he got
well, his courage failed him, and he began to fly off,
and at last bolted without saying all that was expected of him.   While sick he had overflowed with
fine feelings and fine speeches, and when he got well
he said everything but the last important words; in
short, he levanted without declaring his "*intentions.*"
He fled to Paris, and after him flew the family pack
in full cry; he got out of Paris, and made for
Geneva, and they hunted him to Geneva hot foot;
he left Geneva for Como, and they raced him with
a burning scent over the Alps; he ran without
a check to Florence, and they hunted him out of it
to Rome; from Rome to Venice; from Venice to
Trieste; and thence right away for Vienna so close
behind him, that at Vienna they ran into their fox :
and poor Gibby was married to his " girl of the
period " at the Embassy Chapel in great state,
among a lot of people who knew all about it.   " I
have seen many good runs across Leicestershire,"
said Count Landtäg (who told me the story), " but
never so good a run as that; so game a fox, so
staunch a pack, and such fine kill in the open."
The count says, " Gibby had a thought of running
to ground, and turning monk at Rome, that he might
shake off the pursuing lady pack," as the German
politely expressed it; but Gibby's caution saved
him; he dared not trust the serge-frock : so the
petticoats made a prize of him.   Poor Gibby! he is
very happy, I am sure!   A very happy fellow is
Gibby—with his " girl of the period !" '

' And Master Denny seems very happy too,' thought
Martel to himself; ' I wonder whether I know
the reason why? And Miss Palmer?' said he
aloud.

' Well,' replied Denny, while he looked on the
ground so that Martel could not see his face; 'well, you
see, she would never have married Gibby; she could
not make up her mind to say " Nay " to her mother's
wish, nor to say " Yes " to Gibby, who seemed in no .
hurry to ask her. He took it all for granted, you
see, which did not make his chance better, if ever he
had any. And, then, when that unhappy affair took
place with young Gryffyn, Barbara was dreadfully
annoyed at all the ill-natured talk it gave rise to,
and took Gryffyn's part, and vented her vexation
on Gibby, who was not much to blame in the matter.
And so his eyes were opened to the fact that she
rather less than cared for him. And Gibby, who has
plenty of self-respect, and sets a proper value on all
that belongs to him, like a gentleman as he is,
politely made his bow, and they parted much better
friends, and with a far better understanding than
they had ever come to before; and all greatly to the
satisfaction of old Launce, who had begun to see that
it would not do. And you, Martel,' said he, turning
the conversation abruptly, ' when are you going to
be married?'

' I ? Oh ! I am like the fellows of a college, I have
registered a vow of celibacy, to live single and be
comfortable; and when a good living falls to me
from some place in the sky—if I am not too old—I
may follow their example again, and get a dispensa-

tion and a wife to nurse me.   For the present I hold
with them that the marriage vow is a vow of perpetual poverty.   Poor I am ; but I might be worse
off—don't you see ?—so I shall call myself a celibate,
as it were, and take credit for self-denial, don't you
perceive ?'

CHAPTER XIV.

'"Tis great pity
He should be thus neglected   . . . .
This foul melancholy
Will poison all his goodness : for I'll tell you,
If too immoderate sleep be truly said
To be an inward rust unto the soul ;
It then doth follow want of action
Breeds all black malcontents, and their close rearing,
Like moths in cloth, do hurt for want of wearing.'
WEBSTER.

MARTEL had been some time at Finchdale, and was getting sick of it. The work, to be sure, was easy to a man rich in sermons, though in that respect, as he well knew, no two places are alike; and what is best to be said in one place is often best left unsaid in another. He had no more work than was good for him; but he had too much of his own society. Finchdale with the Palmers at home, and Finchdale without them, were as unlike as Brummagem to Paris. His spirits had never recovered their tone, and the monotony of his life was fast reducing them to their lowest level. He had been passing his days in an exalted sphere, and now he had to come down to humdrum. In short, he could not stay at Finchdale; he must leave it or go mad.

But Mr. Palmer could not leave his business in

30—2

Ireland ; and Martel, loath to add anxiety about his
parishioners to the anxiety which he felt about his
tenants, determined, if he could, to find for himself
a substitute on his own responsibility. It was not
easy to do it in a hurry; one would suit the parish,
but would not suit the house or the servants, or the
house and the servants would not suit him ; another
would meet the requirements of the parish and
house and servants, and be satisfied with them in
turn, but would not, as Martel thought, be the man
for Mr. Palmer ; and so on, till Martel became at least
as anxious to get away from Finchdale as he had
been to go there, and all the more so when he heard
that Dicky Gryffyn, who had long been missing
from home, as it were, hiding from his friends and
communicating with no one but his banker, had been
seen on the north coast of Devon. Martel was resolved to go in quest of him, and he must close at
once with some *locum tenens;* but where was he to
be had ?

He was meditating on this one day, as he sat out
of health and spirits, and full of anxiety for his
friend, and regretting, for the hundredth time, that
he had had his wish about Finchdale. He was
roused by a knock and a ring at the door, and presently, to his utter surprise, the servant announced
Mr. de Coucy.

The visitor, as he shook hands, plunged into
apology.

'I was in the neighbourhood, and heard you were
going to leave Finchdale, so thought I would just
look in and say good-bye.'

'Very kind of you, I'm sure,' said Martel, with a look of more surprise than gratification. 'It is a very fine day.'

This cordial remark brought on silence, which Mr. de Coucy at length broke, hesitating and stammering, and slightly colouring.

'He had,' he said, 'heard that Mr. Martel was anxious to get some one to relieve him of his duty; and—and—in fact, he had ventured to come and offer his services.—He had come from the Cadoyer Bounceables.—Yes, it is a long way,' he said, in answer to Martel's questions.

'Have you written to Mr. Palmer?' asked Martel.

'No; I understood it lay with you, and that you were all anxiety to be off.'

'So I am,' replied Martel, who was—for what reason he could not tell, except that he did not like him—as desirous to get rid of this particular man as he had been to secure some successor; 'but, you know, the appointment lies with the rector,' he added.

Mr. De Coucy seemed now surprised in turn, and very uneasy. He expressed many regrets for the liberty he had taken, but he had been led to assume that the appointment lay with Martel, and that he was only anxious to be set free; and so—could Mr. Martel oblige him? He had brought his traps, thinking he would be wanted to stay;—and, most unfortunately, he had sent away the fly—making sure—he was very sorry for his mistake—that there would be no difficulty; and that his services would be—er—acceptable,—and that he would be wanted to take the duty at once.

Martel, surprised before and not pleased, was now astounded and very angry. He had never, in all their intercourse, taken a liberty with Mr. Palmer. He had a horror of liberties, and here he was summoned, so to speak, to give up his parish at once to a man he knew very little about, except that he had done a most cool thing in the most cool way; and this man he was, without notice, to force upon Mr. Palmer, who had never even heard of him.

Yes, there was a bed, Martel supposed; but it was probably damp.

De Coucy did not mind a damp bed—rather liked one. 'But, in a house like this,' said he, looking round and about, 'there is not much danger of damp beds, I should say.'

'Hem!' grunted his reluctant host. 'Have you brought your " testimonials ?"'

'Coming the bishop,' said the other to himself; and to Martel he said, 'No; indeed, you know, I understood the thing to be all in your hands, and that you wished only to be rid of it; and that, as there was no permanency about it, there would be no difficulty. I can, if you wish it, write for my testimonials; only, you know me, and I know you, and, I thought, the writing would be waste of labour.'

'All the same, you had better write for them; it seems the only thing to be done, since you have come without them,' replied Martel, in a very ungenial, grumbling tone, adding, 'I can forward them to Mr.

Palmer; or perhaps you would like to make the application yourself, after the testimonials are come ?'

Mr. de Coucy would like to do so ; he would write for them at once in his own room, if Martel would be kind enough to have him shown to one.

When he was gone, Martel walked about uneasily, pondering his position; and the more he thought about it, the more vexed was he. He had never fancied this man ; quite the reverse. He could not make him out ; the only feature that was clear about him was that he had just done a most impudent thing; and Mr. Palmer always insisted so much on the desirableness of having for a curate a gentleman. Mr. Palmer might think, and most men in his place would think, that Martel had treated him badly in hurrying off and leaving the parish and his house in the hands of the first stray parson he could pick up. Then there was nothing to be said against the fellow but that he could not blush ; they had met at respectable tables, and as to his manners, some folk admired assurance, though Palmer was not one of them. What could he say or do ? He could not turn the man out, and he could not say that he was not a reputable clergyman. There was nothing for it but to write and tell him all about it, and Mr. Palmer must do as he pleased.

Just as Martel was sitting down to carry out this intention, a servant came in for the letters, and this post was lost to him. Immediately after this, Mr. de Coucy entered the room particularly at ease, bland and smiling.

' Were you in time ?' asked Martel.

' I managed to send two lines each to a brace of clerical friends, and, by the way, I wrote to Mr. Palmer to save delay.'

Martel was astounded and inexpressibly vexed. ' How did the man know the address?' he was going to ask, but bethought him that letters addressed to Mr. Palmer had been lying upon the table waiting for the post, and Mr. de Coucy had taken a seat close by. No doubt from them the address had been gleaned by those handsome grey eyes, quick roving under the long dark lashes.

'Sharp fellow ! cool fellow !—rather too sharp and cool,' murmured to himself the curate in charge.

He saw the trick—a dirty trick. It had suited the applicant to date his letter from Finchdale Rectory : this would imply that he was a friend of Martel ; and without involving him in any inexact statement, would serve for a letter of recommendation, which he felt by no means sure of getting from his friend. He had no more confidence in Martel's obliging disposition than Martel had in his position and character.

With laudable precaution, Mr. de Coucy had taken with him in his pocket a note ready written, to be dated from Finchdale Rectory and posted for Mr. Palmer, which stratagem, as we have seen, he put into effect.

Thus he placed Martel on the horns of a dilemma ; he must either show up a brother clergyman and curate, and perhaps injure, more than he thought of doing, a man of whom he knew little good or bad beyond this bit of mingled impudence and sharp practice, or he must run the risk of forcing on Mr. Palmer an unsatisfactory curate.

As these things were passing through his mind, Mr. de Coucy was reading him like a book.

'I see,' said he, with beautiful and not unconsidered candour, 'I see you are not pleased with what I have done. I do assure you, I thought my coming would be a relief to you; and, to tell you *all*, this temporary cure is also a matter of very great consequence to me. I am—there is no use in disguising it—I am in a crisis of my affairs; very awkwardly situated indeed. There is a lawsuit going on that it is of the utmost importance for my family and me to carry out to its termination, which must be in our favour. But my part in it costs me every available shilling I have, and I have just been unexpectedly thrown out of work. I was *locùm tenens* to a gentleman who has suddenly returned to his parish, and whose address I will give you presently. But you see how immensely inconvenient it would be to me, just at this juncture, to be unemployed—and I am not ashamed to say it—*unpaid* —you know.'

'I don't doubt it at all,' said Martel to himself.

'With my last engagement I had to give up my lodgings, and had, in fact, I may say, no place to go to, when, being invited to our friends the Cadoyer Bounceables——'

'No friends of mine,' said Martel aloud.

'Well, *my* friends, then. I heard there, any way, that you were sadly in want of relief at Finchdale.

It seemed to me a special providence in favour of us both.'

This mention of special providences touched Martel. So, when De Coucy went on to say :

' I am really in a very great strait—that is, for some five or six months to come—until this law business is settled—and you know I might be all this time finding a cure ; and if you can help me, as a brother clergyman, to tide over my temporary difficulties by settling me here until Mr. Palmer returns, you will confer upon me an obligation that will make me grateful for ever;'—Martel was silent. De Coucy went on : ' Of course, I feel that I have taken an enormous liberty in coming upon you in this abrupt way, and bringing with me my traps. But misled, no doubt, by the pressure of my needs, I really fancied I was doing you a favour—I did indeed : and for myself, I may say I had not where to lay my head. Of course, my dear fellow, my judgment was warped by my wants ; I see that now, and beg you ten thousand pardons—indeed I do. You will forgive me ?' said he, with great softness of.manner.

Martel was moved ; he forgot for the time his own antipathy and the man's offences ; he was possessed only by a fellow-feeling for a curate in distress, such as he was but too well acquainted with, and on the impulse of the moment he promised that he would do what he reasonably could to put Mr. de Coucy in charge of Finchdale while the rector was away. But he must warn Mr. de Coucy that he would, before long, have to find lodgings for himself—here the long lashes of Mr. de Coucy's fines eyes drooped —for that probably Miss Palmer would be coming home with an elderly relative, Lady Selina Wadhurst, and, of course, the curate, whoever he was, would have to clear out of the house to make way for the ladies.

Of Lady Selina, whom he had never seen, Martel only knew that she was a very 'high-church' woman; in fact, a progressive Tractarian, and, by all account, a most excellent, simple, unselfish person.

Here Mr. de Coucy's fine eyes were turned upwards in pious admiration.

Martel had never seen Lady Selina, but he knew that was her character—a most simple-minded, devoted person—who would be anxious only for what was good and right, though perhaps she might see it through rather highly-coloured spectacles.

If Martel had chanced to look at the handsome candidate for the cure of Finchdale while he was saying this, he would perhaps have caught fleeting over that comely face what looked very like a transient gleam of triumphant cunning, that would scarcely have drawn him closer to his self-invited visitor. But he was looking on the floor, as his way was when the fit was on him to begin a preachment. And if there were anything that might have disturbed his new-born goodwill, it escaped his notice.

CHAPTER XV.

'The most favourite sophism employed by those who seek
to attack and vilify existing establishments —whether ecclesiastical or temporal—is to ascribe evil to institutions, and to
assert that by reconstructing the State you can eradicate the
abuse.   But the stones with which you raise the structure
are infected in the quarry. . . . Princes and rulers, magistrates and judges of the earth, are only men.   The Visible
Church is composed of men, collectively ; man's nature is
unsusceptible of reform.   The main source of evil is inexhaustible.   Plant the *mal seme d'Adamo* where you choose,
the same bitter fruits will always rise above the ground. . .
Seize the lands, rend the mitre, place the priest as the ex-
pectant upon the contributions of congregations : what has
the cause of religion gained ?'—SIR F. PALGRAVE.

Letter from the REV. L. PALMER *to the* REV.
C. MARTEL, *dated from Dublin.*

' MY DEAR DON CARLOS,—

'When a man describes another as "rather
cool," I always think he means to say that he is not
quite a gentleman.   However, as this is to be but a
temporary arrangement, that matters not much.
Well, you offer your hero of romance, Mr. de Coucy,
at the rate of £125 per annum, so long as he may
stay at Finchdale, and lodging in the rectory until

the ladies return to it, subject, mind, to *satisfactory* references. I must not mind want of breeding, if he be not wanting otherwise as a clergyman. I quite understand that you do not vouch for him in any way. It is kind of you to say that you will look after the parish till I land my man.

'When I shall get home I know not; only this I know, that it will be a joyful day to me if all goes well. These fellows in Dublin and Connemara together bother my life out, and yet I cannot grudge any little good that among us we may manage to do; little enough it will be, I fear.

'Barbara is very gay, as, I suppose, you have made out from her letters. She takes to gaiety very kindly, considering how well she does without it at home. I may tell you she gets a good deal of attention. I think I mentioned that she will probably return to Finchdale in a fortnight or three weeks, under the charge of our relative, Lady Selina Wadhurst. I am not sure whether you know her: she is a strong Tractarian, but a dear good woman as ever lived; and most kindly proposes to stay with Barbara, and take care of her so long as I am kept here; they will be sorry to miss you. Colonel Denny, who is here, will, I believe, be their escort to England.

'How glad I shall be to see home again, if it please God! But I must not complain of delay, if I can but do any real service to those poor people in the West.

'With poor old Ireland it seems " *semper eadem*," " worse and worse," as some one here translated it.

And now political economists are talking of—what
do you think ?—just of potatoes *"demoralising"*
the country!   We used to hear of wealth and
wantonness doing that for a people ; but did you
ever hear of a people demoralised by simplicity and
potatoes ?   I think I have you with me when I say,
I would be a bog-trotter, and live on potatoes and
butter-milk in a cabin on an Irish mountain, sooner
then I would be a mechanic and tipple gin and ale
and eat meat three times a day in the filthy, confined,
unaired slums of an English or Scotch manufacturing
town ; I am Wordsworthian enough for that, despite
all the more modern political economists.   Demoralised by potatoes !   What can they mean ?
There was, to be sure, a famine, when the potato-
plant failed ; but the wheat-plant might fail, and
the cotton-plant too—for all our scientific "command
over nature."   Demoralised !   They might as well say
the Irish deteriorated physically on the potato,
when it is notorious as the first of political economists,
Adam Smith, has remarked, that " The strongest
men and the most beautiful women in the British
dominions, are from the lowest rank of the people of
Ireland, whose whole food is potatoes."   If we have
had a famine through failure of the potato, I fancy
the poor French, before the Revolution, were saved
from the regular recurrence of famines by the
potato.

    ' While our later political economists talk nonsense
about Irish potatoes, I do not know that they are
much wiser who talk about the Irish Church.
" Delenda est " is, I fear, a popular cry in England,

at all events among indocile Dissenters and indocile
Tractarians; but, so far as I can see, she is not
unpopular at home, though I think, for all that,
she would be the better for some reforming.

'You see, the Irish is not at all like the English
Church. The English is as Catholic as a Church
can be. It is an offence in the eyes of the bigots
that she comprehends in her communion High
Church, Low Church, and a whole family of Churches,
touching at one end Rome-like Sacerdotalism, and
at the other Independent Congregationalism, and
admitting all the shades of doctrine and ritual that
lie between those extremes; she cherishes in her
liberal bosom Archbishop Sumner, and does not
reject Archbishop Laud. This amicable comprehension,
which binds many over to keep the peace, factious and
self-willed folk describe as "the icy bond of establish-
mentarianism !" and though it is indeed our Church's
glory, these count it her shame, that her Catholicism
consists, not in the counting of noses, but in her
openness to all Christian truth.

'Now the Irish Church is as narrow as her sister
is broad; she is just an antagonist of the Church
of Rome, which is all the world over an Established
Church too, though established on broader and surer
foundations. The Irish Church being narrow has
abundance of zeal, though not always according to
knowledge; that may be mended in these days of
research and new light. Some one said, "The worst
use you can put a man to is to hang him." I say,
The worst use you can put the Church Establishment to is to destroy it. If official epicures hunger

for roast pork, will you let them—more crafty than Charles Lamb's Chinese—burn down *your* house to roast *their* pig ?   Keep the Establishment, I say, and improve her as much as you like ; the greatest improvement would be to enlarge her borders ; to abolish her is to burn down the house.   I would not abolish even the Lord-Lieutenancy ; it would just be handy machinery for securing to Ireland the residence of the royal family, with a train of rich people to spend money and make friends among the Paddies for some months of each year.

'Barbara will have told you the immense success of the Queen's visit.   That she considers her special province, which I must not invade.

'Fancy my having spun this long yarn on politics, which, you know, are my aversion.   Forgive me, and show your forgiveness by telling me all about the parish, like a good Don.   I am, if possible, every day more and more convinced that there is no sphere for doing good like a clergyman's in a country parish—if he have patience, I must add, and is not hampered by irresponsible intruders.   Farewell, my dear Don, or your patience will be exhausted.

'Believe me, yours ever,

'L. PALMER.'

Letter from MISS PALMER *to* MR. MARTEL, *dated Dublin.*

'DEAR MR. MARTEL,—

'The newspapers which I have sent daily, and which I hope you have received duly, will have given you a better account of our grand doings than I could, though I have hurried and scurried hither and thither, late and early, with the rest of the world, to see what was to be seen, getting our carriage crumpled up in the crush.

'On the drawing-room, however, as my special department, I must try my hand, though I shall never be able to give you a just idea of it. We dined early, and at six o'clock started for the castle. I got into a private room, and there sat in quiet for an hour or two. Papa gave me such an account of the crush at the *levée*, that I think he wanted to frighten me out of attempting the drawing-room; but that I was resolved to see, if possible. So I bore with feminine patience the long spell of waiting, thinking "what can't be cured must be endured;" and I was repaid.

'It was a sight! such as I never saw before; nor can I, by description, give you the faintest notion of the beauty and grandeur of the scene. About eight o'clock the company were admitted into the reception-rooms. The night was lovely; all the windows were wide open, and at nine was lighted a very vivid illumination by gas over the castle gateway. Tremendous cheering announced the approach of her Majesty; and a troop of dragoons galloped on to clear the way for the royal party. Three state carriages drove in, followed by another troop of dragoons, and the band struck up "God Save the Queen," with what effect on me you, that know me for a loyal and enthusiastic country girl, can guess.

'Those who had the private *entrée* were first pre-

sented, and then the door of our reception-room was
opened, and one by one we were permitted to pass
through a little scarlet-cloth sort of turnpike-gate,
guarded by two policemen! Our passage into the
presentation-room was so regulated as to allow time
for each presentation without crowding her Majesty.
It was a very large room, nearly square, magnificently
draped in scarlet and gold, relieved by a profusion
of looking-glasses. No one sat. The Queen and the
Prince—that *great* Prince as you, I think, rightly
call him—stood in the centre of the room with
all the royal suite ranged behind in magnificent
array.

'To poor me the splendour was dazzling, and I
confess that, when it came to my turn to advance, I
felt hardly able to move forward. However, as I
could not go back,—like many another brave fellow, I
went on. A couple of *aides-de-camp* shook out my
train at full—and then—and then—I paid my best
homage with all my heart,—dropped my best
curtsey,—another to Prince Albert, and retired,
walking backward; no easy matter, I can tell you,
with a train two yards long to contend with, even if
you have practised it.

'How the other ladies felt I know not; I only
know that I felt as I never did before, when I saw
the Queen of Great Britain and Ireland, the daughter
of a hundred kings, there before me!

'The gathering of rank and beauty, people said,
was amazing. Colonel Denny, who, you know, as
a guardsman has seen so many, is sure that the
Queen never had such a drawing-room at St.
James's.

'The great ladies were dazzling with diamonds; the Marchioness of Mallow was sun, moon, and stars: the most resplendent in beauty was the Marchioness of Oughterard; Lady Letterkenny the next, so their friends say. Among so many, who can tell? I missed the half of those whom I was anxious to see; the thing was on so huge a scale. I missed too what was best of all worth seeing, as I am told, that was, the Queen walking through the length of the rooms, when all was over. I was so anxious to see this that I squeezed into the thick of the crowd for the view, but was not able to bear the pressure; and papa had to get me out to an open window almost fainting, all but gone: so I lost the sight of the Queen as she passed. We did not get home till three o'clock in the morning.

'I stayed in bed till three in the afternoon, and then got up more dead than alive—to go sight-seeing again. Her Majesty's departure was one of the most beautiful spectacles that ever was seen. You know how lovely is the Bay of Dublin: well, the shore of Kingstown was crowded to the pier's point; flags flying, vessels sailing, colours mounted everywhere. We were in the window of the club-house; but others, who were lucky enough to get nearer, had a better view. It is generally hoped that the Queen will come every year in the way she visits Scotland, and that the Lord-Lieutenant's court will be done away with. We are told on authority we can trust that the Queen has expressed herself charmed with her reception; and the lower orders are in raptures with her and her children.

'" What do you say to 'repeal' now ?" a friend of ours asked of a carman.

'"Repale!" said he; "sure we *waked* Repale the night of the illuminations." Are you Irish enough to take in that ?

'Papa and I, who are part Irish, think it one of the best things we have heard. Papa says—apropos of this piece of national wit—he hears Irishmen of all ranks declaring that if that costly sham the vice-royalty were abolished, and a real royal residence of two or three months in the year substituted, the people would be politically content, and the union would be complete. But they are sure that nothing so direct and simple will ever be done, and they are looking out for some outrageously clever trick of statesmanship, as Anglo-Saxon and un-Irish as possible, by which every Protestant will be everlastingly offended, and no Roman Catholic will be won. These speculations papa hears, and I fancy he adopts some of them ; but I dare say he has told you, for he is very full of Irish affairs ; and we both feel just now our drops of Irish blood stirring in us.

'I have lived in a whirl of gaiety, and have enjoyed it very much ; but I shall not be sorry when it is all over. It is very well for a change, but it only makes me sing "Home, sweet home," the more. There, I have my old women and my children, and my music and my books, and my drawing; here I have time for nothing but to stare about me. I believe if I were condemned to this sort of life for a whole year, it would make an idiot of me. Pray when you visit my old folk, tell Jane Bouker I have not forgotten the Irish frieze, and give them all my love; and tell them I shall be heartily glad to see them. Good-bye.

'Ever your friend,

'BARBARA PALMER.

'P.S.—Papa desires me to tell you that he had hardly set foot in Morrison's, before he heard your "Waithurr! waithurr!" "'Iys, sohrr." "Pohnch!" In my haste and egoism, I have most ungratefully omitted to tell you that dear kind delightful Lady Portumna took the responsibility and charge of my appearance at the drawing-room; and being quite at home in such matters, made everything easy and nice for me. But, indeed, I thought so much of the Queen, that I could hardly think of my sponsor or any one else: I quite understand the feeling of the Cavaliers. Now you have heard the last of the drawing-room. I have said so much that I will never mention it again to you, I think. And so I must go to bed, for I am thoroughly knocked up. Good-night.

'B. P.'

So soon as ever the upshot of Mr. Palmer's letter was communicated to Mr. de Coucy, that very instant his deferential modesty vanished as by magic; and with all his old assurance, he begged Martel, in a patronising way, to stay in the rectory so long as was convenient to him; but that he, Mr. de Coucy, was, he supposed, now in charge of the rectory and parish.

To this gracious invitation Martel made no reply,

nor expressed by sign any gratitude ; but packed up
his traps and hurried off, apparently much to Mr.
de Coucy's satisfaction, to make a few visits in the
neighbourhood previous to using his liberty for an
indefinitely long sojourn in the south-west.

Being one day at a town within a few miles of
Finchdale, and having heard of the arrival of Lady
Selina Wadhurst with Miss Palmer at the rectory,
he was on the point of starting for Finchdale to pay
them a brief visit, when, whom should he meet but
Mr. de Coucy, shining glorious in a most elaborate
and artistic suit of the highest known clerical
costume.

Martel, having shaken hands, gently joked him
on his eminently ecclesiastical and even dignified
appearance ; at which he looked grand and grave,
as though so serious a matter was a pretty subject
for jesting ! And when the proposed visit was
mentioned, Mr. de Coucy solemnly shook his handsome head in mysterious disapproval, saying with
emphasis that it had better not be made, in his
opinion.

'As why ?' asked Martel, amazed and almost
angry.

'H'm ! ah, well ! as you ask me—I should say
that you have never met Lady Selina Wadhurst,
and you don't know her ; and, indeed, I must tell
you '—proceeded Mr. de Coucy, with a great deal of
hesitating delicacy—'I must assure you that she is
a very religious person, and of very strict opinions—
and—erh !—erh !' here he hesitated again.

'And what ?' asked the other sharply.

'Well—h'm!—I don't like to say it, you know—but—I fancy—she has heard something about your hunting—you know—or something of that sort,—that has—erh—set her—h'm—against you, I should say. In short, if I were you, I would not go. It would not be pleasant, you know. Lady Selina is a most devoted and exemplary person; but she has her prepossessions: I only mention this to warn you, you know. Do as you like; but I wouldn't if I were you; you know it is going out of your way. Lady Selina will not be long at Finchdale, and there is no occasion for your going while she is there. Believe me, it would not be well to run the risk——'

'Risk! risk of what?' shouted Martel, who had hitherto stood staring at his bland friend. 'Risk of what? I ask you.'

'Oh!—well!—perhaps "risk" is too strong a word; but it would not be agreeable, I warn you. However, I'll say no more; you will only be angry with me: do as you will: only I wouldn't, that's all.'

Martel, of a hasty, irritable temper, red-hot with wrath, declared he would start that instant, and see what all this was about. 'I can't go after to-day; I will go at once.'

'Ah!' quoth the other in a sympathising tone, '*that*, I fear, would be of no use; for the ladies are gone out for the day, and do not return home till late: *that* I happen fortunately to know, for I saw them start. Believe me, my dear friend, it is better as it is. Providence arranges all these things in the best way.'

And squeezing Martel's unresponsive hand, and waving an affectionate and graceful adieu, Mr. de Coucy took his departure.

Martel supposed somebody had been mischief-making, and he could not conceive who, unless it were Mr. de Coucy himself. But he had no time to think about it just then, they were not at home; and at the best he could ill-spare the four or five hours it would have taken to make the visit, so he reluctantly acquiesced in Mr. de Coucy's ' All for the best,' and put off his inquiries to a more convenient season, or, perhaps, some explanation might turn up of its own accord. He would not write to Miss Palmer about it, it would only be bothering her; she was his friend, and as true as steel, he knew. After all, it was probably some mare's-nest of that donkey De Coucy's finding.

CHAPTER XVI.

'A smile that glowed
Celestial rosy red, love's proper hue.'
Paradise Lost, bk. viii.

How very fortunate your father has been tó secure for his parish in his absence so exemplary a young man !' said Lady Selina Wadhurst, as they sat after luncheon, when the servants had left the room. 'So correct in every respect! and so like a clergyman !'

'Yes, indeed, auntie dear'' (the auntie was a fictitious phrase of endearment, for the relationship between the pair was not very near) ; 'yes, indeed, auntie, Mr. de Coucy is very good looking, and very well drest.'

'Yes, my dear, he certainly is very handsome ; but that is not at all what I mean. Good looks are a very secondary consideration, even in young ladies like you, Barbara ; and in a young man of no account at all.'

'I am sure good looks are a first consideration with me, auntie, in every one, old and young ; and I thought perhaps they might be with you, too, for

Mr. de Coucy *is* a very handsome man ; and, auntie
dear, you know it.'

'And you are a very naughty girl, Barbara, and
you know it. What I mean is that Mr. de Coucy is
a thoroughly good Churchman, and dresses like one,
as you remark.'

'Yes,' said Miss Barbara ; 'he wears a longer coat
than Mr. Herbert Spencer, or Mr. Burgoyne, whom
you don't know,' added she, with a smile at her own
recollections. 'He has a better tailor than either
of them, and a better figure ; and is really what
papa, who only knows his name, calls him, a hero
of romance; such beautiful eyes ! and such lovely
lavender French kid-gloves !'

'My love, you are talking nonsense to your
auntie. I have scarcely looked at the young
gentleman.'

'But you do think him very handsome ; you said
so just now.'

'Did I ? But what I admire in him is his devoted-
ness to his work as a parish priest ; and he performs
the service so reverently and preaches such beautiful
sermons.'

'Indeed, auntie, they were two beautiful sermons
that he preached last Sunday. But don't you think
all Dr. Newman's sermons beautiful, auntie ?'

'Dr. Newman's ?'

'Oh, yes, they were Dr. Newman's—word for
word; I know the volume they came from very
well. Papa often reads a sermon from it aloud at
night, making alterations as he goes, as a good
Protestant should do, you know. But Mr. de Coucy

preaches word for word, without any Protestant alteration at all.'

'Ahem! ahem!' said Lady Selina, taken aback ; but she recovered herself, and asked, ' What sermons could be better than Dr. Newman's, my dear ?'

'Oh ! I suppose—as works of literature—none. Papa thinks him by far the most finished writer of divinity now alive, and equal to any of the giants of bygone days; and very practical and sound on MOST points, but not ALL. He is not so *unqualified* an admirer as Mr. de Coucy seems to be. Papa says that all sermons that are written now are just recasts, more or less clever, of old material ; but that clergymen ought to go back to the old mines and dig for themselves; and that *the present century* is for-bidden ground : to borrow from it is stealing, no less ; and THAT, you know, becomes a preacher least of all men, auntie dear. •

'Oh ! my dear Barbara, what an ugly word! Stealing !'

'Cribbing, then, auntie dear ?'

' I don't like that either, my dear. You know,. Barbara, your father uses the old English divines.'

' Yes, auntie ; but not abuses. He just chops them into mince-meat, pops them into Medea's cauldron, and cooks them up anew, for our weaker modern digestions and palates, and all that sort of thing. Who can do any more, when " there is no new thing under the sun ?" least of all in theology, papa says. And, you know, auntie dear, papa preaches very well indeed, 'though I say it, that shouldn't say it.'

' Yes, indeed, my dear, he does preach admirably,

as every one who has had the privilege of hearing
him must say.   And,' added Lady Selina, with faulty
logic, ' that is a reason why you should listen respect-
fully to all sermons.'

' Especially from Mr. de Coucy, or Dr. Newman ;
which is it ?   Whose shall I call them, eh, auntie
dear ?   As Mr. de Coucy *bought* them, perhaps, after
all, I should call them his.'

' Ah ! you are a very naughty young woman,' said
Lady Selina, fondly kissing her, as she passed her
chair.   ' At all events, Barbara, we may judge of the
young gentleman's sentiments and religious feeling
by his choice of sermons.'

' And of his modesty,' said Barbara.

' Certainly, my dear,' said Lady Selina innocently,
in quite another sense. ' I think your father very
fortunate ; and I think myself very fortunate, too.
For, you know, we could not tell whom we might get.
Of course, we ought to be content with any good
clergyman that might be sent to us ; but I certainly
do like a clergyman to appear a clergyman in dress,
and in everything else.'

' And a very smart appearance our clergyman
puts in, to be sure,' said Barbara. ' Did yóu happen
to notice his boots ? He always wears patent-leather,
no less.'

' My dear, I must confess I do not like to see
"home-mission" shoes, and a tumbled neck-cloth,
and hair unbrushed, and clothes that look as if they
were not made for the wearer ; though, I am sure, I
love and reverence all good men ' (and so she did,
with all her heart, good lady that she was). ' But

it is my weakness, if you will, Barbara, to like to see a priest neat and clean, and like a gentleman, too. Ah! those who do so much for us! how can we ever think them well enough cared for?'

To this Barbara made no reply; she was packing up jelly and other crumbs of comfort for some sick friends in the parish.

It somehow so happened that Miss Barbara had not got far into the parish before she fell in with the recent subject of conversation.

'I can't abear this new curate,' said John Bromby, in the servants' hall; 'I seed him just now in the street go and hook himself on to our young missus. I'll be bound for it he was looking out for her.'

'It's rather too soon to begin o' that game,' said the butler.

'I don't know about that,' said John; 'but I know I hate 'im.'

'Oh, I think he's beautiful,' said Susan housemaid, with enthusiasm; 'I never see sich a 'andsome man, never.'

'Didn't yer, though?' said Thomas footman, who was six-feet high, and a beauty too, in his way; 'yer should ha' seen 'im go at Miss Primerose. I thought he wor a-goin' to 'ug 'er in 'is harms. She wor a-passin' across the hall when I fust opened the door to the gent, after the ladies comed 'ome. He took her for Miss Palmer, an' went in a-bowin' an' a-scrapin', an' was a-goin' to shake 'ands wth her like winkin'. Lor', how she did blush—rose-like!'

'I shouldn't a-wonder,' said Susan; 'so should I, if he were to come at me i' that fashion, I know.'

' Don't you wish you may get it ?' snarled Thomas, who had no wish that Susan should be thrown into any such temptation ; 'yer know, real gentlefolk as is strangers don't go a-squeezin' o' 'ands the fust time they meets one another ; they bows an' grins like, that's the ticket with the real sort, that is. This un ain't the right sort, I'll go bail for't.'

' I don't like the gent, by no means,' resumed John Bromby, who was of a jealous turn ; ' I never see un but I should like to pitch into un. Drat 'im, I hate 'im,' said he, rising in wrath. ' What did he go for to give me half-a-crun t'other day, when he had a ride on master's nag ? Gen'lemen ain't so free o' their half-cruns. He's up to some'at, I know.'

' But yer tuk it, John,' said Thomas.

' I couldn't throw it at 'is 'ead, as I should ha' liked to ha' done, I should.'

' Why, what's the matter wi' his money, John ? It's good money ; better nor he is, any way. He guv me half-a-crun for nought, but the brushin' of 'is coat ; an' that's the best thing about 'im, as I know on. I should like some more of that sort, I should.'

' And he gave me half-a-crown,' said Susan, ' for nothing at all that I know of, but just opening the door to him once. I think the man's made of money, I do—and I do like to look at him ; he is so beautiful !' added she, looking as she said it at Thomas, who scowled at her in return.

' Yer like the look o' 'im, do yer ? Then I don't ; an' I don't b'lieve as he's got any money—not he.

Them as has money don't fling it about that-aways,'
said John Bromby. 'I think he's a tailor; that's
what I think. You should see 'im a-hossback; he
is a beauty there! I never see sich a muff i' my
life—never. That poor young Gruffun was worth a
hundred on 'im—so he wor. He worn't so tall-like,
to be sure; he wor a little un—he wor; but he did
look like a man a top of a hoss, that he did. But
this De Choucer, he don't look like a man nowhere;
nor he ain't no more than the ninth part of a man,
if he's that.'

As this last disparaging remark was uttered by
Bromby, Miss Primrose happened to be in hearing;
she was just passing from the housekeeper's room
through the servants' hall.

Bettina flushed up scarlet to the very roots of her
fair hair, or as John Bromby expressed it afterwards,
'she flared up like thatch afire,' and broke in fiercely
as a ruffled dove :

'What's that you say, John Bromby? How dare
you speak of a clergyman and gentleman in that
way! You ought to be ashamed of yourself; so
you ought. What are *you*, to say he is not a man?
There is not so handsome a man, nor so nice a gentleman, within a hundred miles of this, no, nor
within a thousand miles either, be the other who he
may. And you ought to be ashamed of yourself,
John Bromby.'

And as she spoke her blue eye flashed, and her
fair face glowed, and her taper, rounded, lithe form
rose erect and threatening, and no more lovely lass
could be seen within all the distance she spoke of

than Bettina Primrose, when she flounced out of the
room in a transport of anger, to the amazement of
Mr. Bromby, who had never seen her put out before ;
and who being a man of taste, rather admired the
effect of his own evil-speaking, though he could not
conceive what she had to do with the man whom he
so very unreasonably and heartily detested.

Though one be dark and one be fair, there is a
likeness after all between that pretty pair, dis-
similar as they are in many respects. Where the
likeness is, it is hard to say ; but there is one.
Perhaps it may be in the feminine slope and swell
of the shoulders and bust, and in the graceful setting-
on of their small shapely heads. Bettina can wear
her mistress's gowns, and indeed seldom wears one
that has not been hers, for Barbara is very liberal
in the matter of dresses, which, when taken in a
little, fit the maid very nicely. She is of the more
slender, her mistress of the more luxuriant growth ;
but in nicety of proportion, they are much alike.
Man's eye seldom rests on a more lovely pair of
nymphs than were reflected in the large looking-
glasses of that chamber, where, brush and comb in
hand, Bettina stood over Barbara's loosened abundance of hair soft as silk, gossiping as she brushed.

A little tremor of the hand, a faint cough, a little
choking and much hesitation, there was in that fair
maid as she asked her mistress, 'Had she ever
noticed Mr. de Coucy ?'

'Have I ever noticed Mr. de Coucy ? Why, girl,
you know I see him every day in the week nearly.'

'Isn't he handsome, miss ?'

'To be sure he is handsome; every one must see that without much *noticing*, Bettina.'

'Did you ever see such beautiful eyes, and lovely long lashes?'

'I am not in the habit of looking into gentlemen's eyes, Bettina,' said the mistress, raising her own eyes to the glass, and peeping through the rich fall of silky dark-brown hair at the sweet face of her handmaiden, which reddened like a piony in the mirror.

'So *you* think him very handsome, do you, Bettina?' asked the young lady, turning round in her chair, and eyeing that much-blushing damsel with good-humoured mischief. 'Your *notice* has led you to think all that, has it?'

'Me! Miss Barbara,' said the fluttered maiden, half pleased, but trying hard to recover her natural complexion, and to master her rebel nerves; 'me, miss! indeed not I! I hope I know myself better than to think of him, or of any *gentleman*.'

The last word was spoken with emphasis, as she collected her wits.

'You seem, however, to have *noticed* this one pretty closely:—eh, Bettina, have you not?'

'Oh! you don't think so, Miss Barbara, I am sure!'

'Don't I, Bettina!'

CHAPTER XVII.

'Before my God I might not this believe,
Without the sensible and true avouch
Of mine own eyes. . . . . .
. . . . . Is it not like the king
As thou art to thyself ?'
                              SHAKESPEARE.

            'There gushed,
Accompanied with a convulsive splash,
A solitary shriek, the bubbling cry
Of some strong swimmer in his agony.'
                              BYRON.

WINDY, watery, wavy, rocky, dear, delightful Ilfracombe! Magnificent restorer of lost health and spirits! Who, that has ever dwelt upon your wave-beat shore, can cease to remember thee with fond regret? To that sea-girt, stormy haven, though not 'heart-sick,' Martel found his way: as to 'pocket-sickness,' which with him was chronic, he had his doubts about its cure in the fine new terraced town, which has risen up on the old homely spot, under the old name. But he guessed from tidings that had reached him that 'heart-sickness' might have taken Dicky Gryffyn thither, according to the prescription of Mr. Kingsley, whose disciple Dick was.

There one Sunday afternoon, between the morning and evening services, Martel, walking among a crowd of visitors upon the Tors, had given his arm to an elderly lady of his acquaintance, who, between the crush of the crowd and the difficulties of the ground, could not make her way unaided without danger of being precipitated over the cliff. At a steep descent, where the throng was thickest, he caught sight of the very man he wanted. There was Richard Gryffyn passing within three feet of him. Martel tried to catch his eye, but failed; he spoke to attract his notice, but to no purpose. To hail him was out of the question; to run after him was not to be thought of, for the path was at that point especially dangerous, and the old lady on his arm was too helpless to be left for an instant. While this passed through his mind, Gryffyn was gone. It was all terribly vexatious, but unavoidable. Even Dick's address was missed, and he so near! However, Martel had seen him, and knew his general where-abouts, and determined to hunt him out on the morrow, even if he had to ask for him at every house in the town.

The next morning, after an early breakfast, he set out on his quest. The first man he met after he left the house was the doctor, whom he had consulted on his arrival. Martel told him his errand.

'Never mind him just now; he will keep very well for an hour or two. Let him have his break-fast in peace, and do you come with me for a row on the water; it will do you good; just what you want,' said the doctor; 'and when we get back, I'll

help in your search, and we will find your friend
in a trice.'

' May I bathe ?' asked Martel.

'To be sure—from the boat. You swim ?' And
they strolled down to the shore.

The tide was running far out; the rocks stood
uncovered for half a mile perhaps or more; every
rock-pool displayed its many-coloured glories : sea-
anemones and prawns, and sea-urchins and crabs of
several sorts, and other creeping and swimming
things, and plants of a thousand bright hues, and all
the ' gay flowers of the sea,' were bared to the gaze ;
and bared, too, were the urchins of the town. Groups
stark-naked played ' follow my leader' in strings
among the rocks, and swam and dived through the
pools. The sea beyond was calm, all to a strong
ground-swell that storms had sent up from the
Atlantic. The sun was bright, and the sky's deep
blue was reflected in the sea beneath. As the doctor
and his patient arrived among the boats, one touched
the landing-place bearing another acquaintance of
Martel, and sea-birds of several sorts that he had
shot under the rocks, gulls and grebe, and half-a-
dozen cormorants.

' " A gracious, heavenly morning ! I must go and
kill something !" That is what the Frenchman says
for Englishmen like you, destructives that you are !
Fie! fie! Proh pudor !' quoth Martel, shaking
his head, and holding his hands before his face ;
and then to his doctor: 'What with the ceaseless
slaughter of the sea-birds by the men, and the un-
wearied uprooting and carrying off of the ferns by

the women, these popular places will soon be stripped of every natural charm. I never see a lady with a grebe in her hat, but I think her hideous; and I seldom see a fern in a garden, but I wish it may wither and die.'

'Amiable of you too,' quoth the doctor, while the slaughterer laughed.

They picked their boat, a good stout tub, at Martel's suggestion, steady to dress and undress in, and to clamber into. The doctor was no swimmer; but Martel, about two miles from the land, stripped, and being an old water-dog, though he had not bathed for some years in sea or river, had the boat trimmed, and mounting the gunwale, got a good purchase for his feet, and took a header so strong and true, that he clave the clear water as an arrow cuts the air; and so deep was the dive, that the doctor and the boatman had time to wonder whether the diver was ever coming up again. When at last he did emerge, he made an effort to swim about, but was so exhausted, that he had to scramble up into the tub as soon as he could.

'I thought I had missed my way,' sighed he, and lay nude as he was at the bottom of the boat.

All his colour was gone; he was perfectly livid, and his hands were like those of a dead man.

'Don't do that again,' said the doctor. 'Out of health, and long unused to bathing, you made your first plunge too sudden and too deep; circulation was all but stopped.'

Martel had not strength to dress himself for a while, but lay stretched in the sun, waiting for its warmth to restore the current of his blood.

As the boat was rowed towards the shore, he revived, and was beginning to think of dressing, when the boatman called the attention of the doctor to what seemed to be a man swimming between them and the beach.

The doctor had turned to give Martel his clothes, when the boatman exclaimed, ‘He's drowning! I heard him cry; I saw his hands go up.’

It was certain the object had disappeared, and they with rapid strokes were nearing the spot where it had been seen.

While the boatman rowed, the two looked eagerly out, and were sure they saw it reappear for a moment, and then it vanished the second time. The boat flew through the water : presently they were at the spot. The sea was clear, and, save the ground-swell, still as glass; and gazing into it, as the boat stopped, they saw distinctly a man's body standing upon its legs, and swaying to and fro, the head a little bowed and nodding.

‘Put me out an oar,’ cried Martel, and slipped over the side, and this time so softly, that he scarce raised a ripple as he dived.

The water was not above ten or twelve feet deep, as it seemed. He got hold of an arm. The body rose at the touch, for the lungs were not yet filled with water.

How providential was it all! It was well that Martel had not dressed, and it was well that the boat was a stout one, for to get the body on board was not an easy task; and Martel, who had hardly recovered from his first plunge, was quite exhausted when they shipped him. He sat for a minute resting his head on the gunwale of the boat, not able to look what was doing, then forced himself forward to see whether any animation was left in the body. Faintly turning to the face in search of signs, his eye was spell-bound in the first glance; he hurriedly pushed aside the long wet hair to scan the pale features, and instantly fell backwards.

'Richard Gryffyn!' he screamed and fainted.

'If he had recognised his friend in the water, we should have had two drowned instead of one,' said the doctor.

CHAPTER XVIII.

'I firmly believe, and have had such convincing testimonies of it, that I must be a confirmed atheist if I did not, that there is a converse of spirits : I mean those unembodied, and those encased in flesh. From whence, else, come all those private notices, strong impulses, involuntary joy, sadness, foreboding, apprehensions of, and about, things immediately attending us ; and this in the most important affairs of our lives? . . . To see a fool, a fop, believe himself inspired ! a fellow that washes his hands fifty times a day; but, if he would be truly cleanly, should have his brains taken out and washed, and his skull trepanned, and placed with hinderside before, so that his understanding, which nature placed by mistake with the bottom upward, may be set right, and his memory placed in a right position ! To this unscrewed engine talk of spirits and the invisible world, and of his conversing with unembodied souls ! when he has hardly brains to converse with anything but a pack of hounds, and owes it only to his being a fool that he does not converse with the Devil ; for I must tell you, good people, he that is not able to see the Devil, in whatever shape he is pleased to appear in, is not really qualified to live in this world, no, not in the quality of a common inhabitant.'—DANIEL DE FOE.

'There are more things in heaven and earth, Horatio,
Than are dreamt of in your philosophy.'

Hamlet.

'I saw you as plainly as I see you now.'

'Then you have second-sight, and saw my wraith. For on that Sunday I was at Appledore. I drove over here on Monday morning, and I had never set foot in Ilfracombe till about an hour before you found me; the very first thing I did after taking my lodging was to go and bathe.'

''Tis strange! 'tis wondrous strange!' said Martel. 'You and I know that it is true, but if we tell it to any one, he will shake his wise head and doubt our sanity, or give us credit for almost political skill in omissions and colouring. What matters what they think? The meaning of your apparition to me I know thus far; had I not seen it, I should not have gone out at that hour, for my habit is to breakfast later, and then to read for an hour or two. Then I should not have, met the doctor, and I should not have gone out in a boat. I thank the good Providence that sent me to bathe, and that turned me sick, that I might be on the spot undressed and ready for a plunge; two or three seconds more would have finished you, Dicky, my dear boy. And if the doctor had not been with us, it would have been all over with you; as it was, it taxed his skill to the utmost to bring you round; to wait for a doctor would have been death, he says. Dicky, I believe, if possible, more than ever in special providences—ministering angels, if you like—and I am more than ever thankful for them.'

He squeezed his friend's hand, and tears of honest gratitude filled the eyes of both.

After a space of silent thanksgiving, Dicky proceeded to speak of his going to bathe, swimming out from shore, and suddenly finding his powers fail, his legs seemed to drop down, he could not tell how; but he could not get them up again. Some part of the adventure he did not remember very well. He did remember well that *after* sinking, he felt quite happy, sleepy indeed, and with a great wish to lie down, which he could not do : this was all that troubled him. He was gradually sinking into a state of coma, he supposed, and then he knew no more until he awoke in bed, and felt himself swollen, as it seemed, to bursting, and the pain was awful. What he best of all recollected was the sensation of sinking for the first time, and knowing that he was drowning ; it was then he cried out.

'I felt the cold clutch of death upon me,' he said, ' and the first shock was tremendous. In the twinkling of an eye my whole life past was before me clear as the noonday. It seemed spread out to my view in the minutest particulars : I could see myself, and it, as in a glass. I felt, too, the whole and every part; and as I thought of—you know what—I did not care what became of me, and down I went. It takes long to tell, but it was over in the twinkling of an eye. I have no such power of memory now. How is that, Mr. Divine ?'

' Oh ! my dear lad, you only say what thousands have said before you. My idea, or rather the idea that I have adopted, is this, that the excitement of, the last conscious moment of a man in full vigour, stirring his spirit to its depths, brings up all that is buried at the bottom of it. It is not so with most dying men, because they sink by slow decay, and die by inches, and there is not for them the awakening shock of sudden amazement : there is even no vigour left in them for surprise to work upon, they are so weakened by gradual weakness or wounds. You were perishing in your full strength without warning, in an instant, with all your faculties in full force, and the awful suddenness wrought them all into a desperate activity. Often I have had my attention called to this phenomenon of memory, and the more I have heard, and the more I have thought, the more am I inclined to believe that memory is the great evidence of the continuity of our being, that memory is the connecting link of our successive stages of existence, and that no thing and no time can "*erase* the written tablets of the brain :" there is no blotting out of its past impressions, no hope of refuge in oblivion. Let a real *impression* once have been made, things present and the cares of to-day may veil the inscription; but as you, my dear Dick, and many another, have found by experience, the veil may be rent by accidents, and the writing is revealed ; it is indelible, and stands for ever. But I am tiring you.'

'Not a bit. I have the *fact ;* I want a *theory.*'

'Well, "Earth, with daily pleasures of her own," as Wordsworth says, " does all she can to make her foster-child forget his past." But when the veiling light of mortal life is lifted by the startling hand of imminent death, the old writing on the brain comes out again as clear as ever : the page of past deeds done in the body is re-illumined ; things long put by, thoughts, words, acts, re-appear, and all the old scene lives again in memory ; our loves, our hates, our joys, our sorrows—what we have done aright, or done amiss, or left undone that we ought to have done—our sins, our repentances, or our hardening—

all come back in a moment in the crisis, the hour of judgment, when right and wrong are seen in their own colours. And, Dicky, do you ever think how in that day, when all is over with this world, and this mortal has put on immortality, and the spirit is reunited to its old partner and instrument the body to receive the final sentence for things done in the body; did you ever think how, then, " the written tablets of the brain " appear all unerased in witness, and those things which are written in them are according to our works ? " The books are opened; and another book is opened, which is the Book of Life; and the dead are judged out of those things which are written in the books, according to their works." There is the book of *God's* remembrance; and beside it, I think, the memories, the tablets of the brain, of *each man* written over with his own works, the history of his own mortal life, according to that he hath done, whether it be good or bad. My very dear Dick, you have been mighty near finding out the great secret. After life, life again: " Our life is but a sleep and a forgetting." The hereafter of the Blessed I take to be a progress through the many mansions of their Father's house, through the heavens, the work of His fingers, from glory to glory, from star to star in the host of heaven.'

'That is a solid, material sort of hope,' quoth Dicky. ' Where is your warrant, padre ?'

' A text that, for me, sufficiently sums up the proofs and reasonings on the subject, is this : " Thus, saith the Lord, that created the heavens, God Himself that formed the earth and made it. He hath established it. He created it not in vain; He formed it to be inhabited." '

' That is the earth !' said Dick.

' If the earth, why not the stars of heaven, that astronomers tell us are habitable, and not, perhaps, inhabited ?'

' What is astronomy good for ?' asked Dick, with a profound air of practical wisdom. ' The stars may affect us, but we cannot move them ; then why give a life to the study of them, eh ?'

' Because, being habitable, they may be our homes sometime, when we have done with mother earth. Who knows ?'

' Why, padre, you are as material as some of our symbolical friends.'

The padre proceeded :

' The touching and handling of our Saviour's body after He rose from the dead, and His eating of fish and the honey-comb, lead me to infer something (that you call material, though not of the earth, earthy) in store for His brethren, some glorious planet or planets, that have long been in a state of preparation as abodes for glorified bodies. Professor Owen will tell you that you and I have *latent* faculties ; wings, I believe, never to be developed on this planet, but (may I not venture to hope ?), perhaps, hereafter on some other. " The guide of life is probability," says Butler ; and what so probable to me, when I see the stars, as an infinite number of mansions differing in glory throughout the endless spaces of the universe. " We shall be *changed*," and fitted to still higher and higher conditions in

spheres where the Infinite Creator is still better
and better known; in some planets, as Jupiter, say,
or Saturn, where the light may be as the light of
seven days, and to bear its intensity our eyes may
have a smaller pupil, perhaps, or less sensibility of
retina; or, it may be in other cases, a larger pupil
and more sensibility of retina to make less light
suffice.   And after countless changes in countless
centuries, the *material* universe shall vanish in
smoke, and out of it will be developed an *invisible*
universe, and a life for the unseen in the unseen will
ensue.'

'Ah, my old philosopher and preacher! Are you
there again in your "more worlds than one," with
variations and additions? Do you know I feel
happier now than I have felt these three years? I
have had an illumination and a cleansing, even in
this world; and I see things now as they are, and
that all is for the best. That dip under the sea
washed the film from my eyes.'

After a long meditative silence on the part of both,
Dick asked with a smile, as he sat nursing and
rubbing a still aching leg:

'When you soar into your altitudes, padre, don't
you find your wings entangled by the men of
science?'

'Not at all. In the first place, my last altitude,
as you call it, came from the men of science themselves; and, in the next place, I settle myself on this
rock: that for every difficulty they hunt out in a
revelation—not of science, but of morals—there are

ten thousand greater in their own theories. I am immovable on Holy Scripture, until they can find some chart of human life that is not more improbable, that unlocks as many mysteries, and that answers as well the needs of spirits in this earthly voyage. Of our future, we " believe" that there is a " life of " a " world to come "; its precise nature we can but guess at. A great Romanist writer puts part of its felicity in the power of passing bodily through thick walls. Some science says, more prosaically, with Keble's hymn (23 S. after Trinity) that translated to other planets our bodies may enjoy " far greater capabilities of locomotion; that in the planet Ceres a baby might play with a rattle as heavy as a cannon-ball of moderate size ; that an ordinary jumper could leap a house; and a marksman put a rifle bullet in a target twenty miles away." But *I* must *away*, and for the present pass through your door by opening it. I fear I have talked you out of your rest ?'

' Not half enough. Don't go ; you amuse, instruct, and edify me, and leave me a great deal of raw pabulum (dare I say ?) to cook and digest in my solitude.'

' Solitude ! No, you will have plenty of company. By-the-bye, I have not told you that Franklin is here, and Fleming, whom you have heard of as a bold dragoon. You will soon know him, he is very accessible—not to say free and easy—and handsome as a Greek god; but an uncommonly good fellow, a sort of half-brother somehow or other, I don't quite know how, to Miss Fisher, who, by the way, is here also.

You must remember to thank her for calling here to ask after you every day.'

He did not tell his friend that she had waylaid him twice a day beside, to make inquiries about Dick.

CHAPTER XIX.

'What little town by river or seashore,
Or mountain-built with quiet citadel,
Is emptied of its folk this pious morn.'

KEATS.

'Rome flourished when her capitol was thatched
And all her gods dwelt but in cottages :
Since Parian marble and Corinthian brass
Entered her gaudy temples, soon she fell
To superstition, and from thence to ruin.'

T. RANDOLPH.

THE conversation recorded in the last chapter occurred in the early part of the week, and thenceforward Dicky's recovery of strength was unchecked and rapid ; but he resolved that his first going out of the house should be to church.

'Do you know,' said he to Martel, as they sat at breakfast on the Sunday morning, 'do you know —that dive down among the dead men did me a world of good. It has been like a new baptism to me ; it has washed away no end of evil and folly : I feel quite a new man. Let us go to some village church ; I cannot stand the crowds, and the fashion, and the spying, and the party spirit, the " High" and the "Low," that fill these town churches at watering-places, where all the idle congregate to kill time. Why, in South Devon, I had to ask my way to church of a small boy about ten years old; and he answered: "Sir, which church? High Church? Low Church? or Free Church?" If we go to some village, we shall have a chance of getting clear of that sort of thing. I want to be quiet and undisturbed in my prayers and thanksgivings; and I will just send the parson a slip of paper saying that a member of the congregation desires to return thanks to the Almighty for a great deliverance lately vouchsafed to him. Besides I like to see the originality of primitive places. All town churches have a family likeness—even the finest to the poorest.'

'Talking of originality, did I ever tell you my Welsh experiences?' asked Martel. 'You know I came over here from Wales, where I spent a Sunday, and took part in the services at the church I went to. Very queer it all was; the service was what pious scorners would call in pious slang "piebald;" it was half English, half Welsh. I read one of the lessons, the Litany, and the Communion Service in English of course; the rector read the rest in Welsh: then I had to preach an extempore English sermon, and he preached another in Welsh atop of it. Of the congregation, three out of four were Welsh. The two races were all at least as attentive as people are elsewhere; whether they understood what was said or not. It was a case of unknown tongues. The clergyman, I learned, was a Christian-like, laborious man of the peasant class, with a large parish and a very small living. And, as St. Paul wrought at tent-making, and reasoned in the synagogue every Sabbath; so did this Welsh pastor serve his church and hold the plough—till his lands and feed his flock. I, like a stranger wise in his own conceits, took upon me to suggest to him wholly to divide the services, and to perform them in English and in Welsh at different hours; and I appealed cunningly to his strong Reformation principles by asking "How he could read and preach in a tongue 'not understanded of the people'?" But his experience told him that to divide the services would be to divide his people; and difference of race had done too much of that already. No doubt he was right for the present; his system, though as unsymmetrical and as mixed as our morning service, was the one best adapted to the conflicting wants of a mixed, and not amalgamated race; and the stranger critic was wrong, as usual. For my part, I prefer to all others an ordinary English village church such as this we are coming to. I hope I am æsthetic enough to admire the revival of the fine arts, the carving in wood and stone, the painting on wall and on window, the purple and fine linen, the velvet and gold, and so forth; they are charming in their way, and gratify my taste and critical faculties; but they do not move my feelings. A living landscape, a moss-grown church, surrounded by rude and rugged tombstones, and a churchyard not too trim, amid a village of thatched cottages and little garden plots, all telling "the short and simple annals of the poor;" that is the sight that warms my heart. It occasions no wonder, but it creates delight, and would always soothe us into a contented state of mind, if the mind had not by a course of novelties, ostentation, and gross luxury, lost its taste for things natural and simple, and become alienated from the sensible sobriety of Christian content and primitive singleness of heart. How much of it is due to my own native sense of the fitness of things, and how much to early habit, I cannot tell.

> ' " Different people have different opinions ;
>   And some like apples and some like ingions,"

is rhyme and reason, and a very good practical proverb for us all.'

'I wonder,' said Dick, following his own line of reflection—' I wonder how people got on when there was no true religion ?'

'That,' replied the parson, 'is a state of utter darkness that has never existed except here and there now and then just before a crash. The experiment of the French Revolution shows what happens when religious wants are wholly disregarded.'

'Aye; but before that—in the days of old—say before Abraham was called, or before Israel came out of Egypt.'

'God never left Himself without witness, young un, nor men without His light. From the first, He who created the religious want, supplied it—

> " Whether by actual vision sensible
>   To sight and feeling ; or that in this sort ¬'
>   Have condescendingly been shadowed forth
>   Communications spiritually maintained,
>   And intuitions, moral and Divine."

In whatever way made known, God's will was made known to men ; a candle was lighted that should never be put out. It shined now here, now there, as men were able to bear the light of it. God has many ways of revealing Himself. When He lifts up His light it is seen; and when He lifts up His voice it is heard, as he pleases. St. Paul says of the heathen that they did not "*like* to *retain* God in their knowledge,' therefore they had His light; and however little they liked to use the Divine light, they could not quite extinguish it. Speculative science has suggested in a thread-bare sentence, that a wave of sound once put in motion may go on reverberating through the universe for ever. It is certainly so with the sound of Divine Truth; it appears, and disappears, and returns again ; now here, now there, among men, but it never quite dies out with any. It goes on circulating from age to age; it is echoed from nation to nation. "Time is the great innovator ;" by his incessant working changes are wrought in the circumstances and capabilities of men; none in the Light of God, it is like Himself, unchangeable. It may be coloured and made dim by man's inventions, but it can never be clean put out. Could you conceive the traditional story of man with its supernatural element—all that each child of man drew in with its mother's milk, till it became as it were bone of its bones and flesh of its flesh, or rather the breath of its spirit—could you conceive all that vanishing utterly out of the world, gone and no more known ? It cannot be lost; but it can be perverted. The earliest teaching of God's

truth, the Divine spark in man's spirit could not but
survive in man in some form or other.   Memories
connected with it were handed down from one generation to another.   The muse taught them in fable;
the poet, who was the prophet of the heathen, em-
bodied them in his creations; leavened by their
spirit, the heathen philosopher attained to his
measure of purity and gentleness; public opinion,
the mother of laws, was tinged and biassed to better
things by their antique influences; the honest-
hearted among the heathen, who were true to their
lights, were made wiser and purer, and became
centres of wisdom and purity to others.   Thus were
preserved the unseen seeds, which produced a plant
stunted indeed by an ungenial climate and degenerate, yet profitable to the heart of man ; and preparing the ground for the growth of the Gospel.   There
reached and watered the wilderness of the Gentiles
rivulets from the fountain, that slaked the spiritual
thirst of David, Isaiah, and Ezekiel; and from which,
through trackless channels, Job from the East, and
Balaam from the mountains of the East, and the wise
men from the East, drank in their inspirations. When
you find time to give a little attention to this most
interesting subject you will hardly, I think, doubt
that vestiges of genuine religion are discernible in
the literature, and laws, and religious rites of the
heathen.   Religion, rightly understood, is the patron
and friend of science, of taste, and of all improvement.
She made man thoughtful and reflective; and so fed his
genius and quickened his invention; and she has been
by turns in every age and clime the foundress of the

college and the school. Once given in the earliest age of man, with the outpouring of man's children religious ideas have spread from land to land; and I am one of those who cannot believe that there is any race of men which does not retain some spark of Divine light discoverable by those who have patience to search for it.'

'I am sure you are right, padre, about darkness being the prelude to a crash; that much I know. Shall I tell you,' said Dick, 'what were the first words that came into my mind when I came to myself? "I shall not die, but live, and declare the works of the Lord. The Lord hath chastened and corrected me; but He hath not given me over unto death." I feel as men used to feel under the *sortes Virgilanæ*, when Virgil passed for a conjurer; I feel almost as under a vow to take holy orders, and so "live" to "declare the works of the Lord." You see for the last three years I have been the fig-tree, on which no fruit could be found, just cumbering the ground; and I do not think it possible to attain that state of life which I desire henceforth to lead, except in one of those ten thousand privileged parsonages scattered up and down this favoured land: that should be to me as a monastery, wherein I should devote my life to the service of God.'

'I would not for the world seem to hold cheap such a devotion of your life to the best of ends. But I know you will forgive me, my dear young un, if I remind you that you consulted me about taking holy orders before. I then threw cold water on your heat, and you will hardly say that I did

wrong. It is different now; and if you are really
bent on becoming a clergyman, what could I say
against it? But you ought to be aware that not
clergymen alone should "declare the works of the
Lord." As Burke says of primitive and evangelical
poverty, "In spirit it ought always to exist, in the
clergy and in laymen too, however they may like
it;" so we must say of all other Christian duty and
privilege. To me there seems to the full as much
need of laymen to "declare the works of the
Lord" as of clergymen; we want Corneliuses to
love God's people and to build them synagogues.
Should not each man's opportunities guide him in
his choice? I think that God speaks to us now
mainly in providences, and that the special opportunities He offers point out as with His finger to
each of us our proper road in life. You would not
like to be of the Platitudinarian school. To write
sermons without a foundation of study would only
impart to your ingenious and fertile mind a great
facility of producing—vapid nonsense. To be sure
many a congregation, "High" and "Low" or
"Broad," has no objection to the eloquence that
evaporates in vague sentimentality and deals in
unblessed iteration, or to a hearty and loud redun-
dancy that means nothing at all. But how would
you like it yourself? You must be conscious of it,
till you have ruined your mind. They would very
likely "plate" you; but would you be pleased with
your work?'

     ' "There is a book who runs may read,'
quoted Dicky.

'Aye, to be sure, that is verse; but it is not Scripture. That is what the poet says; but what the prophet says is quite another thing: "Write the vision;"—a particular vision—"make it plain, that he may run that readeth;" not, you see, a vast book that is a whole literature in itself, but a certain vision that a man may lose no time in telling.'

'"The Bible and the Bible only,"' said Dick, shaking his head sagely.

'Nay, my young un, the critic is abroad nowadays, and he will tell you that the preacher, who knows the Bible only, knows not even the Bible. We are talking of *preachers* and *teachers*, you perceive; for an unlettered peasant, who can just give a reason for the hope that is in him, may be, and often is, as good a practical Christian as any one. But that is another thing from being "apt to teach," or "rightly dividing the word of truth." I would rather take St. Peter's word than your poet's word, though, by the way, no man demanded more imperatively a learned clergy than did the good Keble: but St. Paul did write things hard to be understood *even in his day;* and yet of the situation, state, opinions, phraseology, and circumstances of those to whom he wrote, every common Jew or Greek knew more than the greatest scholar can know now. No, no, Dick: "Study to show thyself approved unto God a workman that needeth not to be ashamed;" "Give attendance to reading, to exhortation, to doctrine;" "Meditate upon these things." We may not wrest Scripture for want of learning, nor are we oracles to deliver dogmas to be taken on trust, nor

should we ourselves, as weathercocks, turn " High "
or " Low " as the wind of fashion—the *popularis
aura*—blows.   And so, in short, my dear young un,
you perceive that I, knowing my own failing, would
hint that it will take several years' reading to make
you acquainted with the Scriptures you would
expound.   There are fellows who go into the pulpit
knowing nothing, and begging, borrowing, or stealing
everything; but you would not do so.   That is
what brings the pulpit into disrepute; so far is it
from " declaring the works of the Lord." If men
have no brains, they have no responsibility for the
use of brains : you have a head, and are responsible
for the use of it : you have your place, and no doubt
they have theirs.   Now, as a layman, you have a
grand opportunity of doing good service ; that
opportunity is your talent: ought you not to put
it out to the best ᵗinterest ?   It lies there ready to
your hand.   Beside what you have of your own, it
is not too late even yet for you to take Lord Mercia's
agency.   He is the kindest and most hopeful of
men ; he has always maintained that you would
come round to business, and be like your father ;
and he has been waiting for you patiently all this
time.   His agency is, as we may say, in commission
still ready for your acceptance.   Well, *that* I say
is a great opportunity.   If you are the prime minister
of his vast estates, you have as much scope for doing
good as any nobleman in the land.   I am not sure
that a good agent's is not the best life going.   In his
hands what might not great estates do for the
labourer, with profit to the landlord and the farmer !

Only take Lord Mercia's agency with a view to this, and it seems to me that you pay your vow and accept your lot as well as, or even better than, by taking holy orders. In that case your patience may be sorely tried : you would have to go back to college and begin life again, and wait for a living—who can say how long ? Look at me ! In the other case you are a made man. The business of the agency would come by instinct almost to the son of your father. But I am biassed in favour of agents and agencies by certain pet crotchets of my own, so I will say no more to you about it. Consult some one else, like a good boy. But here we are at our walk's end, and you may say, " Open me the gates of righteousness, that I may go into them and give thanks unto the Lord." '

The church stood on an abrupt eminence with a wide sea-view, and our pair, by a steep path clad with evergreens, entered through a lych-gate into the churchyard. There whom should they meet but Messrs. Fleming and Franklin with Miss Fisher, whose father, being an invalid old clergyman, went to a church in the town.

In the village church there was room enough and to spare. But it so happened by chance or management that Fleming, Franklin, and Martel were put into one pew, while Miss Fisher and Mr. Gryffyn were put into another. Dick had forgotten or lost his Prayer-book : he searched his pockets ostentatiously in vain, and had no alternative but to accept the share in Miss Fisher's book, which she offered very modestly. Yet so perhaps there happened soft touches of hands and of fingers, and looks that were moulded to soften, and tones on which memory lingers. All this was almost inevitable; the proximity of a pretty young woman with the wish to be pleased, would produce in any well-conditioned anchorite the desire of pleasing.

The service was ordinary. A lady, the daughter seemingly of the rector, played the harmonium in good time, and the village children sang in good tune; the hymns and tunes were well chosen, and the responses were fairly given throughout the congregation, with the exception of one man, who persisted in making them very loudly in a tone and time quite different from that used by the rest of the worshippers; while another man, his friend as it appeared, was busied wholly in taking notes. The clergyman read fairly, and preached what a party saint, on a pilgrimage of censure, would call a humdrum sermon, implying of course that he could do much better; but missing the pretty obvious reflection—that to be set to preach twice a Sunday to the same people for six consecutive years together would make a difference. Our friends, having ears to hear, found no fault with anything.

The congregation was not large; but as Martel observed, no doubt the church kept up the standard of the little neighbouring Bethel by the indirect influence of her Liturgy and teaching. The Church's service had done good to our friends, as it does always to every one who attends it in a grateful, humble spirit.

'I am not a bit the better for such a service as

that !' shouted the note-taker as he came out of church, looking at his companion with a visage whereon the cardinal virtues were not expressed.

Our party enjoyed his pious emotion, and the day and the scene, which were indeed delightful. The sun shone gaily from the deep blue sky upon the twin deep of ocean, gilding many a sail that flitted over her azure expanse. A light wind blew freshly, bringing fragrance and health from her bosom, rippling her waters and fringing with a thin line of white surf the black bases of the steep shaley cliffs.

Miss Fisher's complexion, usually sallow, was flushed with pink, and her fine grey eyes, always full of sensibility, looked glad and bright as the day. Despite a figure rather angular than un-dulating, and features that, though regular, were thin and sharp, her appearance was thoroughly feminine, that chiefest of womanly charms; and her hands and feet were small and delicate.

Richard Gryffyn had never thought of her as pretty before : why did he now ? Perhaps because her voice was soft, and her manner winning, and her touch very gentle. You will remember that they had been reading and singing out of the same book in church ; Dicky was in a grateful mood, and she was soothing and even flattering in her ways. He was bent on some change of life, and she perhaps might help him to it. The thought did not pre-cisely so shape itself to his mind ; but maybe a suspicion of it was there, all unknown to himself. At least he saw, as he never saw before, that she was gracious and interesting, and, as he condescended to observe also, she was well dressed.

As her relatives and Martel were engrossed with their own talk, the duty of entertaining her was his.

'How bright and beautiful everything looks to-day,' said he to her, as he eyed her cheek, now blooming like a nectarine ready to be gathered.

'Does it?' asked she, with quick womanly consciousness of his glance. 'I thought that with you everything was withered.' And, as she turned upon his her bright eyes, she chanted in a merry, mocking voice :—

> " Out of the day and night
> A joy has taken flight ;
>   Fresh spring, and summer, and winter hoar,
> Move my faint heart with grief ; but with delight
>   No more : oh, never more !"

'Is not that a pretty song?' quoth she, looking at him still with laughing eyes.

And then ensued, on Shelley and on things in general, an enigmatical conversation that was not ill understood by either.

None of the others gave these two a thought or a look ; for poor Dick was set down as hopelessly love-lorn ; and if any one of the three had considered Miss Fisher's situation at all, pity that she was no better paired would have been the feeling with which she was regarded.

'I'll take a little more of that mackerel, if you please—I saw it caught ; and, by the way, I saw Martel start off by the coach. I thought he was going to stay with little Gryffyn ; what's he in such a hurry for?'

This was spoken by Captain Golightly, the next morning, at a late breakfast with Franklin.

' Oh ! he is a restless sort of chap, who never knows when he is well off. He doesn't like to be long away from what he calls his county,' quoth Franklin.'

' What's the county to him ? or he to the county ? He is no county man,' said the captain.

' He is a count, anyway,' said Franklin ; ' he's always about those black squires. I can't think why ; they stick like cobbler's wax together, and hold themselves above the rest of the jackdaws. There is that old Palmer, as proud as a peacock, and Lawrence and Finch Adams are just birds of the same feather ; and Martel is their chaplain.'

' That's all bosh, old fellow, about the squarsons ; they are no more exclusive than other folk,' said Fleming, who had just entered with a cigar in his mouth, which he removed to make his observation. ' Of course there are parsons and parsons, just as there are soldiers and soldiers—and some very shady lads among them, as you know, Golightly ; and barristers and barristers too. There was your learned brother, Franky, that we met t'other day. He knocked his H's about like nine-pins.'

' Well ?' said Franklin, snappishly.

' Well, Franky, my boy, we are a mixed lot, you see, that's all. There's no class boundary but in manners; a duke's grandson drives a coal cart, or a bagman's trap, if he happens to be down in his luck. I have seen that. And an attorney's clerk is the father of a peer if his son happens to be a sharp lawyer. I have seen that too. No one's well-bred, and no one's ill-bred in England, so far as blood goes; it's all money. One Englishman has as good a pedigree as another; if you go far enough back for it. There are many fellows as poor as Job, and as miserable, with lots of grand connections; and there are fellows with lots of money, and nothing else to make them grandees. We have no stud-book, Franky.'

'There is "The Peerage," and "The Landed Gentry."'

'That's it; we are so mixed a lot, that you may trace anybody honestly back to a Plantagenet or a Crusader; but "The Peerage" does not tell how the earl's grandfather was a tinker; nor does "The Landed Gentry" or "The County Families" tell how the squire's great-uncle swept the shop. There is no real difference in England between the People and the Peerage; it is all see-saw, or one down and the other up, like buckets in a well. Money makes the landlord; and the want of it the pauper—that's about it.'

'And what does nonsense make, Jemmy?'

'But it is not nonsense, Franky. There was my own mother—I don't remember her—but I know she was the daughter of a manufacturer, whose father was a common weaver, and a jolly good fellow.'

'But your father! Jemmy,' cried Golightly; why, your uncle is a squire as rich as a Jew, and his family is as old as the hills.'

'I don't know about that, but you see I am healthy cross, anyway,' said the splendid animal, drawing, up to its full height his six feet two of bone and muscle, distributed in perfect proportions ; while his fair face glowed with brilliant health and a smile of exquisite good nature. 'Now,' continued the tall Jemmy, 'a German nobleman's stock for twenty or a hundred descents are all in the stud-book, just like a race-horse's. There is a difference between a man and a horse in England. In France Martel's father was a real marquis of the old French stud-book ; and in England he taught dancing. But, mind you, he could not lose his birth and breeding, though he did turn dancing-master. Perhaps it is because they knew his father that Palmer and his lot stick to old Marty.'

'And perhaps it is because he is "tufty,"' suggested Golightly.

'Not he ; as he says, he must play second fiddle to somebody, wherever he goes, if he has no money ; and as he finds the Palmer set pleasant fellows, he plays to them—that's all. "I am not a gentleman myself, but I know one when I see one," is what he says about it.'

'And he's not a bad judge,' said Captain Golightly : old Palmer and his friends Finch Adams and Lawrence are not of a bad sort.'

'You don't know them, 'Lighty.'

'Though I don't *them*, I know that, Franky, my boy.'

'Aye ; you know a great deal, both of you. The barrack is the place for knowledge.'

'You see, I sit and think, Franky,' said Fleming, with complacency—' sit and think as I smoke my five-and-twenty pipes a day, in country quarters, when there is no hunting. And, as for old 'Lighty, I dare say he does just the same; though he is a family man.'

'No, no, Jemmy; my wife won't stand all that; so I cultivate my mind with novels, you see. She puts me up to the right sort, you know: Thackeray, D'Israeli, and Bulwer Lytton—" tip-toppers"—don't you perceive? I take it they know a thing or two. But, holloa! I say, Fleming, do you see that?' cried the Captain, breaking off his home reminiscences, to call his companion's attention as he threw the stump of his cigar out of the window.

'See what?' asked his friend.

'Why, there's your old governor toddling down to the beach; and very well he goes—for him.'

'Well: what of that?'

'Don't you see who's with him? Your half-sister, man, Miss Fisher, and Dicky Gryffyn! my boy. Dicky's getting better! Dicky will soon be well! Let us go down and join them, or, no; we won't spoil sport! if they have your consent, Jemmy, they have mine.'

'By-bye, Franky,' said the long lieutenant, firing a parting shot as he left the room; 'by-bye, Franky, and remember,—" worth, not birth;" "money maketh manners," and "manners maketh man," as we were taught at Winchester. Ta! ta!'

'It is astonishing how nearly a blockhead may blunder into truth,' said Franky; '*Old wealth* is "Aristocracy," with Aristotle, you know.'

Golightly looked as though he did not know; and Franklin laughed.

CHAPTER XX.

'Mercy, guard me!
Hence with thy brewed enchantments, foul deceiver!
Hast thou betrayed my credulous innocence
With visored falsehood and base forgery?'
MILTON—*Comus.*

'I HAD the pleasure of meeting often many years ago Admiral, then Captain, De Coucy; but I have scarcely seen him since. May I ask if he is in any way related to you, Mr. De Coucy?'

'My uncle,' replied De Coucy.

The inquirer was the Lady Selina Wadhurst, thin, short, spectacled, and formal, always handsomely dressed in black or grey silk of prim old-world fashion. She was the daughter of a cabinet minister long dead, and was an ardent and self-forgetting lover of all goodness, especially when it appeared in the form of churchmanship, most of all in the guise of High-churchmanship.

If there be truth in the old proverb, Mr. de Coucy's ears must have tingled and burnt as he made his answer. For at that very moment a conversation concerning him was carried on in a very pretty parsonage not very many miles off.

The Reverend Stephen George Lawrence had a fine taste, understood horticulture, and could lay out grounds to perfection; he had also the means of indulging his taste. His rectory was in size more suited to the living, which was very small, than to a childless clergyman of ample private means—something over two thousand a year, and sociable and hospitable habits. But he did not enlarge his house; he utilised and beautified it. He put every hole and corner to use, and made the whole convenient and snug; and then adorned it so, that his little baby-house was to a person of nice perceptions far better worth seeing than many great show-houses. The grounds were small, and the place was confined; but it adjoined the churchyard. He pulled down the needless, ugly churchyard wall of red-brick, and grew ivy upon its ruins and upon the church tower, which was ill-proportioned. He took in hand the churchyard and gardened it, and made the church and rectory one of the prettiest sights in the neighbourhood. He and his wife went much to great houses, and entertained their owners at his small one, in which, however, he outdid the grandees by its cosy, well-judged, well-drilled arrangements, and the completeness of its appliances. Each guest knew that his or her special likings, whatever they might be, were pretty sure to be remembered and attended to at the Lawrences'; so that every one felt at home with them in the enjoyment of his own peculiar comforts. Mr. Lawrence's horses and carriages and servants were all good and serviceable. It need hardly be added that he and his wife were both good financiers, and experienced people of the world.

'My dear,' said the Reverend Stephen to Mrs. Lawrence, 'I wish you would drive over to-day and call upon Lady Selina Wadhurst at Finchdale ; you know she has charge of Barbara while Palmer is away. And to say the truth, I don't like the look of that young man they have about them, whom Palmer has got for curate there.'

'I shall be very glad to call upon Lady Selina ; but, Steenie dear, don't you think it would be well for you to call upon the curate, as a politeness to Mr. Palmer, you know, though you don't like his look. Somebody, I forget who, told me that he was a very handsome young man.'

'And Barbara is a very handsome young woman, with a very handsome fortune,' replied Steenie. •

'And if he should happen to have one too, Steenie, I think it might do very well.'

'He looks to me much more like a fortune-hunter than a man-of-fortune,' retorted Steenie.

'Well, my dear, Lady Selina will see to that.'

'That is just what Lady Selina will never do. You know how she threw away her own young daughter, with her forty thousand pounds, on that grey old Puseyite, whose father dealt in tenpenny nails. Her extravagant Church opinions blind her to all other considerations ; and this handsome fellow is just the man to make a fool of her. His clothes are all of the very latest and most pronounced eccle-siastical cut, with a coat down to his heels, and all in perfect keeping, I am bound to say, and uncommonly well-made too.   He must spend a deal of time and money upon his costume.   Altogether he is got up with much more finery than a gentleman such as Arthur Clifton is, with all his nonsense, would ever think of.   And his manner is as foppish as his dress ; in short, I believe the man is an impostor or a Jesuit.'

'Oh! Steenie dear, I wish you would not talk in that way, and use such words.   It is such a bad fashion you have got into : nobody talks about Jesuits now.'

'No, my dear, of course not.   Now that the real thing has come among us, I know it is bad manners to mention the name.   Never speak of present company, eh ?'

'But, Steenie, you are always so suspicious and so severe.'

'If you mean that I like a direct man, and a direct way of speaking, I do.   I'll have nothing to say to a set that is delusive or elusive.'

'Or abusive,' suggested the lady.

'They are very often that too, but in a sly, indirect way.   Be his sentiments what they may, I tell you this young man is an adventurer ; I dare say he is a swindler.'

'Is he so *very* handsome, dear ?   You have not told me that.'

'Yes ; he is *very* handsome.   I have scarcely ever seen a handsomer man.'

'In what style, dear ?'

'Tall and dark——'

'Why, that is you, Steenie.'

'Pale, with dark eyes and long eyelashes,' continued Steenie, unheeding his wife's flattering interruption—'a sort of clerical corsair, with an expression at once devout and sentimental—just the man to take in a woman.'

'Thank you, my dear; I am sure you mean to attribute good taste to us. Is he gentleman-like ?'

'No; I don't think he is; he has too much manner.'

'I should like to see him and judge for myself. Where did you see him, dear ? And what is his name ? I don't think that I have heard it.'

'I did not catch his name; I only saw him for a minute or two at the inn at Lobthorpe. He was with Lady Selina and Barbara in the carriage; and he was so handsome and attentive, and so outrageously clerical and new, with his lavender kid-gloves and all the rest of it, that I took particular notice of him, and arrived at the conclusion that he is a humbug, if not worse.'

'That is so like you, my dear. You make me quite curious to see him. I wonder whether I shall agree with you.'

'Not very likely,' said Stephen grimly.

'That is just what I want to know,' said his wife.

'Well, I'll do you the justice to back you against any detective in a matter of that sort, if good-looks are put out of the question.'

'I do not know that I can thank you for the compliment,' said the lady; 'but I will call upon Lady Selina, and perhaps I may see this clerical Adonis. You will come with me, my dear ? And will you call upon him, Steenie ?'

'I will go with you; but I certainly will not call upon him, unless he turns out very different from that which I take him to be. I should not like to see poor Palmer's nest rifled while he is away.'

'Do you know, Steenie, I think our pretty Barbara a young lady well able to take care of herself.'

'So did I, till that affair of young Gryffyn.'

'I just fancy Barbara singed her fingers the least bit in the world, while she was manœuvring to catch him for her cousin, Kitty Fisher; that is my idea of it, Steenie. Little Miss Barbara is very fond of managing. If she had given him a thought for herself, she would not have been so open and careless. As she ran so much in his way on her cousin's behalf, I don't wonder she found the little man agreeable. He is short, to be sure, and freckled, and far from being the handsome man you describe the new curate to be; but Mr. Gryffyn's expression is very animated, and that grows often to be more interesting than mere beauty; and his manners are very good indeed. I wonder where he got them ?'

'In France, no doubt. You know he was sent to Nancy, where the old-fashioned high-bred people are most to be found, and Lord Mercia, who is at home in France, gave him introductions; otherwise they are not at all accessible.'

'How kind of Lord Mercia! But he is always so kind! Though his kindness does not always turn out so well; but it has done wonders for young Gryffyn: and indeed I think Barbara's scheme a very good one for both the lady and the gentleman.

Dear Barbara is really a very warm-hearted girl, and has quite a genius for match-making, I suspect.'

'I more than suspect that another person has it too,' quoth the husband.

'Thank you, my dear; you are full of compliments to-day, though I don't understand you. I know you mean to be civil. It seems to me that *you* want me not to make, but to mar a match.'

'I detest match-making, and adventurers and impostors, and believe this man to be both; and I have the greatest regard for Palmer and his daughter, as you know.'

'But Lady Selina——'

'Ah, nonsense! You know Lady Selina as well as I do, and what she is capable of. Why, if she takes it into her head that he is a man of her school, she would think she was doing God service, and the best thing she could for Barbara, by forwarding a match with him, if he had not a penny, as I fully believe he has not. Did you ever see a man, with his dress, and turn-out, perfect, that was not either an adventurer or a bankrupt, or on the high road to become one?'

Steenie was pacing the room with his hands stuck deep into his pockets, as his manner was when angry. Mrs. Lawrence blandly replied:

'I know, my dear, how terribly severe you are. It is very wrong; indeed it is. So to disabuse your mind, will you please ring for the carriage? We will go and inspect this phœnix at once. I am very anxious to see him, and quite prepared to admire him for all you say.'

'Humph!' grunted her lord, ringing the bell.
'At best, I believe he is a Jesuit in disguise.'

'Well, you know, the Jesuits are very self-denying
people.'

'Yes ; if self-denial means a determination to have
your own way at all costs.   Charles the Twelfth of
Sweden, and Louis the Eleventh of France, and
Pope Gregory the Seventh, were very self-denying
men after that fashion ; but I should not like to
have stood in their way.'

'Oh, my dear! when you begin to talk history,
you talk such nonsense ; I perfectly detest history,
and I don't believe a word of it.   The Jesuits are
very zealous anyway ; and zeal is a good thing.'

'Yes ; in a good matter.'

'They are all earnest and conscientious.'

'Conscientious! earnest! zealous!   Yes! "*quite*
saintly*," of course!   "Saints!" who canonised them?
their party, to be sure, just to exclude others; a
trick as old as the eternal city.   Zealous indeed!
Why, so was a Spanish Inquisitor; so was a Red
Republican ; so is a Thug.   Zealous indeed! so was
Robespierre, and an ascetic to boot.   Zeal! aye;
"they compass sea and land to make one proselyte ;"
and what then ?'

'Oh! my dear! I must leave the room, if you will
go on in that strain,' said the lady.

'If your friends, the Jesuits, these admirable
men,' proceeded the irate husband, 'as they style
themselves in their "Thrasonical brag," were to get
the upper hand—well, I know a little, I guess a

great deal, and can jump to a pretty sure conclusion
—as to what they would do with the like of me.'

'Then, Steenie, do to them as they would not do
to you.'

'You are very good,' replied Steenie, 'but I
could not stay in the Church of England, that's all.
I should be in pocket, too, by resigning my living
and going to live at Kingston near Dublin, or even
at any English watering place, though I should hate
the life there.   I think the amount of this living is
a proof that I undertook its duties for love and not
for money.   But, if I lost all that I have of my own
besides, I would resign just the same.'

'I know you would, Steenie, if you thought it
right,' said his wife, soothingly. 'No one that knows
you can doubt it.   I have heard you say a thousand
times that all your property belongs to the Church.'

'So it does, to the Reformed Church, while I am
its servant; and that is the reason why I would
take care that it should not belong to a Romanised
Church, of which I would never be the servant.
Your zealous gentlemen would hardly fill up all the
small livings in out-of-the-way country places like
this.   Zealous gentlemen, I observe, do not go out of
reach of society.   I do not hear of small livings in
the Collieries being filled by "zealous" gentlemen, as
a general rule, though some splendid fellows live and
die there, whose names do not get into the papers.
Instead of your zealots flocking to those neces-
sitous and benighted parts, I hear complaints of a
dearth of ministers, and invitations to zealous men,
which are not accepted.'

'I wish you would have done with your zealous men; I am sick of them,' said the wife.

'So am I. How it will all end I cannot imagine. First we had ecclesiologists and church politicians; then we had architects, these did some good; and now we have lawyers and church politicians again, who make the Church like a ship with sea-lawyers among the crew; and we are coming to men-milliners like this man at Finchdale.'

'Well, my dear, I can't stay to hear you. Nobody but you says these harsh things now. I shall go and put my bonnet on. The carriage will be round directly.'

This worthy pair, not long afterwards, were with the Lady Selina in the drawing-room at Finchdale; when dressy Mrs. Lawrence, holding up her hands, exclaimed—

'So this gentleman is a nephew of Admiral de Coucy!'

'Yes,' said Lady Selina, 'I heard it from himself not three hours ago.'

Here Mrs. Lawrence shot at her husband a triumphant glance that said, as plainly as eyes could speak—'You see how very wrong you were.' And then remarked aloud, 'How curious it is that one meets with friends everywhere! Admiral de Coucy is a very dear friend and a constant correspondent of ours. I was going to write to him this very day. Now I shall have the pleasure of telling him that his nephew is for a time our neighbour, and how delighted we shall be to show him every attention in our power.'

Her letter drew a reply by return of post from the Admiral, who wrote :—' I had but one brother ; and he had no son ; the person you mention must be an impostor.'

' I told you so,' said Mr Lawrence.

CHAPTER XXI.

'Sweet Echo, sweetest nymph that liv'st unseen
    Within thy aery shell,
      By slow Meander's margent green,
And in the violet embroider'd vale
    Where the love-lorn nightingale
Nightly to thee her sad song mourneth well :
Canst thou not tell me of a gentle pair,
    That likest thy Narcissus are ?

    ' O, if thou have
Hid them in some flowery cave,
    Tell me but—where,
Sweet queen of parley, daughter of the sphere !
So may'st thou be translated to the skies,
And give resounding grace to all Heaven's harmonies.'

MARTEL, having scent of a cure to his mind, had left
Ilfracombe for Cornwall in quest of it, and was
staying at a little seaside place beyond the Fowey.
He had travelled far on land to that out-of-the-way
inaccessible parish, starting at four o'clock in the
morning, had caught the rector at breakfast, and had
returned at six in the evening, thoroughly worn out.
He was now sitting in the window of his lodging
gazing on the esplanade, where the visitors were
enjoying a late promenade.

'What an echo you have here!' remarked he to the landlady.

'You may say that, sir! we hear all that goes on, and many things that we are not supposed to hear— a deal of love-making you know, sir,' replied she unscrupulously. 'No one would think, sir, that he could not say a word on those far beaches there, but it all comes to our ears!'

It was indeed a gossiping window for any one, who, without wishing to be a listener to secrets, was a curious observer of life and manners, while the view was as lovely as any in fair England. To sit in that window and rest would have been the thing most to Martel's taste, if he had not been so very tired. As it was, he was thinking of going to bed, when his ear was caught by these words—

'Old Palmer, you know, is safe in Ireland.'

Martel thought he was dreaming, and rubbed his eyes.

The voice went on :

'Nobody knows how long he'll be there. He's looking up some tenants in the West; it's like enough they'll shoot him ; the best thing they can do ; proud, greedy aristocrat!'

Now Martel was awake in earnest, and heard as plainly as ever he heard anything in his life, another voice not unlike the first reply :

'Well, what'll that do for us? I don't see.'

'Don't see!' repeated the first voice. 'Why, don't you know Jack has made the daughter head over ears in love with him—ready to say snip to his snap, or to jump down his throat, for the matter of that ;

and he's going to run away with her, or she with him, I don't know which—that's all. Do you see now, old Buzzard ?'

'But is he sure of any tin ?'

'As sure as acres are acres and dirt is dirt.'

'Do you mean to say she has agreed ?' asked voice number two.

'Planned it all herself, sir ! that is, I don't 'xactly know what the dodge is, but she will do anything that he tells her.   Handsome chap, Jack, and no mistake ; no girl can say nay to' him.   Uncommon fine physiog ! Tip-top education, and all the ticket, goes down amazingly with the swells, especially ladies that like Psalm-singing. Jack must make hay while the sun shines. He may get the small-pox.'

And at that enemy to Jack's beauty the amiable pair laughed.

It was beginning to grow dusk, and Martel, from his post of observation, could but just make out the outlines of their figures ; indeed he could scarcely trust his eyes or his ears.   He had thought he must be dreaming ; but sight and hearing were too sure. You might have knocked him down with a straw. But there was no time to throw away in wonder ; something must be done, and done at once. And his first step was to go after the conspirators and find out who they were.

They entered an inn.   He followed them.   They sat down in the coffee-room, and called for brandy and water.   He followed their example, taking his seat not far from them.   Then they lit cigars, and, between smoking and sipping, talked at intervals in buzzing whispers, of which only just enough reached his ears to let him know that they were still on the old topic; and that an elopement was decided on, and arranged for, and was to come off immediately ; though no day was named audibly.

The men were dressed like gentlemen; and somehow neither of the faces seemed quite strange to him. Wondering when or where he could have seen them, Martel heard number one again refer with unctuous admiration to the gay marauder's beauty, and its fascinating effect.

'Handsome Jack ! Handsome chap ! People do say, 'specially the girls, who are the best judges—do say that he is 'mazin' like me ; they'd hardly know one from the other.'

' He is a beauty then !' retorted number two. ' But if you come to likeness, he has a deal the most family likeness to me ; so says every one that ever I heard speak about it:—though I'm not going to say that I am so pretty as you are,' he added, grinning.

This playful part of the dialogue seemed to give Martel the clue he was seeking. Observing closely the men, as they spoke, he was reminded of Mr. de Coucy ; and then at once there flashed across his mind the memory of the agreeable and well-informed clerical tourist, whom he had seen driving triumphantly away in Mr. Finch Adams' carriage with Mr. Finch Adams' guineas in his pocket ; while again he seemed to see the ingenious and ingenuous salesman of the unfortunate Captain Browne.

Sure enough there they were, that precious pair,

the Reverend Adolphus John Williams, *alias* Green, and Captain Browne, or his active representative; and, aided by the hints with which their conversation had furnished him, Martel saw in each very clearly a family, but not flattering, likeness of the well-favoured Mr. de Coucy, *alias* ' Handsome Jack.' They were probably brothers; they were palpably swindlers.

To frustrate the conspiracy which Echo had so strangely revealed, and to save, if possible, his friends from the hands of these rascals, Martel had played the uncongenial part of a detective to some purpose. He now retired and ordered a fly to take him to the nearest station, five miles off, by six o'clock the next morning.

The only move that seemed to be open to him was to get to Finchdale before the attempt at abduction, and then by some means, or by any means, to prevent it. This, if he were not *too late*, he felt no doubt about.

He did not believe one moment, for all he had heard, that Miss Palmer was in any guise or degree a consciously consenting party to this pretty scheme. She was too good and too clever to be suspected upon any evidence of such cruel folly. But she might be the victim of some atrocious fraud. That man De Coucy, if he were, as Martel could not doubt he was, the 'Handsome Jack' of the plot, was an adroit intriguer, a hypocrite, and a swindler, capable, as Martel had proved, of any deceit.

Oh! how Martel wished now that he had shown him up at the first. He felt a partner by his stupid

silence in all this mischief. No doubt the whole
thing had been planned before he applied to Martel;
the heiress had been marked down by this brotherhood of villains, and 'Handsome Jack' was the bait
to catch her. The man was as plausible as he was
unscrupulous, and well-favoured as he was un-
principled.

And yet, as Martel turned the affair rapidly over
and over in his mind, it appeared certain to his
judgment that these infamous scamps must have
overreached themselves. That they believed in their
own success seemed clear; but they must be the
dupes of their own vanity—their natural craft was
dulled by their ignorance of the principles and feelings of people of honour and integrity. The
question then was—how was he to act? or rather
was he to act at all?

The idea of these fellows succeeding was so pre-
posterous that it seemed absurd for himself and in-
sulting to the Palmers that he should move at all in
the way of crediting so scandalous a bubble. He
would make himself ridiculous. And what a compliment to Miss Palmer! 'It would serve me right if
she never spoke to me again; only she would know
that I never doubted her. The expenses of the
journey too, for such a "tale of a tub!"'

But, after all reasonings, hopes, and beliefs, there
was still the palpable fact, made known to him in a
specially providential way—and this appealed to the
strongest persuasions of Martel's mind, made
stronger by his recent experience at Ilfracombe—the
undeniable fact that these two unscrupulous men

35--2

were leagued with that handsome villain in some plot against Miss Palmer which they believed to be now on the point of succeeding. He could not doubt the testimony of his eyes and ears as to the reality of the conspiracy ; and had he a right, for fear of ridicule, or even blame, had he a right to slight the special providence that had revealed it to him ? Not to speak of the vast debt he owed the Palmers for kindnesses received by him, and the many more intended by them—there were no people in the whole world whom he so loved and revered. The right thing was to go, and go he would. While he believed absolutely in Barbara's sense and goodness, he believed no less in De Coucy's hypocrisy, treachery, craft, and experience in mischief, not to speak of his dangerous personal gifts, and the no less dangerous aid of these two audacious adventurers.

Revolving these things incessantly on his bed, he turned over and over, feverish and sleepless, though sore weary, racked with various doubts, and stimulated to a painful state of nervous irritability. And when the well-feed servant came to call him at three o'clock in the morning for his early drive to the train, he left his couch not only not the better, but very much the worse for the few hours that he had passed in it.

CHAPTER XXII.

·' At no time of my life have I been a person to hold myself polluted by the touch or approach of any creature that wore a human shape. On the contrary, from my very earliest youth it has been my pride to converse familiarly, *more Socratico*, with all human beings—man, woman, and child— that chance might fling in my way ; a practice which is friendly to the knowledge of human nature, to good feelings, and to that frankness of address which becomes a man who would be thought a philosopher ; for a philosopher should not see with the eyes of the poor limitary creature calling himself a man of the world, and filled with narrow and self-regarding prejudices of birth and education, but should look upon himself as a catholic creature, and as standing in an equal relation to high and low,—to the educated and uneducated, to the guilty and the innocent.'— DE QUINCEY.

'I ALWAYS go against the clergy ; they are so unpopular,' drawled one fashionable dandy to another in a first-class carriage, wherein Martel had taken his place with the vain hope of getting some sleep.

His constitutional irritability, quickened by want of rest, was nettled by this depreciatory remark, made before one of his cloth.

'Shall I tell you why they are "unpopular," sir ? asked he.

The other lifted his eyebrows and shook his head, as, with the least possible labour to himself, implying that he had no curiosity on the subject.

'Because,' proceeded the curate, 'because, sir, they are supposed to take the part of rich men, like you. If they were to stick to the text "Do not rich men oppress you?" and ring changes upon it, instead of varying the note with "The powers that be ordained of God," they would be popular enough to win even your vote and interest!'

'I have not the pleasure of knowing who you are, sir,' lisped the dandy, who was the eldest son of Sir Hurleigh and Lady Olivia Burleigh.

'My name is of no consequence,' said Martel. And the dandy bowed assent with a humour that charmed the parson, who replied, 'But I know who you are, sir—a member of Parliament and a representative of us little folk, if you will permit me to claim that honour. As one grateful for your condescension, I would beg in return for it to be allowed to invite your notice to this sentence of Lord Plunket, in regard to us poor and "*unpopular*" priests : "It has been well observed by an eminent historian, Dr. Robertson, that the influence of the priesthood is most strong when united with the discontented portion of the population; but that, when allied with the governing powers, their influence is proportionally diminished." I always carry that sentence about in my memory, and I beg to place it at your service, sir.'

No reply or notice was vouchsafed by the young member, whom Martel knew well enough by sight as the son of a county baronet and the grandson of a duke, who was Lord-Lieutenant of the county. As heir of these ancestral honours, he threw up his chin, fixed his eyes upon the roof of the carriage and wrapped himself in sublime silence. And Martel, cooled by this ebullition, though he could not yet get the sleep he sought, was soothed by the sweet morning air, which blew in freshly through the open windows.

When the train stopped and a fresh ticket was to be taken, the careful traveller, finding that sleep would not visit him, as he had hoped, in a first-class carriage, took a turn in the second class, seeing that no thirds were attached to that train.

'For what are we waiting?' grumbled he on the platform, addressing no one in particular.

'Ministers, sir,' a sharp, flashy, commercial-looking gentleman volunteered, in the tone of pompous rebuke.

'Ministers, eh?' quoth the other, staring. 'These are your Poloniuses, are they? Not very worshipful to look at, anyway.'

'They have inscribed their proud names in the history of this great commercial country.'

'Proud! are they? Why are they proud? They will soon be turned out for their pride,' snapped the cleric.

> ' "One crowded hour of glorious strife
> Is worth an age without a name," '

replied the trader poetically.

'Oh, you are for capping verses, are you?' quoth the cleric. 'Have at you, then :

"'Half ignorant, they turn an easy wheel,
And set sharp racks at work to pinch and peel.
Why are they proud?   Again I ask aloud,
Why, in the name of Glory, are they proud?"'

'They are proud, sir, to be our servants, sir, and do our work, sir; and I, sir, am proud of the way they do it; though you do call it "pinching and peeling,"' the other replied, taking off his hat and standing with it in his hand bareheaded before his servants.

'Servants, no doubt, and in fashion,' replied the caviller; 'imperious, I may say imperial.   The Twelve Cæsars, I call them.'

'There are only eleven.'

'Never mind, any one of them thinks himself equal to two; I'll be bound.'

'They seem to have "pinched and peeled" you, sir,' sneered the man of commerce, smugly looking at the other's clerical cut with non-conforming eyes.

'Pinched me!   Peeled me!   Not a bit of it; "Cantabit vacuus coram latrone"—a cut-purse can't pick an empty pocket, you know.   So I'll just keep my hat on head, and keep my head warm.'

'And I take mine off, sir, to gentlemen whom I respect, I may say revere—great men, sir! orators, sir!'

This was uttered 'ore rotundo' with a dignified judicial air.

'Orators! are they?   I do not like the men,' replied the parson: '"They are Philistines, and speak the language of Canaan."'

'Why, what have you to say against them?'

' You have said it: they are orators.'

' And what's the matter with orators ?'

' Only this, that they do for mobs, gentle and simple, what favourites are said to do for princes.'

' What's that ?'

' Tickle 'em, sir ! tickle 'em !'

' How tickle ?'

' Many ways.'

' Name one :'

' Well : they are too fond of the ephemerous tales.'

' The female's tail!—What's that you say ? These gentlemen are no more fond of petticoat government than you are : let me tell you that, whoever you be ; an' I don't know, an' don't care—with your tails and your nonsense and rubbish.'

' No doubt, my friend, but you mistake me. My " *ephemerous* tale " means only a little fable with an excellent moral, of course, but with just a spice of malice in it—not more than enough, you know, to poison men's judgment against fair discussion. It is what Mr. O'Connell, who knew its use, called "A very good fib, if it lasted a week ;"—only fib is not the word he employed, he called it by a plainer and uglier name.'

' Rot your fibs and fables, *I* don't want to know about fibs and fables. I want to know what you mean by 'femer's tale; that's what I want to know.'

' It is an old trick ; and as these fellows are keeping us waiting, I'll give you an old example of it, if you will listen : When a great part of the Roman legions were ready to mutiny, a private soldier mounted the shoulders of his comrades and addressed himself to the army with all the vehemence of natural emotion: "You have given liberty to these miserable men," he said, pointing to some criminals whom they had rescued; " but which of you can give back life to my brother ? Who can give me back my brother ? He was murdered last night by the hand of those ruffians who are kept by the general to butcher the poor soldiery. Tell me, Blæsus" (for that was the general's name), "tell me where thou hast laid his dead body ? Even an enemy does not grudge the right of burial. When I have tired myself with kissing his cold corpse and weeping over it, order me to be slain upon it. All I ask of my fellow-soldiers, since we both die in their cause, is that they would lay me in the same grave with my brother." The whole army was in uncontrollable uproar, resolved to do the man justice at all hazards and all costs ; when—upon inquiry they found that he never had a brother. It was all an *"ephemerous tale,"* but very effective for *oratorical* purposes. That is your *" ephemerous tale."* '

'Oh ! I see, sir,' said the hearer, chuckling at the fraud; 'I see you mean a little spouting and bounce !'

'I mean spouting that is very inexact, and statements altogether unfounded.'

'Oh! sir, I adore Freedom. I would not have liberty of speech trammelled—not by no means.'

'Aye, *you* love Freedom ; and so do I, sir—but what sort of Freedom ? Do you mean freedom of thought ? I also am for freedom of thought—very much so. Or is it freedom from the trammels of truth you mean? Is it there you are? Avaunt! Avaunt!'

'Good Heavens!' cried the other, looking aghast.

'What's the matter, man? Are you ill?'

'My purse is gone! and ten guineas in it!'

'You don't say so! some one has taken a "liberty" with you, and made "free" with your purse. This station is a very "free" place—quite a temple for the adorers of "liberty." You see, sir, while you kept your hat in your hand, you did not keep your hands in your pockets. But look out: the train is starting; your baggage is in. If you don't mind you will lose your train and traps, as well as your purse.'

'Get in, sir,' says the guard, and shut the door upon him.

The guard whistles; the train moves.

His tormenter shouts in at the window:

'" Who steals my purse steals trash ° ° °
But he, who filches from me my good name——"'

'Blow me! if I don't crack his saucy nob, or knock his eye out!' was the traveller's vow, as he snatched at his umbrella to shy it at his adversary's head.

He was balancing it for a shot, when its handsomely-carved ivory handle caught his eye; he calculated the cost of its silk: sound commercial principles prevailed, and he did not throw good silk and ivory after the lost gold. He kept his umbrella, and Martel kept his head unbroken, and his eye in it; but his friend piously commended him to the vengeance of Providence.

Before long his own train carried him away.

Into the compartment which held him entered at

268 THE BLACK SQUIRE.

the first stoppage, pushing his way with a swagger, a private soldier. To whom a handsome gentleman, well dressed in black—apparently a solicitor—said, reprovingly :

' I think you have mistaken your carriage ; this is a second-class carriage.'

' I know it,' said the soldier. ' I am in her Majesty's service ; we travel in what class we like.'

' Not with your officers, in the first-class,' said the elder.

' Erhm ! no. I belong to the second-class of society.'

' So much the worse for you, my friend,' put in Martel.

' Why so ?' asked the elderly gentleman.

' Because the second-class pays for all ; all the direct and all the indirect taxation falls upon it.'

' How is that, sir ?' said the elder; ' the more a man's income, the more he pays.'

' Aye, when you can get at it; but "flesh and blood " will not let you, we are told on excellent authority. When men count by hundreds, there is no mistake; when they count by hundreds of thousands, we are told they take their bill, and for one hundred, write fifty ; and for two hundred four-score. " Any statesman can govern a country in a state of siege," and any Chancellor of the Exchequer can finance with an income-tax.'

' You seem to know all about it, sir ; perhaps you'll tell me why.'

' Because the weight of the income-tax falls upon that most helpless class of persons, whose incomes range from two or three to six hundred a year; and these, though generally well educated and intelligent, are politically ciphers.'

'Indeed, sir? How's that?'

'On account of what they have, or what they want, for themselves or their children. They are too isolated and too dependent to make head against a government, however oppressive and rasping.'

'They have votes, sir; which those below them often have not.'

'But those below have brick-bats to break ministers' heads; and those below can form mobs, which those above cannot. Your modern minister is most amenable to the reason of mobs, and sees great weight in a brick-bat.'

'You know a great deal more than I do, sir,' said the lawyer to the curate; and to himself: 'Low, radical parson! of all radicals the vilest,' muttered this legal friend of prescription and of the law's delay, sidling off as far as he could.

'We protect the government,' said the soldier, with not unbecoming dignity.

In course of time these all got out, and parted friends, for all their professional difference of opinion.

Martel, having had his turn of first and second, now took a ticket for the third class of society, as the soldier had it; whereinto entered six navvies.

'Anybody object to smoking?' asked one, with chivalric courtesy.

'You are more polite than most folk, to ask the question,' said our friend, always ready for a talk with any one.

'I like to do as I would be done by,' replied the navvy; and, no one objecting to it, he lit his pipe.

He had finished it, and no one else was smoking, when a young 'gent,' velvet waistcoated, ringed, and curled, entered and without ceremony commenced smoking, and puffed his clouds of smoke into Martel's face; who turned to his friend the navvy, and said:

'You see?'

'That don't make it right,' quoth the navvy, whose manners and sentiments were in all respects above those of the 'gent.'

With beer aboard he and his partners might have been 'rough;' but it is something to be courteous and considerate when sober.

After a while the company was changed. Fustian took its departure, and was replaced by broadcloth. The clergy of the lesser sort affect third-class carriages and Australian meats, and would be ranked by the soldier in the lowest class of society.

One of those who entered now—a sad invalid evidently—turned to another ruddy with health, saying:

'You are a clergyman, I presume?'

He nodded assent.

'And you have a country cure?'

'A small one.'

'Aye, I thought so. Look at me. Did you ever see such a wreck? And I dare say I am not older than you are. But I have for twelve years worked single-handed in a large town parish; and here I am, prematurely worn out and turned out to die, just as I have gained experience and am fit to be most

useful! Oh! but I see my error too late—too late!
It comes of the false ambition instilled into me by
men whose circumstances were far other than mine.
I have not used my reason as God willed; I have
been set on to do too much. The doctors told me I
was killing myself. I had no right to do it, of
course; it was suicide. At last my body struck
work, and now I have to give up everything. Like
the man who tries to do a large business with a
small capital, I am ruined. God did not call me to
ruin and to make myself useless. He needed not
any special measure of work from me. What He
required was that I should employ such talents and
means as He gave me for the general good, and for
my own good, in sobriety and moderation. What
was really given me to do was what He made me
equal to, and no more. I have attempted more, and
have of course done less. If my time were to come
over again, I would not so overmark myself, nor
suffer rich men, rolling in wealth, to use me up and
throw me aside like a sucked orange!'

'You are beneficed?' asked Martel of the
speaker.

'Yes, I am beneficed, as you call it.'

'I am not even that,' said Martel; 'and you see
I am not a chicken; but

> '"I am shepherd to another man,
> And do not shear the fleeces that I graze."

I have tried town and country, and would put
my experience as against yours, thus: I have as
little as possible allowed other people to think for

me, though I am but a "journeyman parson," as the farming folk word it. With the exception of one short period, my way of looking at my work has been this: Say you have many miles before you with but one horse. You must not exceed six miles an hour, if you mean to get to your journey's end. If you have plenty of relays of horses, you may travel twelve or fourteen miles an hour, if you like. That is just the difference between a rich and a poor clergyman. The poor man is vain, if he wantonly copes with the other; he is weak if he suffers himself to be bullied or tricked into competition. Excuse me, sir, but you have let other people think and feel for you; and the end of it is they have ridden your horse with their spurs—which is never fair play.'

'But the bishop encouraged me,' said the poor invalid. 'He said the Church needed extra work.'

'If he had made over four thousand seven hundred of his five thousand a year for the maintenance of extra workers—whether he would have done a wise thing I may doubt; but I am sure that his practice would have squared with his counsel.'

'Would you say with Talleyrand, " *Surtout point de zèle?*"'

'I fear I must say that long and close observation makes me sure that very much which passes under the name of "zeal" is the indulgence of egotism and self-will, and the reckless gratification of a thirst for excitement. Talleyrand, I suppose, was a man who knew good work, and how to get it. My dear sir, when a man begins to build he should count the cost, whether he be able to finish. Re-member that, though to a poor clergyman—as to a rich one—is considerately allowed three months' holiday in each year by the law of the land, on the plea' that nature needs rest and recreation—the same plea which allots the long vacation to lawyers, and a still longer vacation to legislators—yet, for all that, there is also a law of the purse, which allows the rich and forbids the poor parson to take the re-laxation which the law of human nature and the law of the land prescribe. It is not only that what is commonly called "work,"—meaning mechanical routine, or labour intellectual, such as due study and sermon-writing,—calls for cessation and a change; but even garrison duty and the monotonous stationary business of a sentinel keeping watch and ward over some "remote, unfriended, melancholy, slow" village outpost exhausts vitality and requires relief. Prolonged from year to year without intermittence, it sours the mind with discontent, or plunges it into the depths of despondency, and renders a man unfit for his duties, or too often tempts him to support his sinking spirits by stimulants, under whose influence he is lost. Vacations and recreations are wrong for all, or necessary for all. In the system of nature there is no respect of persons. It is not so with systems ecclesiastical. If a man has a private fortune or a living of two thousand, or one thousand, a year, he leaves his parish and goes to Rome for a year when he is tired of work. And where is the harm? His friends will sing his praises, and say he is giving himself body and soul to his calling, and needs rest and a change. Only—the man with two hundred or one hundred a year dependent on his health must beware of letting his rich neighbour cut out the work for him, or make the running : he is carrying extra weight. A man riding his one horse will not ride against another who has two or three, if he does not wish to be soon brought to a standstill. Pardon these rural illustrations. I hope you will yet recover and profit by them. Remember, "Those also serve who only stand and wait." And let me, on my own comfortable experience, recommend an entire change and a lounging watering-place, with good sea air and no duty. But keep clear of the Church politics and squabbles of those idle places.'

The invalid, who saw that our friend loved talking, and thought that perhaps he might by chance know something, then asked his opinion about sermons :—

'It has become,' said he, 'the fashion to laugh at sermons; but I assure you I have not found it a laughing matter to produce two sermons a week. They say people go to sleep, and do not attend, and so forth ; but they criticise and find fault, any way.'

'As to attending, I don't know what they do attend to. Attention is trouble, and people don't like trouble. They pay their guinea and go to the opera, and then they talk through all the music, and do anything but listen and attend. I wonder what they do in the House of Commons nine nights out of ten ? We know a certain great rhetorician ceased to attend a certain great annual dinner where speeches were wont to be made, because while he spoke the company would talk, and talk so loud. I believe that people listen as well to sermons as they do to anything else. And I maintain, too, that sermons, such as they are, do a world of good. They provoke discussion, and half the outcry against them is secretly prompted by sly folk who do not like discussion. Sermons help to keep the moral air sweet; they prevent stagnation; they do in an orderly way for religious thought once a week what the press does for political thought every day. Gag the press, and we know what the end will be. It is a like end that those have in view who would gag the pulpit. In country parishes, that is throughout the greater part of England, the pulpit is the only awakener of religious thought—I would almost say of thought at all. It is a great aid to the digestion of Holy Scripture. You don't like a man's sermons; well, your disapproval sets you thinking. The preacher is the angel that troubles the pool, that you may step in and be healed.'

'I'll tell you,' said the invalid, ' what, as a clergyman working single-handed, I felt grievously, and that is the length of the morning service. But, when one speaks of it, the answer is a personal sneer—"Shorten your sermon; leave out your sermon." No one complains of the length of the prayers, but one does complain of the repetitions. Some parts are simply repetition. Being pruned of those repetitions, the whole would be more complete, continuous, consistent, and uniform.'

'That,' said the ruddy rural cleric, who had been

a silent listener hitherto, and looked rather bored by what he heard—'that,' said he, 'would make the service like some beautiful statue which I have read of, that was left to the tender mercies of critics, who met, hammer and chisel in hand, and chipped off a bit here and a bit there, till nothing was left but a dummy.'

. 'Three services, however beautiful and complete in themselves, huddled together into one, without method or adjustment, can hardly with justice be compared to the unity of a beautiful statue,' replied the invalid.

'It is not only,' said Martel, 'that the morning service is full of—may I say *forbidden* or vain?— repetitions, but the language of the Prayer-book is often fatiguing to read. It has none of that flowing rhythm in short sentences which is one of the thousand perfections of the English Bible. Some of its sentences, as in the General Thanksgiving and the Prayer for all conditions of men, are half a page long; and to keep up the voice throughout them at the end of a long service is a great strain on the strength of an average middle-aged man. You and I, sir, who, besides administering Holy Communion, have had in the course of one day to read, as in Passion Week, 250 or 300 verses of Scripture, besides the morning and evening, the baptismal, marriage, and burial services, with preachings and churchings, we know something about it. Your don in Convocation knows nothing—nothing whatever. He never did the work, and he never means to do it; and so he is able to believe himself when he says that the morning service is "*not* too long" and is not marred but is beautified by its—I will not say "vain"—repetitions. The dignified clergyman is like "little Jack Horner;" he has "put in his thumb and pulled out a *plum*, and says, What a *good* boy am I!" His conscience is quite at the service of other people; and how morbidly sensitive and scrupulous conscience becomes in the matter of duty when another is to do it—need I tell you ?'

' My horse and your spurs again,' said the invalid, laughing; and added, ' I should think you preach extempore, sir ?'

' When I talk, yes; and that is always, you will say.'

' No, no.'

' Yes, yes; too true, sir, too true. But I hope my long tongue has helped to make short your journey, though sleep would have served you better. This is, I think, your station. Good-bye, and better *health* to you. Try the sea-shore, and keep clear of Church schemes and Church parties.'

As this one got out of the train, another clerical came up to the window.

' Ah, Martel ! is that you ? Can you tell me of a schoolmistress ?'

' I thought your school was to be made over to the Government; your curate thought so, any way.'

' Oh, no! I could never feel it right to let my school out of my hands.'

' Then you are coming into residence ?'

' Well, no; I can't do that, on account of health.'

' You remind me of Lever's Irish P.P. who sent a

message to his black sheep, fighting in the Peninsula: "Tell Mickey Free I have my eye upon him." You know you have been non-resident these three years, and mean to continue so.'

'No; not non-resident.'

'Why, you live three hundred miles from your parish.'

'But I am not non-resident.'

'Not non-resident!'

'Not legally, you know. I have no license; the bishop does not require it: so I don't consider myself "*non-resident*"—not legally "non-resident."'

'Then you are illegally non-resident; at least, you are three hundred miles from the school that you have your eye on. "Tell Mickey Free I have my eye on him,"' he shouted after him, as his friend went away.

'What a queer thing is conscience!' was his reflection. 'This fellow has a living of twelve hundred a year, and is a leader in the Low Church party, and is really a good man. How funny!'

END OF VOL. II.

BILLING AND SONS, PRINTERS, GUILDFORD, SURREY.